"Gail Sattler's funny and endea
favorites of mine. You'll soon be

The Rock Harbor

"I've been a Gail Sattler fan for a long, long time, so I wasn't at all surprised to find myself laughing out loud at her snappy dialogue, cheering every lovable character . . . and missing them when this entertaining, uplifting story ended! Better ink your return address stamp, because you're not gonna want to let this one get very far from your 'keepers' shelf. *Take the Trophy and Run* is one of the most enjoyable novels I've read in ages!"

—Loree Lough, best-selling author of
84 award-winning books, including *An Honorable Man*
(#3 in the First Responders series)

"A colorful, light-hearted romance filled with quirky characters. Just the kind of book I love to read. Gail has produced another winner in my opinion."

—Lena Nelson Dooley, author *Maggie's Journey,*
Mary's Blessing, and *Love Finds You in Golden,*
New Mexico, a Will Rogers Medallion Award winner

GAIL SATTLER

A *Bloomfield* Novel

TaKE the tRophy & Run

B&H
PUBLISHING GROUP

Nashville, Tennessee

978-1-4336-7729-8

Published by B&H Publishing Group
Nashville, Tennessee

Dewey Decimal Classification: F
Subject Heading: MYSTERY FICTION \ LOVE STORIES \
FAIRIES—FICTION

1 2 3 4 5 6 7 8 • 16 15 14 13 12

Dedicated to the real "Stan the Mechanic."
I love ya, Dad.

If you were a gnome, where would you go?

While most people have heard stories of world-famous traveling gnomes, the truth is that most gnomes spend all their "lives" in the gardens of their owners, where I'm sure they are very happy.

But I suspect some gnomes out there wish they could travel, only they don't have the means to jet off to foreign and exotic destinations.

I hope this inspires all the gnomes lovers out there who can help their gnomes to travel—even if those gnomes don't go very far from their own back yard. But no gnome gnapping allowed.

Winning isn't everything.
But losing isn't so great either.

Dear Reader,

Have you ever felt trapped in a difficult situation that seems to be spiraling out of your control, even after you've sought God for help? Then, when at last you see all the pieces finally fitting together and things are going the way you want, something happens and your world turns upside down, again, and you wonder what just hit you?

In *Take the Trophy and Run*, Amber Weathersby tries to find answers that just keep evading her, and time is running short. Even though her oldest and dearest friend is with her at every twist and turn, she is too afraid of potential risks to ask for help.

But God doesn't want us to be alone. He instructs us to bond together, to give help to those who need it, and also, even when it's hard, to accept help when it is freely given.

I'm glad you've joined with me to share the adventures of Amber and Stan as they strive to find the treasure they seek, even though they are striving for a different prize.

Gail Sattler

CHAPTER One

Amber Weathersby stepped back and rested her fists on her hips. "What do you think? Is it too much?"

Kathy tilted her head, tapping her finger to her chin as she studied Amber's garden gnome standing proudly in the middle of Amber's kitchen. "I'm not sure. Does my son know why you borrowed his sombrero? He's had it since he was a child. Are you sure nothing will happen to it?"

Amber bit back a grin, keeping her face turned toward Stan's small sombrero, which sat atop the gnome's head. He had told Amber exactly what he wanted to see happen to it, but couldn't tell his mother. For some reason, his mother considered it much more special than he did.

Amber pressed one hand over her heart. "I plan to take good care of it." At the end of the party, she planned to carry out Stan's wishes. Someone would either step on it or run over it with their car.

"You do such a great job displaying the trophy every year. The ceremony wouldn't be the same without you. None of our ceremonies would."

Amber smiled. "Creating all the displays for the garden club is so much fun. I love doing this, no matter what the occasion."

Not only was it fun, it was the difference that kept her business alive and food on her table. For the last five years she'd loaned her custom-designed garden gnome to the club for the spring celebration. Then, for every other occasion or party, the garden club purchased a selection of specially designed ornaments from her, raffling them off when the party was over.

As well, with the start of each new growing season, every member purchased a new Bloomfield Garden Club ornament from Amber, a new design every year. For the garden club, it was the most important time of the year. When the new growth sprang forth, the garden club celebrated with The Spring Fling.

Not only was the Bloomfield Garden Club her best customer, the prominent members were also good clients, and almost everyone in the garden club was a good friend.

Her membership had nothing to do with her gardening skills. Whenever she attempted to nurture outdoor plants, her garden either turned yellow and limp or became an artistic arrangement of petrified sticks. Nothing had the color or vitality promised by the little plastic tags that came with the plants.

The only plant that had lived a happy and full life was a potato she'd dropped out of her grocery bag. It had bounced into the flower bed by the front door, where she'd accidentally stepped on it, sinking it into the soil. Then, being out of sight, she'd forgotten about it until it mysteriously sprouted into a plant that eventually grew cute little white flowers. It was the first plant she'd grown successfully from scratch.

The only reason she'd been allowed to renew her membership at the garden club after killing off her entire garden and part of her neighbor's was because Stan found enough spare parts in his auto repair shop to rig a timed sprinkler for her. She'd made him a deathbed promise not to second-guess the sprinklers and never manually water anything in her garden ever again. Because of Stan, she'd kept a few hardy plants alive, even if they were a little burned from too much fertilizer.

Amber extended her arm and opened her palm toward the gnome, who proudly held the annual trophy. "Pamela says the winner of the best early garden for The Spring Fling contest is Becky. I think the Mexican look will work well with the colors that are blooming in her yard. What do you think?"

"I think Becky cheated. She's gloated for weeks about her secret formula for some kind of new fertilizer she's been using. I don't know what she's doing, but it can't be legal."

"I don't think there can be such a thing as illegal fertilizer."

Kathy made an undignified snort. "Becky found it, and she's been using it. No one can grow such full roses so early. It's not right. Not even Libby's roses are so lush this early in the season. I plan to talk to Libby about that."

Even in the garden club, jealousy still reared its ugly head. Amber patted Kathy on the shoulder. "I thought you and Becky were friends."

Kathy made a grunt that sounded like a growling dog. "We are friends. But we'd be better friends if she shared her fertilizer."

Amber bit back a grin. "Then figure out your own secret formula and maybe you'll win next year. But for this year, it's time to get going. The ceremony can't start without the trophy. Stan will help me set up everything at Becky's, and then we'll meet you at the clubhouse. I'll see you there."

"HOW'S THIS?" STAN WILSON forced himself to smile as he moved Amber's gnome for the fifth time, hopefully placing it at the angle she wanted.

"No, a little to the left. You've got him too close to the tree."

"Like this?" He nudged it exactly two inches then stepped away.

"That's better. People will take pictures of Gnorman and he can't be half in the shadow as the sun moves."

The lecturing face of their former science teacher flashed through his mind. "It's not really the sun that moves, it's the earth that . . . Norman? You named a garden statue?"

"Yes, but it's not what you think. It's spelled with a *G*. Then an *N*. Gnorman the Gnome."

Stan shook his head and jerked his thumb over his shoulder at the gnome in question. "You can't spell Norman that way. It's not right."

"That's the way it's spelled. Live with it."

"That's ridiculous."

"He's custom-designed to hold the trophy, so he's very special. Since he's special, he had to have a special name, and Gnorman, with a *G*, worked."

Stan stared at the little gnome who had been a fun tradition of the routine for the annual contest. Stan's tiny sombrero made the small man-like statue as tall as Stan's knees. Or was that gnees? He shook his head. He'd never known the gnome had a gname . . . er . . . name. Norman. No. Gnorman.

Stan shook his head once more to clear the gnocking . . . knocking . . . in his brain. "I give up. Gnorman, it is. Why is he all dressed up this year?"

"Do you remember a few years ago in the newspaper they had a story about a garden gnome who was kidnapped and became a world traveler?"

"Yeah, that was quite a story."

"Exactly. I think Gnorman would want to travel, but he can't go very far. After all, he has responsibilities. So he'll do the next best thing. He'll wear your old sombrero and the poncho I made for him, and he'll think he's gone on vacation to a beautiful exotic place."

Stan had never thought of Mexico as exotic, but then again, he'd never been there. "I think it's you who really wants to take a vacation in Mexico. It's not that expensive. Why don't you find someone to run your store and go?" Stan held his breath, waiting for her reply. In his dreams she would say she would love to go to Mexico but didn't know who she could ask to go with her on such short notice, and of course, he'd volunteer. He'd volunteer to go anywhere with Amber, even if it was just to the next county.

"I can't."

"Why not? I'm not saying to close the store and disappear. Just that you should hire someone to run things for a few days and have a nice holiday."

Her eyes widened, and he knew she was thinking about it. But instead of the smile he expected, along with her softening and changing of her mind, her expression tightened. She looked away. "I can't do that."

Stan opened his mouth to argue with her, but she turned back to him and gave him that look she'd used since they were in their teens that always froze him solid.

He wanted to tell her that he'd go with her, separate rooms, of course, and if she couldn't find someone to run her store, he would have one of his mechanics do it. Jordan wouldn't be much help if people asked for help on matching colors for the decorative items she carried, but Jordan certainly could be polite to customers and work the cash register. Most of all, knowing Jordan and his wife had a baby on the way, Jordan would really appreciate a few additional days of work to earn a little extra money.

From the look on her face, she'd shoot down any suggestion he made. Even though they'd spent most of their time together when they weren't working, it really wasn't appropriate for them to go on vacation together, no matter how good buddies they were. All things considered, people would be bound to think the wrong thing. He would never do anything to tarnish Amber's reputation, and most importantly he would never do anything to damage their friendship.

He raised one hand in surrender. "Even if you don't take a vacation, I still think you work too much. You need some time off."

Amber planted her fists on her hips and gave him the look. He forced himself not to cringe. She'd worked on that look to get her way back in the days when they reached puberty and he grew taller than her. A dozen years later it still worked. He wondered if she practiced in a mirror and if she used that look on anyone else.

She narrowed her eyes. The look intensified. "Unlike you, I don't have people working for me, so I have to work six days a week unless I shut down for a day, and I can't do that."

He wanted to tell her that, of course, she could. If she didn't want Jordan, he could loan her one of his other two mechanics. But that look kept his lips sealed.

Plain and simple, Amber worked too hard. Saturday was the busiest day for both their businesses, but Stan only worked Saturdays to give his employees weekends off to be home with their families. Unlike Amber, he took two days off—Sunday and Wednesday, and he could be flexible. "If you won't take the time off to go on vacation, how about if you take next Wednesday off and we'll go do something fun. Just something local."

Her face paled. "I can't."

"Why not?" He stood still, waiting for a reason, but instead of explaining, she lowered her head and dug around for something in her purse.

Gathering more courage than it took to tell Andy Barnhardt that he needed a new transmission, he stepped forward and stood close enough that she couldn't ignore him. "You haven't answered me. What aren't you telling me? I thought we told each other everything."

"I . . ." Her voice trailed off as she pulled her hands out of her purse and began to close the zipper, but her hands shook too much to pull it in a straight line, and it jammed.

He stepped back. "Amber? What's wrong?" He didn't think taking a day to goof off with him was such a scary proposition.

"Nothing," she mumbled without looking up at him, which told him that something was indeed wrong. "We'd better get to the party. We don't want them to wait for us to announce the winner."

Stan suspected that everyone knew the winner anyway, the way the members gossiped. Every year the garden club did the same thing; they served tea and some bad pastries made by one of the ladies in the group while Amber set up her gnome in the winner's garden. This year, instead of setting up tables and chairs in the courtyard at the amenities building at Lake Bliss Retirement Village, which they used as their clubhouse, he'd insisted on going with Amber, using the excuse that he was entitled to help since it was his sombrero.

They drove the four blocks in silence. As he expected, when they joined the party already in progress, everyone stopped talking and stared at Amber. Pamela Jasper, the president of the garden club, waved to her and then stepped up to the makeshift podium.

"May I have your attention, please?" Pamela shouted, not having the benefit of a microphone, as if anyone in the group would dare talk during a moment like this.

The hush spread like oil leaking from a filter that hadn't been tightened properly. Amber grinned from ear to ear while Pamela called out, "The winner of this year's Spring Fling Early Bloomer contest is . . . Becky!"

Everyone, except Stan's mother, clapped enthusiastically.

"Now let's all go to Becky's and continue the party!"

The whole garden club, complete with spouses, friends, and guests, prepared themselves to change locations. A few headed to their cars, but most of the members picked up their teacups and walked the short distance to Becky's house. Stan could imagine what their mismatched group looked like to the people on the street who weren't members. Including the guests for today's party, there had to be over a hundred people in their group.

Considering that some of the garden club members were elderly, they made the distance in pretty good time.

Everyone gathered in a semicircle in front of Becky's garden.

Pamela made her way to the front and faced the crowd. "Here we are! Congratulations again, Becky. It's that time we've been waiting for all year; it's my great pleasure to award you The Spring Fling trophy." She smiled and clapped her hands, encouraging everyone to do the same. "Becky, please come forward."

The crowd separated to allow Becky to join Pamela.

Pamela turned to Amber. "We're getting pretty excited to see our faithful little friend. Where is he?"

Despite the heat of the warm spring day, a chill rushed up Stan's spine. He knew exactly where the gnome was supposed to be. He'd been the one to put him there.

He turned to look at Amber at the same time as Amber turned to the center of the garden.

Her purse dropped on the ground and a bunch of girl stuff bounced out. Amber gasped and pressed her palms to her cheeks. "Gnorman! He's gone!"

Chapter Two

Amber stared at the place in Becky's garden where Gnorman had stood holding the trophy. Stunned, she pressed her hands to her face until she felt a gentle tugging on the hem of her blouse.

"Amber?" She looked down at Becky's young niece, whose eyes were wide. "You dropped your purse and a bunch of your stuff fell out. Want me to help pick it up?"

Without moving her head, Amber scanned the ground. Sure enough, half the contents of her purse lay strewn about her feet.

Out of the corner of her eye, she registered Stan approaching from his position beside the end of Becky's fence.

Quickly hunkering down, Amber grabbed the most embarrassing items first. "Yes, thank you, Sasha. A man should never see the contents of a woman's purse."

Little Sasha nodded and giggled. "My mom says that when she's got a chocolate bar and doesn't want Daddy to find out. You don't got any chocolate, but you got some good gum."

Amber dearly wished her last piece of Wrigley's was a big-gie-sized Three Musketeers. There probably wasn't a better time for chocolate than right now. Everyone would ask her where Gnorman and the trophy were, but she had no clue. She had to find him, and fast. Even though Gnorman had made a place for himself, and for her, in the garden club, the most important absence wasn't really the ceramic gnome, but the trophy that she'd strapped to his hand.

As she reached to pick up her lip balm, Stan's black leather shoes blocked her hand's trajectory. She withdrew her hand, tilted her head back, and looked up, way up, at Stan, who looked down at her.

Usually when they stood side by side, she had to look up at him anyway, since he was nearly six feet tall and she was merely five and a half feet. But kneeling on the ground, she felt even smaller than usual beside him.

Stan crossed his arms over his chest. "What's going on? The gnome was here less than half an hour ago."

Amber stood, checked around them to make sure no one was close enough to listen to their conversation, and then stepped a little closer to be sure. "It's obvious someone's taken him. I can't figure that out. He's just a garden gnome. I wonder if it was a bunch of teenagers up to mischief, but a garden gnome isn't something I can see a bunch of kids stealing."

Stan shook his head. "I don't know if any of the local teens who usually pull pranks like that would be out of bed this early on a weekend. Besides, if you're thinking of the same group as I am, most of them have relatives in the garden club, and they wouldn't dare steal your gnome. They'd get off lighter if they'd stolen a car."

Amber turned to look at her aunt's vintage Cadillac. "Except Aunt Edna's car. That one's pretty untouchable."

Stan squeezed his eyes shut and sighed. "Please, I touch that thing way too often. It's almost impossible to find parts for it. I've actually wished someone would steal it." He shook his head. "Never mind that. We need to find out who took your gnome."

They both scanned the crowd. "It can't be anyone here. When we got to the party, everyone here was there."

Stan lowered his voice to barely above a whisper. "That's not necessarily true. This is quite a crowd. If anyone disappeared for five minutes, which is all it would have taken if they had their car parked half a block away, no one would have noticed they were missing. It wouldn't have been hard for anyone to sneak off for five minutes. The courtyard was a huge free-for-all."

Amber glared at Stan. "Sneaking off to a car sounds rather devious."

He grinned. "Not really. It's just good planning."

"Good planning? Are you speaking from the voice of experience?"

Stan's ears turned red. "Let's save that conversation for another day. All I'm trying to do is consider all the possibilities."

While Amber really wanted to hear about Stan's misadventure and why he'd parked his car a block away from some unnamed event, and why she hadn't heard about this story until now, this wasn't the time. Again, she scanned the crowd. Looking from one person to the next, her attention stopped on her Uncle Bill, her Great-Aunt Edna's husband. Bill had no interest in the flowers. Instead, he watched the food for the luncheon being unloaded from a small line of cars.

"Oh dear," Amber whispered to Stan. "I hope Aunt Edna doesn't catch him breaking his diet."

Before she could say "transfat," her aunt appeared in the distance, lips thinned and jaw clenched, using her cane not to help her walk, but to move Libby out of her way, as she quickstepped toward her husband.

Amber cringed, having been poked with Edna's cane a few times herself. "Does that cane ever touch the ground, or does she just use it to clear a path?"

Stan shook his head. "I've never seen it touch the ground. I think she doesn't want the end to get scuffed. It's amazing how she gets around at her age."

"Seventy-five isn't as old as it used to be. Aunt Edna does aerobics three times a week, and I hear she uses bags of fertilizer for weight lifting."

Stan cringed, and Amber would have cringed, too, if she wasn't concentrating so much on not appearing nervous.

"Let's go talk to Becky," Amber said. "I don't want to be anywhere near this."

Stan simply nodded and followed her to the circle of people who tried to console Becky that the trophy that should have been the centerpiece of her yard for the season had vanished.

If Amber worried about how to break into the conversation, she shouldn't have. The second everyone saw her, conversation dropped like a bale of hay off the end of Jackson's baler.

Becky stepped forward. "What are you going to do? Everyone knows I won The Spring Fling Early Bloomer Award, since it will be published in the newsletter." She smiled widely. "I would have loved to have the trophy in my garden, but now this will bring more publicity to my garden than the trophy. The little gnome though . . ." Becky gave a loud, sad sigh. "He's become such a fun tradition of The Spring Fling party, we've got to find him. I know he's one-of-a-kind. You must be so upset." She lowered her voice to barely above a whisper. "If we find him at Bethany's house, I'll just . . ." She let her voice trail off, then cleared her throat and smiled at the gathering crowd. "We all need to find out who took Amber's little Gnorman."

Amber wanted to remind Becky that since Bethany wasn't a member, there was no way that the town pack rat could possibly have known where the semifamous gnome would be. Even if she did know, Bethany would never steal anything. She just liked to buy more than she needed, and her yard and living room were a testimony to that. But before Amber could open her mouth, Naomi, who happened to be Bethany's mother, complete with one of her flamboyant hats, joined them.

"If you ask me, I think Tom took Gnorman. He's been trying to get Becky's attention for years, but she never takes him seriously. This would make her notice him."

Not very subtly, they all turned to Tom, who was talking to Andy, who was pointing at Aunt Edna's car and shaking his head.

Amber shook her head. "I don't think so. I don't know Tom that well, but he seems quite honest, and this doesn't seem like something he would do."

Libby elbowed Amber in the ribs. "What about Andy? With one arm raised, your little gnome would make a good outside perch for that ridiculous parrot of his."

Pamela spun toward Libby and waved one of her hands, flashing her multicolored nails dotted with rhinestones. "Andy is quite mischievous, but do you really think he would do something like this, even as a joke, with something as special as The Spring Fling trophy?"

Libby narrowed her eyes and glared at Pamela. "So you're admitting he did it?"

Pamela glared back. "I'm not admitting a thing. I think you're more likely to hide the gnome and trophy, then call it a joke."

"Well!" Libby stiffened and raised her nose in the air. "I refuse to stand here and be insulted."

Before Amber could tell the two alleged friends to stop squabbling, Libby stomped off to join the people organizing plates and utensils at the food table.

Stan raised his palms toward the group. "Ladies, please. We're not pointing fingers. We're trying to figure out who could have done this." He turned slightly and took hold of Amber's elbow, causing her to flinch. "I think Amber and I need to check out Gnorman's last known location."

"Ohhhhh . . ." Elsie, the garden club's most senior member except for Aunt Edna, drawled. "Are y'all looking for a l'il ol' clue?"

Amber squeezed her eyes shut. "Elsie, that is the worst fake Southern accent I've ever heard."

The other ladies gasped at her reprimand, then Elsie chuckled. "Sorry. I was trying to get into character. You know. Like method acting."

Pamela's eyebrows arched. "You mean like from one of those mystery detective TV shows? Are we looking for clues? Like Lana did it with her paintbrush in the garden?"

Becky's eyes widened, and Amber could almost see the gears turning in her head. Becky broke out into a conspiratorial grin. "Or Stan did it with the wrench in the cul-de-sac."

Stan's grip on her elbow tightened. "Do they really think I would do something like this?"

From the widening eyes of everyone in the little circle, Amber could see that no one thought Becky's joke was funny. The air went still in their little circle.

Pamela crossed her arms over her chest and narrowed her eyes. "Becky! No Clue jokes. This is serious," she hissed.

Becky shrugged. "He's the first person I could think of with a wrench. That was a real weapon in the real game, you know. Not a paintbrush, which is all Lana would have." She turned and glared at Pamela.

Amber lowered her head and pinched the bridge of her nose. "This isn't a game, and no one was murdered. My gnome and the trophy are missing, and we've got to find them."

A slight pressure on her elbow encouraged her to walk away from the group of women.

"That's right," Stan said over his shoulder as he guided Amber to a vacant spot. "We'll figure this out so they aren't missing for long. Excuse us, please."

———— ♆ ————

STAN GRITTED HIS TEETH.

Amber's membership with the garden club already rested on shaky ground, and this wasn't doing anything to help her position. It was a natural and expected prerequisite that members of the garden club be . . . gardeners. The only reason Amber had a garden at all was because of the sprinkler system he'd rigged for her. Prior to his handiwork, the only plant she'd grown successfully was a potato, which he didn't even know flowered. She'd almost cried when they'd dug it up. Then she couldn't bring herself to eat the potatoes it had grown.

He didn't know why a person who could become emotionally attached to a vegetable would want to be a garden club member, but he didn't need to know the reason. He only knew that she desperately wanted to be a member, and that was good enough for him. The novelty of her gnome displaying The Spring Fling trophy every year was a major component of her continuing membership, so he would do whatever it took to get the gnome back.

Stan turned slightly, guided Amber to an unoccupied spot under a big tree, and released her.

"I don't know about you," he said, "but I really think it had to be a member of the garden club who took your Gnorman."

"I agree."

Together they scanned the crowd.

Even though his garden was nowhere near the level of Becky's, he had enough plants strategically placed that he qualified for membership. He knew most, but not all of the other members, especially the newer ones.

"I can't tell if everyone is here," Stan said. "I wish I had access to my membership list."

"I know. But there are more people here than just the members. There's a lot of guests because this is the second biggest event of the year for the club."

Stan ran his fingers through his hair. "This is scary that I know this many people. There's more people here than at a usual Sunday service at church."

Amber sighed. "I know. And like you, I don't think anyone here could have done it, but there's no one else who would. Does that make sense?"

Maybe not to anyone else, but he knew what she meant.

Stan searched through the crowd one person at a time. Simply, there was no one he considered suspicious or capable of pulling a stunt like this in the group. Many of the women he knew were members of the garden club so they shared a lot of friendly news, otherwise known as gossip, and most of the men who were here only came for the food.

Stan grinned, thinking that not only did he also enjoy all the great food while he was at a garden club event, most of the older ladies heaped leftovers on him to take home. As one of the few members who owned a large pickup truck, he often hauled heavy stuff for anyone who needed help, and sometimes that included transplanted trees. The ladies were appreciative, and he had enough homemade meals in his freezer to last him awhile.

Amber turned to him and ran her fingers through her hair, messing it up and making him want to pat it smooth again, until he decided he liked it slightly mussed.

"I can't think of anyone here who would steal the trophy," she muttered, "especially when one of the members is the chief of police. Have you got any ideas?"

Stan opened his mouth to respond, but when she looked up at him with those gorgeous green eyes, his words caught in his throat. Amber's eyes were the color of deep jade, and from as far back as he could remember, that had always been his favorite color. For years he'd wanted to buy a jade ring for Amber, not just because of her beautiful eyes, but because he wanted to treat her special. The only reason he held back was because she would never accept such a thing from him.

Their mothers had been best friends, so close that they'd had a double wedding and bought houses next door to each other. They were even pregnant at the same time, so Stan and Amber had known each other since they were born. Whenever he did something to annoy her, she threatened to show their friends pictures of them as babies, one shot in particular where she had a cute little dress on and he only wore a diaper and one sock.

Growing up, he and Amber had spent time together almost every day of their lives, including after they went to school and met other friends. Even now, as adults and no longer living next door to each other, they still saw or talked to each other nearly every day.

Every time he tried to buy her something nice, she got angry with him for spoiling her, so now all he could purchase for her were birthday and Christmas presents. But if one day she would accept a "just friends" gift for no special occasion, a jade ring would be his first purchase.

For a moment his heart went cold, remembering the day when her parents decided to leave Bloomfield and move to Chicago to live closer to Amber's grandmother because of her failing health. It had been the most unsettling time in his life until Amber told him she'd decided to stay in Bloomfield. Once the decision had been made, she'd leased a small townhouse, opened her little store, and joined the garden club. They both loved small-town life.

Stan continued to look down into her eyes, unable to break contact.

The reason he'd joined the garden club wasn't because he loved gardening so much, or, like most of the other male members his age, that he could get a lot of good, free food. It was because Amber, knowing her lack of gardening skills, had been too afraid to attend the first meeting alone, so he'd joined to go with her.

Getting his thoughts back to the issue at hand, Stan turned and watched another group of people milling around Becky's yard at the spot where Gnorman had been and shaking their heads.

At some point everyone there had checked out the empty patch of grass and no doubt wondered the same thing: who took the gnome, and where was the trophy?

He sighed. Watching the crowd was getting them nowhere. "Maybe we should walk around and talk to people."

Amber's posture sagged. "If that's what you think will help. I'm sure that's all everyone's been talking about, and they'd just love to repeat themselves to us."

He shrugged his shoulders. "We've got nothing to lose." Or rather, nothing more to lose.

Amber straightened her purse strap on her shoulder. "Okay, let's see if anyone has any better ideas than we do."

Stan clenched his teeth so he wouldn't say his thoughts out loud; ten times zero was still zero.

CHAPTER Three

Amber dragged her feet as she approached her store. She'd been unable to sleep, worrying about Gnorman and the trophy. While she already missed her little gnome, it was more important to find the trophy.

For now, everyone they'd spoken to felt sure that Gnorman, along with the trophy, would be returned within a day or two, after whoever who had taken him was satisfied with their practical joke. But after thinking about it all night, Amber wasn't so sure this wasn't more personal.

As she inserted her key into the lock, her hand stilled. Next to the lock, a white envelope stuck out from between the door and the frame, held up by the deadbolt.

Leaving the key in the lock, Amber shifted her purse and tote more securely onto her shoulder, pulled the envelope from its hiding place, and ripped it open.

She gasped at a message constructed of words and letters cut from a newspaper and sloppily pasted onto a plain piece of paper. Blobs of dried glue containing colored donut sprinkles and what appeared to be coffee stains at the bottom of the page added to the note's mystery. Amber held her breath and read.

Gnoman has been gnome gnapped. you must not interfere with his journey until all conditions are met. gnoman must stay where he is for four days. then you will receive another note. if he is moved, i will find him and he will be harmed! this is a warning. do not interfere or you will be very sorry.

Amber flipped the paper over for more, but it was blank.

No demand for money had been made, no conditions to be met had been listed, nor had there been any mention of the missing trophy. The note also failed to mention Stan's hated sombrero, although she didn't know whether that was good or bad.

In case she had missed something, she read the note again, halting on the word *journey*. Every gnome owner in the world knew about the famous gnome who disappeared from his owner's garden to become a world traveler with photos of him at many popular tourist destinations around the world mailed back to the owner.

Then, as suddenly as he disappeared, he mysteriously returned to his home unharmed and none the worse for his adventure. Airlines and travel agencies had picked up on the story, and a number of them still use a gnome in their advertising. Now, years later, the trend of disappearing gnomes was old news, and garden gnomes around the world were safe.

Amber slipped the note under her arm, picked up her purse and tote bag, and went inside. As soon as she turned off the alarm, instead of her usual routine of dusting the displays, she headed for the phone and dialed Stan's auto shop.

She didn't give him a chance to finish the usual spiel of greeting before she blurted out, "I just got a ransom note for Gnorman, except there isn't a ransom."

"What are you talking about?"

"I also have a clue. The Gnome Gnapper loves coffee and donuts."

A silence hung over the line, then he sighed. "That means pretty much everyone in the garden club."

Amber stared at the note in her hand, feeling her enthusiasm deflate. "I guess." It wasn't like she could look for the donut with the missing sprinkles to lead her to her missing gnome. "This note is so strange. I'm not sure what it's really saying." Just as she opened her mouth to read it to Stan, the other line on her phone lit up. "Can I put you on hold? I have to take another call." She pushed the hold button and was halfway through the greeting for her store when Naomi's voice interrupted her.

"I found your gnome," Naomi said, her voice trembling with excitement. "He's here beside the fountain. I don't know how he got here, but when I went outside to water my hanging fuchsias I saw him. Someone must have put him there in the middle of the night. I have to tell you I love the little costume you dressed him in. I'll get someone to help me take him over to Becky's yard right now. I thought you should know that."

"No!" Amber nearly shouted into the phone, then pressed her teeth into her lower lip and lowered her tone to a normal speaking level. "I'm sorry, I didn't mean to deafen you. You can't move Gnorman. I just got a note that says I can't move him for four days or something bad will happen. It doesn't say what, but I don't want to find out the hard way." She squeezed her eyes shut, not sure if praying about a ceramic statue was something God wanted to hear, but she muttered a quick prayer of thanks that he'd been found, then cleared her throat. "Does he still have the trophy strapped to his hand? Or the sombrero?"

Amber closed her eyes to picture the section of the retirement village where Naomi lived. Each ground floor suite had a small backyard with short fences dividing each unit from the other. The rear of the properties opened to the community's common ground, where Naomi and a few other residents maintained a garden with a small fountain that backed up to the center's small golf course. She could almost appreciate the irony of the situation—the garden club held most of their meetings at the Lake Bliss Retirement Village amenities building, which was across the complex from where Gnorman had been found.

"The trophy is gone," Naomi said, "but a picture of it is taped to his hand. I don't know why you're talking about a sombrero. He's wearing a hat that matches perfectly with his Pilgrim costume. He's absolutely adorable."

"That's not the costume I put on him. Tell me, is there a note anywhere?"

"I don't know. Let me get my binoculars."

Amber gritted her teeth while the phone clunked in her ear. She had no idea why Naomi would have binoculars, nor did she want to hear what Naomi used them for, but she was glad they were handy. Naomi's footsteps echoed, followed by the shuffling of Naomi pushing the curtains aside, then the mini blinds clattering as Naomi pulled the string to raise them up. Amber couldn't help it, she shifted her weight from foot to foot at the sound of Naomi's footsteps getting louder as she returned to the phone.

"There's an envelope in his other hand. I thought it was part of the costume, but maybe it's not."

"Don't move him. I'll be right there." She hung up the phone as quickly as she could without slamming it in Naomi's ear, grabbed her purse, and ran for the door.

At the moment she touched the handle she remembered about Stan, whom she'd put on hold. She nearly tripped as she turned around and flew back to the phone.

"That was Naomi. She found Gnorman. He's at the retirement village. I have to go."

"I'll meet you there." A click sounded in her ear before she could tell Stan that wasn't necessary.

She didn't need Stan's help moving Gnorman, because Gnorman couldn't be moved. The issue wasn't Gnorman; it was the garden club's trophy, which had been engraved with every winner of The Spring Fling contest since its inception thirty-something years ago, before the club bought a computer for record keeping. The Spring Fling trophy was as important to the garden club as the Stanley Cup was to the NHL, except the Bloomfield Garden Club's trophy remained small with only one name added yearly, versus the names of every player on the winning team. Because the names were engraved on the trophy, the club used it as their permanent record, which made the trophy irreplaceable.

The year she had joined the garden club she'd been entrusted with having the trophy engraved, adding the new winner's name, then placing it prominently in their yard on a pedestal. One of the older ladies had accidentally dropped the pedestal the day of the party, and it had been a last minute inspiration to get Gnorman and strap the trophy to his hand, having her garden gnome triumphantly hold it up rather than trying to balance it on a rock. Everyone loved her idea so much it became a tradition.

Until the note, she might have considered Gnorman's disappearance as a prank, but now she wasn't so sure. If this was personal, then it was no longer a game. She wanted to recover Gnorman, but her main responsibility was to recover the trophy.

And recover it she would . . . if none of the well-meaning elderly residents of the Lake Bliss Retirement Village community got to Gnorman first.

EVEN THOUGH AMBER HADN'T told him where to go at the retirement village, Stan didn't have any trouble finding her gnome. Nowhere in the whole town of Bloomfield did news travel faster than among the residents of the Lake Bliss retirement community.

The crowd of people gathered around the fountain told him where to find Amber's gnome. As soon as he saw the little gnome, he knew why. It was a strange thing for the thief to do. The thief had changed the gnome's costume.

He had to admit, he liked it better than Amber's Mexican costume, but he wasn't about to tell her that.

"Hi, everyone. Is Amber here yet?" he said as he reached for the gnome to pick it up.

Like iron filings around a magnet, a sea of wrinkled hands surrounded his arms, halting his movement.

"I'm sorry," one of the elderly ladies said. "Naomi told us that Amber said not to move him."

"Why not? I was just going to take him and put him in Becky's yard, where he belongs."

Before the woman could answer, he saw Amber running at top speed across the grass.

"Stan! Don't touch him!" she hollered at the top of her lungs, waving her arms in the air.

At the sight of Amber approaching, the hands retracted.

She didn't wait to get her breath back before the words tumbled out of her mouth. "The note said not to move him, and that there would be another note here with further instructions."

Stan turned his head to the gnome at the same time Amber grabbed a small envelope that had been tucked in the gnome's hand. In a split second she tore the envelope open and pulled out a piece of paper to read it.

The envelope dropped to the ground as Amber's face tightened. One of the ladies tsked, picked the envelope up, and tucked it into Amber's purse.

"This one has the same bottom line as the other one. It says that he's got to stay here for four days and no one is to move him." Her hand dropped to her side. "That's it. Nothing about what this person wants or what I have to do to get the trophy back." She turned and scanned the crowd. "Do you hear that, everyone? Please, no one move him. I have to get the garden club's trophy back. I don't know what to do, so we have to do what this person says."

Most of the people surrounding them nodded. Others scrunched up their faces, like they were thinking of how to solve the problem, but coming up with nothing.

Stan turned to look down at the little gnome, his painted smile showing him blissfully unaware of the trouble surrounding him. "I guess all we can do is wait out the four days, but on the third night, maybe we can do a stakeout and see what happens. If whoever did this is going to move him on the fourth night, then we'll be ready."

"But four days is such a long time. We've got to do something." She bent and touched the gnome's new jacket. "This is really well fitted, almost like it was tailor-made. You have to admit that he's an odd shape and size. I don't know anyone who is capable of doing something so intricate except for one person—the town seamstress, Zoe."

Amber fumbled inside her purse, pulled out her cell phone, and snapped a few pictures of the gnome in his new outfit. "I think I'll make a stop on my way back to the shop and see what she says. I'm sorry you had to come all this way for nothing. You should get back to work."

Stan felt his jaw tighten. He didn't know Zoe well, and he didn't think she was the type to pull this off, but the facts spoke for themselves. "No way. She went through a lot of trouble, so I have a feeling it's not going to be that easy. I'll go with you for backup."

Amber didn't argue with him, so he followed her to Zoe's house and stood beside her as she knocked on the door.

Zoe opened the door without looking first to see who it was.

"Please come in." Zoe stepped aside for them to enter. "Have you had any luck finding your gnome?"

As Zoe looked into Amber's face, Stan studied Zoe. Nothing about her revealed any guilt or signified that she was trying to hide anything. Her concern over whether or not Amber had found her gnome seemed genuine.

"Yes," Amber replied as she walked into the foyer. "Naomi found him at the retirement center and called me." She reached into her pocket for her cell phone and flipped it open. "The strange thing is, he's not wearing the costume I put on him. Instead, he's wearing a costume that looks like it was made by you." Amber held her phone open toward Zoe.

Zoe's brows scrunched in the middle. "I remember that little costume. I made six of them for a display at the museum last year. I'd made rag dolls and dressed them up as Puritans for a Thanksgiving display. I heard it was really popular. Then, after everyone recovered from Black Friday, they gave the dolls back to me. I didn't have anything I could use them for, so I sent them to the consignment store."

"I don't understand. How could that jacket have fit Gnorman so well?"

Zoe smiled ear to ear. "When I asked what size they needed for the dolls, they said about the size of a garden gnome. So I went to Victoria's house—remember she won last year—and measured your little gnome and used him as my model."

Stan gritted his teeth. "That means everyone who has been to the museum last fall has seen this outfit, and there are five others like it."

"I'm afraid so."

Amber glanced out the window. "You said you took them all to the consignment store. Maybe we can go there and see who bought the dolls."

Stan checked his watch. He'd told Mark that he would only be gone for twenty minutes and he'd already been much longer. He wouldn't make his staff work overtime, so he would have to work late tonight to catch up on the lost time to have his customers' cars ready for them to pick up in the morning.

But this piqued his curiosity. Someone had gone to a lot of effort to play hide-and-go-seek with Amber's gnome, and even though it was probably childish, he wanted to be the first to find out who it was. Although, if he had to admit it, he liked the idea of helping Amber find out who had pulled off this caper.

It seemed more challenging than some of the other things he'd helped her with. A few years ago he'd rigged up a timer for her pottery oven so her creations would be finished when she got into the shop in the morning without being left sitting in the hot oven all night. He still didn't understand how one could overbake a statue, but he didn't really want to know the details. He only needed to know that Amber needed his help.

More recently he'd tried to help her conquer her fear of heights and took her on the Ferris wheel the last time the fair came into town.

He smiled at the memory of Amber holding onto him as if her life depended on it while their car swayed at the top, screaming into his chest so loud his ears rang for a week. To calm her down, he'd kissed her, and it was a moment he'd never forget. Since then, he'd wondered what he could do to make that happen again, a difficult task without a Ferris wheel.

Finding out who bought a bunch of dolls was so easy it would almost be cheating.

Almost, but not quite.

"Let's go. I'll drive."

CHAPTER Four

"I love that color on you. It really brings out the green in your eyes."

Amber smiled weakly at her friend's comment, ran her hand down the jade-colored shirt, and continued dusting her display of smoked-glass butterflies.

"Thank you. I got this at the consignment store. I didn't know how much nice stuff they had in there."

One of Sarah's brows quirked. "Consignment store? Once I heard you say that you would never buy anything from there in case someone came in to your store and saw you wearing their old clothes."

Heat flooded Amber's cheeks. "I might have made too quick a judgment call on that. Tessa told me that she never takes anything into the store that shows any signs of wear. All the clothing people bring in for consignment is required to be nearly perfect, or she says she tells them to take it to Goodwill instead. She says most of the clothes in her store are things people bought either without trying it on at a department store, or got as a gift so they couldn't take it back, or something they wore once for a special occasion and don't want to wear it again in the same crowd."

"That's nice that you changed your mind, but I sure would like to know why you went into the consignment store in the first place."

Amber sighed and then turned to her best friend. "I guess by now you heard that we found Gnorman by the fountain. Stan and I did a little detective work that took us to the consignment store. When we arrived, there were only five dolls instead of six. We asked Tessa who bought the sixth doll, and she said the strangest thing. A couple of weeks ago she was straightening her display and noticed one of the dolls was missing. Where the doll should have been, someone had left an envelope with money and a typed note saying they didn't have time to wait in line, so they left the money and ran out."

"That really is strange." Sarah crossed her arms. "There's never a line at Tessa's consignment store."

Not only had there not been a line during the entire time Stan and Amber had lingered in the store, but not a single other person had come in. "I didn't mean about Tessa's store not having many people in it at a time. I meant, doesn't it strike you as strange that the note would have been typed? What did this person do, not want to wait, go all the way home, type a note, and come back? That would have taken ten times the amount of time of just standing in line. If there was a line, which there probably wasn't."

Sarah's mouth formed an *O*.

"That's right. Someone had planned to buy the doll before they even got to the store. Tessa says it was the exact change for the right amount, including the sales tax. Someone didn't want to be seen buying the doll, and now we know why."

"You have to admit, that's pretty clever. But at least we know that the person isn't a thief."

"Not a thief?" Amber crossed her arms over her chest. "Of course the person is a thief. He or she stole Gnorman and the trophy."

Sarah waved one finger in the air. "It's not really stolen. They're just leading you on a rabbit trail. Maybe this is just a bad practical joke."

Amber turned and stared blankly out the window so she wouldn't have to face her friend. "I'm afraid it might be more than that. I think someone has something against me, and they're trying to get me kicked out of the garden club."

She heard Sarah's quick intake of breath. "What are you talking about? Why would anyone do that? I'm sorry to say this, but your garden isn't exactly competition to anyone else wanting a prize."

"I didn't tell anyone, but the day before The Spring Fling party, someone egged the front door of my store and dumped a soft drink all over my car. Those are usually things someone does if they have something against you."

Sarah's brows knotted. "Who has something against you? What have you done?"

"That's the thing. I have no idea. It was annoying to clean up the mess, but taking Gnorman and the trophy is serious. The garden club entrusted me with that trophy and it's gone missing, with a great public spectacle, while I was responsible for it. If I can't get it back, they'll kick me out of the garden club. Even if they don't kick me out right away, they won't renew my membership."

The question was almost written across Sarah's forehead, but she didn't say it. *Why is being in the garden club so important?*

It was a question Amber wouldn't answer . . . ever. She couldn't explain her situation and she didn't want to involve anyone else in the mess she'd been dragged into. Not Sarah, and especially not Stan. She hadn't told him about what happened because he would try to help her, and even though he helped her with so much, she wouldn't accept his help on this.

"Let's just say I must be a member in good standing, so I need to get that trophy back."

Sarah's expression told her that she wanted to ask more, but for now she would wait until Amber was ready to talk. That wasn't going to happen. Amber had dug herself into a hole, and she had to get out of it by herself.

Sarah's expression softened. "I'm sure you'll get it back. Word around town is that Stan's been right there with you following every lead since it disappeared."

Amber sighed. "You know Stan. He always likes to help." She didn't know how he knew, but every time she needed help with something, no matter how minor, he showed up, volunteering to fix whatever was wrong. A few days ago he'd even helped her restring her guitar, making sure he trimmed every end piece that she usually left sticking out. She still couldn't play the guitar that well, but it sure looked good. "I don't know why he does all those things. Maybe he doesn't have enough to do."

"He certainly does. When's the last time you tried making an appointment to get your car fixed?" Sarah's voice lowered to a whisper, even though they were the only people in the store. "He doesn't do favors for everyone. Just you." As she finished her sentence, Sarah gave Amber a big, exaggerated wink.

"Stop that. Stan and I are just good friends—like I'm good friends with his mother. Kathy's been helping me learn how to make my own jam this year."

"Really? Stan's favorite jam, or yours?"

"I said stop it. I need your help to figure out what to do next. How can I find out who bought, and I use the word loosely, that doll with the Pilgrim costume? Or better yet, how can I find out who put Gnorman beside the fountain? That's a pretty public spot."

Sarah shook her head. "Not really. Most of the people who live at Lake Bliss go to bed early. That's the thing with retirement communities. They're past the late-night party stage. It's an adults-only complex; no one under age fifty-five is allowed to live there. During the daytime there are enough people milling about so that most ignore what everyone else is doing. My guess would be that whoever put him there did it in the middle of the night. Didn't you say that Naomi phoned you in the morning?"

"I had a feeling it would come down to this. Since the note said we weren't to touch him for four days, on the third night— that would be Wednesday—I need to do some surveillance and see who takes him away."

"Sounds like a plan." Sarah grinned from ear to ear. "I think you know what this means."

Amber squeezed her eyes shut. "I know. I'll call Stan."

STAN COULDN'T BELIEVE IT. He was humming. Humming. While planning a picnic lunch. Or rather, a picnic midnight snack.

He changed his tune to "The Teddy Bear's Picnic."

He'd asked Amber out for dinner a few times, and every time she'd turned him down. Not maliciously or to reject him. She simply didn't take him seriously.

This time they would share a more intimate meal than if they went to the Fancy Schmantzy on Main Street.

Thinking of the Fancy Schmantzy, his hands stilled in the middle of his grocery list. He couldn't remember the real name of the one high-class restaurant in town. Ever since he was a kid, the place had been called the Fancy Schmantzy. A storm had blown a tree into the sign, and since everyone knew the place by its nickname, Fred and Rita, the couple who owned the restaurant, never replaced the original sign. Now, a generation later, no one could even remember what the real name was.

The name didn't matter—only that it was a classy place to take a date. Not that he'd ever taken Amber there. But one day he would. They would share fresh baked bread before their meal, and afterward they'd order some fancy coffee and dessert, all while sitting at a dimly lit private table, with soft music playing in the background to enhance the mood.

Amber often complained about the ordinary brown color of her hair, but he liked it—not too dark, not too light, with a slight curl. She'd have it clipped up with some kind of barrette with sparkly stones on it, which would set off the sparkle in her jade-green eyes. Although she didn't know it, Stan considered her very pretty, and when she smiled she had the cutest dimples.

He forced himself back to the project at hand. Tomorrow night they couldn't light a smoky candle between them because they had to stay hidden, which meant their only source of light would be a small flashlight, with minimal usage. The music, instead of soft classical violins, would be chirping crickets and the splashing of the fountain in the distance, and maybe the croaking of the resident bullfrog. It would be almost like surveillance from *NCIS*, staking out a crime scene.

Stan stopped writing his grocery list and looked out the window in the direction of the Lake Bliss Retirement Village. It wasn't really a crime scene because no one had actually gone to the police station to report this to Bubba, maybe because he was at the party and already knew, at least unofficially. If anyone did report the disappearance, he wasn't sure how it would be classified. A missing gnome was more of a prank than a crime, although technically the gnome had been stolen. Was gnome gnapping a felony or a misdemeanor?

Stan shook his head. This wasn't Chicago or Los Angeles

or Miami or any of the big cities where felony crimes happened. This was Bloomfield, USA, where the city council proudly boasted having a flower of some kind on every corner. That wasn't really true, but they liked to think so.

He didn't want his evening with Amber to be laced with foreboding. He wanted to make it calm and relaxing, like a date.

If he were going to take Amber out on a date to the Fancy Schmantzy, he'd wear his best suit, maybe even a tie, and he'd polish his shoes. He didn't know what she'd wear, but he imagined a nice dress and matching strappy shoes that showed off her cute little toes.

But not tomorrow. Technically it was spring, but it still got cold out at night. Instead of their best clothes, they would be wearing heavy jeans layered with a T-shirt under a sweatshirt, bundled up in padded jackets. Plus he'd pack a quilt in the toolbox in the back of his truck, just in case.

He couldn't hold back a grin. In a way, he hoped they would get cold, just so he could snuggle with Amber under the blanket.

Stan shook the thoughts from his head and continued with his grocery list. He planned on making nice meaty sandwiches on those fancy rolls she liked, with thick mayo, cheddar cheese—sliced himself, not the processed stuff—and crispy lettuce. Instead of the rich dessert they served at the Fancy Schmantzy, he bought easy-to-eat chocolates, and he knew exactly the kind Amber liked best.

He also planned to bring a big thermos of coffee, only because Naomi had agreed to give them a key to her townhouse in case they had to use the facilities in the middle of the night.

It was going to be perfect. Nothing could go wrong. He had everything planned down to the last detail, including a spare battery for his camera that was currently in the charger.

He'd been planning for two days, and he was going to do everything he could to make the night just right, for however long it took, even if that meant all night.

He actually hoped it would be all night.

Just as he folded the paper and tucked it into his pocket, Stan's cell phone rang. His heart picked up in speed. It was nearly midnight, much too late for anyone to call unless something was wrong.

His dread changed to amusement when he read the caller ID. It was Amber, probably just making sure he still planned on keeping watch over Gnorman until someone arrived to spirit him away. It would feel good to tell her that he was not only nearly ready, but that he also had a surprise for her.

"Hey," he drawled as he answered the phone, mentally kicking himself at the sappy tone of his own voice.

"It looks like we won't have to do the surveillance tomorrow night. Naomi just called. She looked out the window on her way to bed, and Gnorman is gone. The note said four days, but I'm thinking whoever did this took him away early, probably guessing what we had planned. So it looks like we're back to square one."

Stan pressed his hand over the list in his pocket. He still felt like asking if she wanted to have a midnight picnic anyway, but he couldn't think of a reason to justify it except that he was an idiot. "Now what?"

She sighed, such a sad and lonely sound, and it made him want to run over to her house and make it better. "Now we wait. Again. The first note said we'd get another one, so there's nothing else we can do."

"There has to be something. How about if I come by your store tomorrow for lunch, and we can talk about it."

"I guess. Sure." She sighed again and went silent.

Not the most enthusiastic response, but she hadn't turned him down. So it wasn't a total loss. He even felt himself smiling. "I'll be there, and I'll bring lunch. See you tomorrow."

CHAPTER Five

Amber flinched as the bell above the door jingled, signaling someone's arrival.

She knew who it was. She hadn't been able to get him out of her mind. It wasn't something she could put her finger on, but he'd sounded strange when she phoned last night to cancel their spy mission. Almost like he'd sounded disappointed, which she couldn't understand. So far, he'd been everything he'd always been—a good friend who always came when he thought she needed him. For some unknown reason, something had changed since the day before. His response had made it sound like finding Gnorman had become personal to him.

"Hi, Stan," she muttered, knowing he'd again left his employees to run his repair shop while he came with offers of help. Despite knowing he planned to drop by, she still wasn't ready for him, and she didn't have a single idea worth discussing. "I'm sorry but . . ." her voice trailed off as she turned toward the door.

Instead of Stan, it was Pamela who had entered her store.

Pamela, who had an envelope with Amber's name on it in her hand.

Pamela held out the envelope. "This was on the ground in front of your door. I thought it might be a ransom note, so I brought it in."

The second Amber had it in her hand, she ripped open the top. Just as she grasped the letter inside, the door opened again. This time it really was Stan.

"It's another note," she said as she pulled the letter out of the envelope.

Instead of dropping it, this time she tucked the now-empty envelope under her arm and unfolded the letter. Pamela shuffled beside her while Stan stood behind them, reading over their shoulders.

Just like the last one, this note was constructed of words and letters cut out of the *Bloomfield Gazette*, but it wasn't as sloppy.

Gnorman was feeling very bereft.
he didn't like the fountain,
so he left.
he wanted something
adventurous, more than a
plank.
anyone who opposes him
will walk the plank!

Amber gritted her teeth at the bad poetry. "Gnorman didn't like the fountain? I don't understand what's going on. They didn't mention the trophy. I hope whoever has done this hasn't lost it." Her heart stopped for a second. "Or broken it."

Behind her Stan grunted and mumbled the words of the note, half reading them out loud. "Except for being cut out of the newspaper again, this note is quite different from the last. This one isn't the perpetrator giving us instructions. It seems to have gone into some kind of storytelling mode, like they've personified Gnorman. Strange."

Amber noticed that the word *strange* came up a lot recently, but it fit.

She read the note again. Unlike Stan, she read silently, then turned around to face him as she spoke. "You're right. I wonder what this means, trying something *more adventurous*. Walk the plank? That sounds like something out of *Pirates of the Caribbean*."

Stan's eyes lit up. "Yeah. But Jack Sparrow never walked the plank. He dove off of it. Then do you remember when he—"

Amber waved the note in the air. "Never mind Captain Jack. You're getting distracted." She lowered it and pointed to the part about walking the plank. "What does this mean? Why is someone doing this?" Although, the more she thought about it, there was only one reason that made sense.

Her membership to the garden club always stood on shaky ground. Initially Aunt Edna had convinced the board to approve her membership even though, at the time, the only live plants in her yard were a patch of Forget-Me-Nots that had spread from her neighbor's yard. For the first three years the voting committee approved memberships, approving hers only after her aunt reminded them what a delight it was for the winner of the spring contest to have Gnorman in their garden holding the trophy for the whole season. Her garden now supported many flowering plants, thanks to Stan, but it remained very basic, and not all that colorful. Only by the grace of God, and Gnorman, was her membership renewed every year. Without Gnorman, Amber had serious doubts that her garden would be approved. Even if they found the gnome with the trophy, enough damage had been done because of the disruption to the garden club's biggest celebration of the year that she couldn't be sure of her renewal. If the trophy was returned broken, or not returned at all, not only would her membership not be renewed, she'd be kicked out in disgrace.

She had no idea who, or why, but it appeared someone wanted her out of the garden club.

The best laid plans . . .

Had fallen short.

Amber turned to Pamela standing silently beside her. If anyone could help in a convoluted situation such as this, Pamela could. Pamela always had her fingers in many pies, and even though some people found her annoying, and even a busybody, everyone knew that Pamela's efforts often resolved most issues, especially issues that weren't her own.

"You're always a great . . . problem solver. What do you think?"

Pamela's brows knotted as she reread the note. "This says that Gnorman wants adventure, and it mentions walking the plank. My first thought is to look for a pirate ship."

"Here? In Bloomfield?" Stan rubbed the back of his neck with one hand. "We're slightly landlocked."

"I know that. But I read in the *Gazette* yesterday that the Bloomfield Cinema started running a pirate movie, I can't remember the name. On Sunday a few people came in dressed as pirates, which apparently raised some eyebrows. If we have pirate fanatics among us, maybe they know about a pirate ship where Gnorman would make someone walk the plank."

For lack of anything better, even though it wasn't really much of a clue, at least it was the start of one. Besides, a bad idea was better than no idea.

"Ronnie works at the theater every night," Amber said. "She's a garden club member, and she was at the party." Most important, Ronnie wasn't on the garden club's operating committee. Amber felt safer talking to Ronnie than Ronnie's mother, Minnie, who was on the board. She also knew Ronnie better than she knew Minnie. "I'm sure she'll want to help find Gnorman. If she remembers who the pirates were, I'm sure she'd tell us. I think talking to them would be a good idea."

Pamela beamed. "I think that's a great idea."

Amber bit her lip to hold back a grin. Of course she did. It was her idea.

Stan checked his watch. "It'll only take us ten minutes to get to Ronnie's place. We're good."

"How do you know where Ronnie lives?"

"I don't specifically, but I know her car, and I know which driveway it's in. I passed it on the way here."

Pamela also looked at her watch. "I can stay here and watch the store while you two go."

"Two?"

At her question, Stan grinned. "I have to be back in twenty minutes so Hank can go for lunch. I think that gives us enough time. Let's—"

Amber held up one hand. "I know," she grumbled. "Again. Let's go."

Just as Stan predicted, they made it to Ronnie's house in plenty of time—eight minutes, to be precise. Knowing that Ronnie worked late to clean up the theater after it closed, Amber felt hesitant about knocking until she heard Ronnie singing one of the songs they'd sung at church last Sunday—a little off key, but probably better than Amber could have done.

When Ronnie answered the door her cheeks were a bit pink, but she welcomed them in anyway.

Amber got straight to the point. "I heard that you're running a pirate movie at the theater, and you had a few pirates in your midst on the weekend."

Ronnie nodded. "Yes, we did. It was a little unnerving. I actually thought they were going to rob me, you know, with their masks and swords and all. But then two of them had a sword fight and one of the swords broke. So I knew they were only plastic."

One of Stan's eyebrows quirked. "Sword fight?"

"I know. But once I saw how much fun they were having—I mean they weren't even paying attention to me at the counter—it was a lot of fun to watch. They drew quite a crowd."

Amber's heart quickened. "Then a lot of people saw them. Do you know who they were?"

"No, they were high school kids. But I heard one of them use the name Tyler."

Great. Tyler. One of the most common names of the generation. "Did you hear any other names? Did you see if any of them were with anyone you know?"

"Sorry, no. It was kind of hard to hear with all the yelling 'Ahoy, mateys' and people cheering them. Why are you asking?"

"We're looking for a pirate ship somewhere in town because we think that's where someone put Gnorman, my little gnome, and the garden club's trophy."

Beside her, Stan checked his watch.

Ronnie nodded. "Yes, I remember them going missing at The Spring Fling party. Wasn't it nice that Becky won?"

Amber made a perfunctory smile. "Yes, she deserved to win. And we want to get the trophy back to her. Thanks for your help. I've got to get back to the store."

As she reached Stan's car parked behind Ronnie's in the

driveway, she turned to ask if any of his customers had teenage boys named Tyler, but Stan was nowhere to be seen. She almost started walking back to Ronnie's door, just in case he went back inside and she didn't notice, when he appeared at the side of Ronnie's house.

"Where were you? I thought you had to get back to let Hank go for lunch?"

He jerked his head toward Ronnie's backyard. "I wanted to check and make sure that Gnorman wasn't back there. It was a long shot, but that's probably why we came here instead of just phoning. We have to go after the long shots, because we don't have any short ones."

Although she knew he was trying to be funny, Amber didn't laugh at his joke. "And?"

"Nothing. I'll drive you back."

The drive was short and silent. When she returned to the store, she quickly thanked Pamela, who disappeared on her quest of whatever it was Pamela had been doing that day.

Of course, because Amber hoped to spend most of the afternoon in silence thinking about where Gnorman and the trophy could be, and where in town there could possibly be a pirate ship, she had more shoppers and browsers than she'd ever had in one day for this time of year. Most of them expressed their shock at the way Gnorman disappeared, but none of them had any suggestions or ideas. Because everyone in the building wanted to talk to her, and because she had to put back everything Pamela had picked up and replaced crooked, she closed up much later than usual.

She almost made it out the door when the phone rang. Since she was already late, a few minutes more wouldn't matter, so she picked up the phone.

"Gardens and Gifts Galore," she muttered, giving up on trying to sound cheerful. "How can I help your garden glow?"

"Amber, it's me, Ronnie. I'm at the theater. I don't know how this happened, but Gnorman is here, in the lobby. He's dressed up like a pirate. And he's got a note in his hand."

"I'll be right there." Amber hit the autodial on her cell phone to call Stan—and ran.

Chapter Six

A mber stood opposite the theater, waiting for a break in the traffic so she could run across the street. Of course, if Bubba caught her jaywalking, he'd stop and give her a stern talking-to, which would completely waste the time saved by not walking to the corner and crossing at the intersection. She checked both sides of the street for his blue uniform, and once assured he wasn't in the vicinity, she ran across the street at the next opening in traffic and headed for the theater.

The marquee emblazoned with the neon letters spelling out "Bloomfield Cinema" came right out of the fifties. Unlike the sign at the Fancy Schmantzy, this one hadn't been touched since then, with the exception of changing burned-out light bulbs. The ancient structure stuck out from the building like a large awning over the ticket window and sidewalk except, instead of being only a thin covering, it was about six feet thick.

She smiled, remembering trips to the old theater with the youth group from church. Once, because neither she nor Stan were really interested in the movie, they'd gotten distracted by the multitude of small lights on the underside of the huge protruding sign. The rest of the group had gone inside, but they'd stayed outside looking at the lights under the awning, comparing them to the stars in the sky. One thing had led to another, and they'd agreed that not even an astronomer could count the stars, which were infinite in the heavens, but they could actually count the lights.

They'd missed the opening of the movie but knew there were exactly 468 light bulbs on the underside of the Bloomfield Cinema sign.

Amber jogged to the ticket window where Ronnie's father sat reading a book. Before she could explain why she wasn't buying a ticket, he raised one hand and pointed with his thumb over his shoulder toward the door. "Stan's already here. They're in the lobby waiting for you."

She nodded her thanks and went inside.

Just as retro on the inside as out, the walls were a mixture of golds and browns, completed by a high valance ceiling painted in the same tones. To her left, at the concession stand, Minnie measured butter to pour into the popcorn machine. Amber waved to Minnie, who smiled and waved back as Amber continued walking.

To her right, a rail portioned off the area where people entered the lobby from outside, where she would have been if she'd actually bought a ticket. At the end of the section cordoned off by the rail stood a young man wearing black slacks and a uniform golf shirt that matched the décor. Movie posters decorated the theater walls and doors, but unlike the new, multiplex mega theaters in the cities, this building housed only one theater. One poster highlighted the current feature, which was the pirate movie she'd heard about, and a couple foretold upcoming movies. Another, covered with some kind of plastic preservative, looked like it had also come from the fifties with a picture of some handsome man and beautiful woman. She had no idea who they might be, but she was sure her parents, or more likely her grandparents, would have known.

Beyond the entrance to the theater, the water fountain protruded from the wall. Amber looked past the opening to the stairs leading to the balcony. It was a place she'd never been, and never would go. Whenever the youth group had gone up in the balcony, Stan had stayed with her in the lower level, not making fun of her intense fear of heights. The rest of the group had thought it very romantic, but Amber knew it was just Stan being kind.

Behind her, a few patrons had already arrived early for the movie. Unfortunately, none of them dressed as pirates.

But there was one pirate in attendance.

Gnorman.

Not a Pittsburgh Pirate, but the classic kind. A blue vest with a bright red hat, along with a pirate's eye patch complimented a child's plastic sword in his raised hand, where the trophy should have been. Standing beside Gnorman were Ronnie and Stan, neither of them dressed as pirates.

Unaware of Amber watching, they both gestured toward Gnorman as they talked, not paying attention to anything going on around them.

Stan looked like he did most times she saw him at the end of the day, like he'd just crawled out from beneath a car, and given the time, he probably just had. Grease streaked his dark brown hair, and his usually clean-shaven chin sported a five o'clock shadow, probably because it was now nearly seven.

She had to smile. All their lives, from the playground to school to youth group outings, and even college, Stan had always saved the dirty jobs for last in the day. He'd been clean as the proverbial whistle at lunch; by the end of the day, he looked like he'd been rolling in the pit under the hydraulic hoist. Today must have been quite a day fighting his mechanical demons.

Ronnie, on the other hand, hadn't yet started her workday, and she was the opposite of Stan—perfectly groomed with her short black hair combed gently over her ears. Unlike the young man at the end of the rail, Ronnie wore no uniform, but instead a dated outfit Amber could only describe as old film star casual. Her perfection made Stan look even less so.

Ronnie laughed at something Stan said, reached to brush something off his shirt, and rested her hand on his forearm as she spoke.

Amber felt her smile fade. She cleared her throat and began walking toward them.

The second they saw her, Stan reached up, about to run his fingers through his hair, froze, then rammed his hands into his pockets. "Here he is. I can see the reference to walking the plank."

One of the few early customers walked toward the concession stand and started checking out the snacks for sale. "I don't think you need me," Ronnie muttered. "I have to get to work. Excuse me."

As she left them, Stan pulled his hand out of his pocket, plucked the envelope from Gnorman's hand, and gave it to Amber.

After she ripped it open and pulled out the paper inside, Stan shuffled closer to read the note over her shoulder.

Amber sniffed. Usually by the end of the day she could smell the fruits of his labor on him, but today he was especially potent. "Nice. Ode de Oil. Tough day?"

"It's actually Ode de Transmission Fluid. My day isn't over yet. I have to go back."

Guilt roared through her. "I'm so sorry. I shouldn't have called."

He looked down at her and smiled. "It's okay. I want to help you find Gnorman. With the way this has been shaping up, it's really piqued my curiosity. Finding Gnorman dressed like a pirate makes me picture Captain Jack, and I'm ready for an adventure."

"You know what happened to the curious cat, don't you?" She couldn't help but smile back at him. "Speaking of pirate adventures, do you remember back in middle school when you thought it would be a great idea to build that raft and sail across Lake Bliss?" They'd found out the hard way that all the sticks they'd gathered and woven into a makeshift raft wouldn't stay together with the constant jostling of the two of them laying on it, paddling with their hands.

Stan broke out into a laugh. "Yeah. We nearly made it half way across before it fell apart. What a couple of drowned rats we were that day."

"That's for sure." They'd never been so glad for the swimming lessons they'd been forced to take as children, together of course. They'd learned the hard way how much harder it was to swim in clothes than a swimsuit. Amber's smile dropped as she thought more about what had happened that day.

She'd been wearing shorts and a T-shirt with flip-flops, which had floated away, but Stan had been wearing full jeans and sneakers. When waterlogged they'd become very heavy, very fast, making it impossible for him to swim. The scariest moment of her life, more scary than being at the top of the Ferris wheel, had been watching Stan sink while frantically trying to tug off his sneakers in the middle of the lake. She'd treaded water for all she was worth to keep both of them afloat until he managed to loosen the laces enough to get his feet out of his sneakers. Suddenly the thought of being a *drowned rat* wasn't so funny anymore.

She pushed the thought of losing Stan from her head to concentrate on the new and less dangerous adventure at hand—the new note.

Again, this one was made from words cut from the *Bloomfield Gazette*.

avast! me hearty and scurvy knave!
i have the treasure, hidden in my cave.
you will never catch me, i will win this race.
this is my adventure, so revel in the chase.

Stan reached out to steady the paper. "Scurvy Knave? I think someone reads too many bad adventure novels. But the poetry is kind of creative."

She read the note again. "I just noticed something. This one is different. The others were worded so someone else is talking about Gnorman, but this one is worded like he's talking to us."

"You're right. What do you think that means?"

She had no idea, but one thing she did know. They were no closer to getting the trophy back than they had been before they found Gnorman again. She looked down at her little gnome, attired like a semifamous pirate. "My best guess is that we're supposed to leave him here. I hope this 'revel in the chase' doesn't mean what I think it means."

Stan reached down and tapped the tip of the plastic sword with his index finger. "I have a bad feeling that it does." He sighed. For the first time since the debacle in Becky's garden, he sounded tired. "I guess we'll just have to follow him, wherever he goes. For now, we have to do it their way. But don't worry. Whoever is doing this is bound to either get tired of it, or make a mistake. Besides, how long can it possibly last?"

CHAPTER Seven

Stan wiped his hands on the rag, then shoved it in his pocket. "We've been friends since high school. Do you think I'd cheat you? You really need a new alternator."

Hayden clenched his teeth. "This is going to be expensive, isn't it?"

"Let's define expensive." Satisfied his hands were clean, Stan pulled the keyboard toward him, typed the password, and called up his estimate calculator. "It's less expensive than replacing your transmission, and less expensive than if you'd blown a head gasket. The way it's running, you're lucky you made it here."

Hayden sighed again. "I know I don't have a choice. Go ahead and fix it. Do I get a courtesy car?"

Stan looked through the window of his lobby to the parking lot. This was Bloomfield. Of course he didn't have courtesy cars. The only vehicle in the lot that didn't belong to a customer or his mechanics was his pickup.

He turned back to his friend. "Why do you need a courtesy car? You live within walking distance to work."

"I'll walk to work." Hayden's frown changed to a grin. "But I have a date tonight and I need a car."

Stan gave his friend a light punch on the shoulder. "Dude." It was good to see his friend dating. Shortly after they graduated from college Hayden had met Marissa and married her after a whirlwind romance. The quick marriage ended with a quick divorce when Hayden caught Marissa cheating on him. Hayden was a good guy, and he deserved to find a woman as faithful as he was, who would share his life. "Anyone I know?"

Hayden looked out the window, down the street. "Actually, yeah. You know her pretty well."

Stan ran through a mental list of women Hayden might want to date that he knew well. If he had to think of dateable women, he'd pick a woman with a good sense of humor, someone sensible, honest, trustworthy, and of the same faith. Of course having a good job would help.

So he ran through a mental list of the women their age at church.

The first woman who would be a good one for his friend was Amber.

He imagined Hayden taking Amber out for dinner. He grinned, picturing Amber bartering with Hayden over who got the crust from the home-baked bread that came before the meal. She'd win, obsess about putting too much butter on it and eat it anyway, the whole time complaining about putting ten pounds on her butt. Two minutes later she would take another piece and say she was going to jog around the block when she was finished eating, then not do it. They would laugh at each other's jokes and have a great time, and Hayden would take her home.

Stan's smile faltered.

Hayden would want to kiss her good night.

His eyes narrowed. "Who?" he asked, knowing his voice came out clipped, but he didn't care.

Hayden's brows arched. "Your cousin Crystal. That's okay, isn't it?"

The picture of Amber smiling faded to his cousin's face, then merged back to Amber. Instead of looking at Hayden, he turned to his computer and called up his inventory list to see if he had the right alternator for Hayden's car, or if he would have to order it. "She's a good choice. Crystal's not seeing anyone right now." Neither was Amber. Which suited him just fine. Although he didn't know why the thought of Amber and Hayden together bothered him. Hayden was his best friend, and he wanted to see his best friend happy, especially after his short and unhappy marriage. He also wanted to see Amber happy. He and Amber had been friends since forever, and they'd seen each other through all their low points, as well as their high points.

He waited while Hayden removed his key from his key ring. Stan tagged it, then stuck his hand in his pocket and pulled out his own keys. "You can borrow my truck," he muttered while twisting his key off the ring. "Make sure the gas gauge is in the same place when I get it back tomorrow."

Hayden accepted the key and attached it to his own ring. "Thanks. I really appreciate this. How are you going to get home tonight? I guess Amber can give you a ride. I hear you two have been spending a lot of time together lately trying to find her gnome. I wonder where he'll turn up next after the theater, and what he'll be wearing."

In Bloomfield news traveled fast, which Stan had always found amusing. Until now.

"I don't know why this town has a newspaper. Does anyone need to read it?"

Hayden shrugged his shoulders. "Sure. It's got lots of good stuff in it."

Including lots of words that were currently being used to make ransom notes that didn't have a ransom.

One corner of Hayden's mouth turned up. "They have a contest going at the *Gazette* to see who guesses the next outfit."

"Did you enter?"

"Yup. I think next time he'll be a ninja. Crystal thinks he'll be a pilot."

And Stan thought Gnorman should just be a gnome, holding a trophy in Becky's garden. "You go have a good time with Crystal. I'll call Amber and see if she can give me a ride." Maybe once he was home she'd wait while he had a quick shower, and they could go out for supper. Where he'd let her have the crust with all the butter she wanted. And hopefully she would wear her favorite purple sneakers, because this time, before they got back in the car, they were making a trip around the block.

AMBER DUMPED THE WATER out of the spaghetti, set it back on the stove, then nearly jumped out of her skin when Stan appeared beside her.

"What are you doing here?" she gasped as she pressed her hand over her pounding heart.

"I live here. What are you doing?"

She glanced at the clock on Stan's stove, then back to Stan. For someone who could shower and get dressed in the amount of time it took her to boil a pot of noodles, he looked good. He'd picked a nice pair of dark jeans and a button-down shirt instead of his usual casual evening attire of sweat pants and his favorite holey T-shirt. Not only was he clean and well dressed, but he smelled good too, like some kind of woodsy soap and shampoo.

"I made supper. I can't believe you're down here already.

Did you even get wet?" Yet, as the words came out of her mouth, she knew he had. She'd heard the water running, and all traces of grease were gone from his skin and hair. If it wasn't her imagination, he'd also shaved.

He looked good enough to be in a magazine, or on the cover of one of the romance novels she liked to read.

Instead of fantasizing about Stan smiling from the cover of a book, she stirred the sauce and turned off the heat. "Everything is done. How did you get ready so fast?"

"I don't know why you say that. I also don't know why it takes women so long to shower and get dressed."

Amber spun around so fast that her hair flew into her eyes. "How do you know how long it takes a woman to shower?" She stood, pointing at him with the spoon, not caring that a drop of red sauce landed on her sock while she waited to hear who it was that had showered at his house. She just might have to claw the woman's eyes out.

His eyes widened. "I don't know. Movies, I guess. I also remember my mother tying up the bathroom. When I was in college I had to get up extra early to shower before her or there was no time, and no hot water."

She felt herself sag. Kathy was safe.

"What? Why are you looking at me like that?" He blinked, then walked to the cupboard, took out a couple of plates, and returned to stand beside her.

"Nothing," Amber mumbled as she piled a couple of helpings of pasta onto the plates Stan held over the stove.

The concept of Stan being so familiar with a woman that she would use his shower nearly made her heart stop. She didn't like to think of Stan that way, but he was quite a handsome man, and he was out there in the dating universe.

Some women might not have thought that a mechanic was a very glorious profession, but no one knew Stan like she did.

He was smart, funny, and a good businessman, even though he wore streaked blue coveralls instead of a three-piece suit. He ran his business at a reasonable profit, but with compassion when he knew someone was faced with a costly repair. He set his standards high, and his customers and his employees all respected him.

He also had his standards for dating set high, waiting for the right woman whom God would one day put in his path.

They never talked specifically about such things when they were together, but the topic of what happened behind closed doors had come up at the single adults group at church. While it had been an embarrassing conversation for the group, it didn't take a rocket scientist to see that Stan was saving himself for marriage, as was she. Of course, neither of them ever having a long-time serious relationship made it so much easier to stay away from temptation. As for her, she'd never even been inside a man's house without a group, except for Stan's, because that didn't count.

He continued to hold out the plates. "I told you we could go out and it would be my treat," he muttered while she spooned the sauce on top of the noodles. "You didn't have to cook."

"Look at the time. Even though you were fast in the shower, if we went out we'd only be leaving now. Instead, we're ready to eat."

He grumbled something she couldn't hear as he set the plates on the table, then folded his hands on the table and waited.

Amber also folded her hands, but she wasn't ready to bow her head. "Excuse me? I didn't hear what you said."

"I said if we went out we would have had something better than plain old spaghetti."

"Spaghetti is good. It's also fast, easy, and inexpensive. Besides, it's not the weekend."

"Hayden is taking Crystal out tonight. It's okay to go out for dinner on a weekday. Everybody's got to eat."

She looked down at her spaghetti, trying to imagine Hayden and Crystal together, but she couldn't. Stranger things had happened. "Good for them, I hope it works. What about us? Are we going to eat?"

His cheeks reddened, which she thought adorable, despite his crabby mood. She'd always thought it was cute that Stan was one of a few men she knew who blushed.

"Sorry." He cleared his throat and made a short prayer of thanks for their food, but instead of starting to eat, he played with his spaghetti, pushing it around on his plate.

"You look like something's bothering you, and I doubt it's about your friend and your cousin."

He was silent for a few seconds before putting the fork down. "I heard that the *Gazette* is having a contest about Gnorman and what kind of costume he'll have on the next time he turns up. That makes me think someone at the newspaper might be behind this."

Amber's fork froze an inch from her mouth. "Are you kidding me? Don't you think it's a little farfetched that Randy, Bailey, or Jayne would do such a thing?" Although a publicity stunt or conspiracy made to increase circulation was certainly better than the alternative that had been rolling around in her head.

"Think about it. If the contest boosts sales, that will also get more advertising revenue, which is where the big money is."

Amber lowered her fork. "While entertaining, I don't think it's likely. Although we do know that whoever is doing this at least takes the newspaper."

"That's no help at all. That's pretty much the entire population of Bloomfield. Like you said, it's probably someone in the garden club."

She didn't want to think that, but she couldn't help it. She didn't know what she'd done to make someone want to get her kicked out in disgrace, yet it was happening. Only no one knew she would lose more than just her membership.

She raised her head to make eye contact as she spoke. "I know we're starting to get desperate for a real clue, but I don't think it could be any of them. I don't think anyone else who works at the *Gazette* is in the garden club, so that's a dead lead."

"The other day you made a comment about someone wanting you out of the garden club and it's really bothering me. Why do you think someone would do that to you?"

"Because I can't even grow vegetables, never mind flowers. I don't belong in the garden club."

"You've got a nice enough garden that meets minimum standards, and everyone likes you."

"No, there's someone who very obviously doesn't like me."

He sighed. "I don't think that—"

The ringing phone interrupted Stan's words. He shifted in his chair, pulled his cell phone out of his pocket, greeted the caller, and turned to Amber. "Yes, she's here."

Amber froze as she watched Stan nodding while the other person talked. "We'll be right there." He flipped the phone shut, returned it to his pocket, and stood. "That was Tucker. Tonight he's on duty instead of Bubba." Stan grinned. "I'm on his speed-dial in case something goes wrong with the police car. Anyway, he was doing his rounds and he says there's an envelope stuck in the door of your store. If we get it now instead of morning, maybe if we get to where it says Gnorman is going to be, and if they're still there, we'll catch them in the act."

That was a lot of "ifs" but it didn't matter. Amber stood so fast she nearly knocked her plate off the table. "Let's go. And this time, I'm driving."

CHAPTER Eight

B ut this note doesn't say where he will be. It just says what kind of costume they've put him in." Amber held up the note so Stan could read it over her shoulder. "This isn't any help."

there's something funny
going down.
it might be that gnome man's
a clown.
when the day is done,
he'll make a pun
and everyone else will
have lots of fun.

Stan groaned. "Does someone think they're being funny? Is this a hint that we're just a couple of Bozos?"

Amber lowered the note and turned to him. "Are you kidding?"

His blank expression told her that he wasn't.

Amber glanced down the block, as if Gnorman would just be there, waiting to be discovered. "Did Tucker have a time frame? Did he say how long it was from the last time he looked at my store door to the time he found the note?"

"No. I think he'd just started his rounds. That means it could be anytime from when you closed and left to when he phoned."

Which really wasn't long. She'd driven to Stan's shop, picked him up and gone to his house, made a pot of spaghetti, and they'd barely sat down to start eating. It hadn't been even an hour.

She looked up at the sky. It wasn't dark yet, so likely whoever had slipped the note there hadn't yet put Gnorman in his designated location for the night.

"What's the matter? Are you locked out of your store?"

Amber spun around.

Libby stood at the edge of the sidewalk, holding the bright red leash that secured her little dog. Amber smiled. No matter how rotten she felt, seeing Libby's cute little miniature schnauzer always cheered her up.

"No, I just needed to stop by." As she spoke, she ran her finger along the paper in her hand. Libby was always good at solving problems, making her wonder if she should tell Libby about the new note. For a second she considered Tobie. Schnauzers, even little ones, were known for their noses, possibly little Tobie could help sniff out Gnorman's current location.

She hunkered down to pet Tobie, and without Libby seeing, put the note under the dog's nose so he could sniff it.

Above her, Libby smiled. "Tobie and I were just at the dog park and we're on our way home for supper. We're a little late today. I was busy making my cinnamon pecan coffee cake, but you know Tobie. He just had to have his daily constitution, and I needed my walk for the day too."

At the word *constitution*, Tobie's stubby little tail started to wag. He ignored the paper and turned around to look back toward the dog park.

Amber stood. "I should let you go. Have a nice evening."

Instead of leaving, Libby rested one hand on Amber's arm. "I know you've been stressing about the escapades of your little gnome. Can I give you some of the cinnamon pecan coffee cake I just made? It's still warm. You know I don't eat the sweets myself, but I like to have something on hand for guests."

Amber opened her mouth to decline Libby's kind offer, but beside her, Stan's eyes lit up.

"Cinnamon pecan coffee cake?" She could almost see his mouth watering. "Really?"

Amber forced herself to smile. "That would be wonderful. We'd love to have some of your yummy cake."

"Then come with me." Libby waved for them to follow her, but Stan touched Libby's shoulder, stopping her before she started walking home.

"We've got Amber's car. I know you're getting some exercise for you and Tobie right now, but how about if we give you a ride the rest of the way."

Libby waved one hand in the air. "Nonsense. You two can take the car to my house, and I'll walk Tobie the rest of the way home." Before Stan could protest, Libby resumed her walk.

Amber couldn't help but grin. "I guess that's decided. Let's get in the car and go. It's not far, she'll only be ten minutes behind us."

Guilt washed over Stan's face. "I feel like I'm being rude. We can't let her walk while we take the car."

"We're not being rude. She's out walking her dog, and she's now walking half a block ahead of us. If you want to walk with her, go ahead. I'll meet you there."

Stan glanced back and forth between Libby and the car, shrugged his shoulders, gave Amber a quick wave, and jogged off to join Libby.

Good ol' Stan.

Amber got back in her car and drove the few blocks to Libby's house, making sure to wave as she passed Stan and Libby, chatting as they headed to Libby's house.

Walking down the path to Libby's house, Amber sighed as a case of the warm fuzzies enveloped her. She adored Libby's house. The stately but homey two-story red brick house had two immaculate white columns in front for the porch. In large beds surrounding the porch, colorful azaleas bloomed. Two huge old oak trees in the front yard shaded the front of the house when the sun was up, keeping it cool until later in the day.

Of course the best garden was in the back. That was where Libby kept her roses and all the other summer blooming flowers, behind the house, out of the hot midday sun. Like the Lake Bliss Retirement Village, Libby also had a fountain in the middle of her garden. It was an ongoing but fun argument for the community to say which fountain had come first.

Since this year Becky had won the now-missing trophy, Amber hadn't seen Libby's early garden. Libby was never shy about showing off her prize roses, just like most of the people who were on the operating board for the garden club. Amber didn't think Libby would mind if she went into the backyard to see what Libby had planted this year.

The clever secret latch for the gate wasn't really so secret, and she pulled the right board to gain access. The large fence provided not only security for Libby's little dog, but Libby valued her privacy. Amber only went in because Libby had invited her. The yard, including the magnificent garden, was Libby's haven.

Sure enough, Libby's spring garden was awash with color. Before checking out the flowers, Amber stood still, closed her eyes, and inhaled deeply, wanting what she could never have—to enjoy the beautiful fragrance of all the gorgeous blooms in her own backyard, just like this.

After a few deep breaths she opened her eyes and turned to the corner where Libby grew her favorite roses, a brilliant yellow blossom, rare, and difficult to grow. Amber couldn't remember the genus except that it was a number. It was an ongoing joke at the garden club that the year Libby turned the age of her favorite rose's name, there was going to be one very big party.

Strangely, if she had to guess Libby's age, she would have said that Libby was older than Kathy, and that party still hadn't happened.

She turned and made her way to the corner when a small outcropping of a hideous combination of clashing colors stopped her in her tracks.

The click of Libby's gate echoed, followed by a symphony of yipping.

"Amber? Where are you? Tobie led us to the back, so we knew you were here. I can make some tea and we can . . ." Libby's voice trailed off. "Oh! How did your little gnome get here?"

———— ❦ ————

STAN CLEARED HIS THROAT. "I don't know what to say. He's kinda . . ." Words failed him.

"Ugly?" Amber replied with more of a question than an answer, but they obviously shared the same opinion.

Libby dropped Tobie's leash and plunked her fists on her hips. "You have to get him out of here. He clashes with my Forty-Niners. He's absolutely garish." Libby's face skewed with clear distaste at the gaudy mismatch of Gnorman's bright clown costume with the blended milder tones of her valued roses.

Tobie, however, had no hesitation. He walked up to Gnorman, sniffed him, shuffled into the right angle, and raised one hind leg.

"No!" Amber screeched, and she ran to the dog. She scooped Tobie into her arms and backed up a few steps without putting him down.

Libby's cheeks turned as pink as the flowers beside the house that Stan couldn't remember the name and pulled her dog out of Amber's arms. "I'm so sorry. He's a feisty little fellow, as you know. Your Gnorman doesn't belong here, so Tobie needs to show Gnorman who's boss."

Stan bit his lower lip. That wasn't the way Stan showed his employees at the shop who was the boss. He merely signed their paychecks.

While Amber stood there gaping, Stan went to the gnome and pulled yet another note out of his hand. Just like the others, it was constructed from words cut out of the *Gazette*.

for now, Gnorman is not on
the run
he is stopping to have
some fun
so do not be a party
pooper.
Bring out the balloons,
it will be just super!

Libby tapped one finger to her chin. "This poem has kind of a lilt to it, don't you think?"

"Never mind the prose. What is this note trying to say?" Stan clenched his jaw. "I've always hated clowns. Now I hate them even more." He turned to Amber, still staring at Gnorman's brassy outfit. "Have you ever enjoyed a clown?"

Amber shook her head. "I've never liked slapstick. I can't see anything funny about people falling or doing things that would normally hurt."

Libby absently patted Tobie while she spoke. "Amber, dear, clowns can be funny with their outlandish shoes, tooting horns, colorful costumes, and painted faces." She then frowned at Gnorman. "Except for that one. He certainly isn't funny, at least not in *my* garden."

While it was true that clowns did have painted faces, Gnorman didn't. The only coloring added was a sponge cut into a round shape that covered his nose. Amber approached Gnorman, poked the sponge, and swiped her thumb across his cheek. "At least they didn't paint his face. That stuff is hard enough to get off of skin. I don't know if that would have damaged his paint." She extended one hand toward Gnorman. "I'll get the trophy back. I promise I will." If it wasn't his imagination, Stan thought he detected a break in Amber's voice, like she was trying not to cry.

Libby nodded. "Of course you will. But what are we going to do right now? Whoever put Gnorman here wasn't thinking very clearly."

"Why not?"

"Because I have a dog." Libby grinned ear to ear, accenting the laugh-lines at the corners of her eyes. "Naomi didn't catch whoever is doing this while he was in her territory, but Tobie and I certainly will."

Stan kept his lips sealed, not wanting to mention that whoever put Gnorman in Libby's yard had obviously done so despite Libby's watchdog wannabe. However, if Libby had taken this as one-upmanship between herself and Naomi, this was something he could use to their advantage. Still, he would have preferred to do his own surveillance, but he didn't want to be the one to cause the dog to bark, then ignore the dog's barking when the Gnome Gnapper really showed up for what was turning out to be a series of middle-of-the-night rendezvous.

"Let's go inside. I'll start some tea, and we can let Tobie do his doggy duties."

He pressed his fingers to the small of Amber's back to guide her toward Libby's house. "That's great, but if you don't mind, if Amber can loan me her car keys, I'd like to go home and get some chicken wire to put around Gnorman first."

CHAPTER Nine

Amber took advantage of a slow morning to once again go over her financial statements.

Nothing was any better than last week, but at least it wasn't any worse.

Only because she hadn't been kicked out of the garden club, the home base of all her best customers, yet.

In what she knew was a futile effort, she'd placed an order that she couldn't afford to include a stock of nongardening craft items, praying she could expand her business before she lost it all.

She'd taken a gamble, except it was probably already too late. Soon it would be time to pay the piper. Or, she could make another appointment for a loan at the bank, and be turned down again, just to be sure.

Amber lowered her forehead to the desk and covered her head with her arms. She didn't know how, but she'd made it through the recession. She'd gone down to her last penny, but her financials had hovered just barely above going into the red.

She'd thought she was safe. Recovery was slow, but it was recovery. A few more years, and she could have her loan paid off. Her parents, if they had still been alive, would have been proud of her.

But three months ago Uncle Henry had called in her loan. When she hadn't been able to get another loan from the bank, he'd said he'd give her two years to pay off everything she owed him, but one late payment and she would forfeit and have to liquidate in order to pay what she could, which wouldn't cover the loan. The worst condition of the loan said that if her business failed she would move to Chicago and work for her uncle until he saw fit that all the money, plus interest, was paid off to his satisfaction, and Uncle Henry set his own interest rate. Everything had been fine and fair while her parents were alive, but when the economy took a nosedive and people stopped buying luxury items, her profit margin plummeted to bare survival. With careful planning and a lot of cutbacks, she had survived. Until her uncle decided to play dirty.

The bank didn't consider a craft store hovering on the edge of going into the red in a failing economy a worthwhile credit risk, plus she was locked into her lease for another four years.

Even though her uncle had doubled the interest on the loan, with her steady stream of customers from the garden club she was able to make it if she lived on macaroni and wieners. Her car, paid off and an old beater with the minimum insurance, was cheaper to keep running than pay delivery fees on her orders. Stan, of course, kept her old car running in tip-top shape, and even though he didn't know why she insisted on keeping the old thing instead of getting something newer and in better condition, he never complained.

But if the board members of the garden club kicked her out for losing their historic trophy, that portion of her client base would be gone. Losing that chunk of income would be the straw to ultimately break the camel's back. Everything she'd worked for in the last five years since she'd opened her business would be gone. She'd have to close her doors and declare bankruptcy to get out of the lease. Then she'd have to move to Chicago, if her car made it that far, enslaved to work in a cubicle in a high-rise office tower in downtown Chicago until her uncle released her from her contract. Or he would make her manage one of his stores when she would rather be managing her own. Uncle Henry wouldn't give her the loan without that codicil, and his lawyer had drawn up the contract, so she doubted she could take it to court. Even if she did, Uncle Henry had more money for lawyer fees than she did, so her chances for winning would be slim. Bottom line, either way, she lost. She couldn't be late for a single payment.

She didn't hate Chicago; she'd even been there once. It was a nice city. But it was big, with crowds and noise and traffic jams and construction and tall buildings and bad air, and everything else that went with a big city. She'd been born and raised in small-town Bloomfield, where everyone seemed to either know each other or at least recognize them in passing. A person could walk to the shopping center, or work, if they wanted to, and probably know most of the people they saw well enough to at least chat with them, unlike a big city sea of nameless faces. Her friends were in Bloomfield, and even if she didn't have any close family left here except for Great-Aunt Edna and Uncle Bill, she had Stan, who was better than family.

Bloomfield was too big to realistically know everyone; after all, the population, according to the sign welcoming visitors to their small city, boasted 9,978 people. Most people still waved to each other even if they didn't know one another's names.

In her mind's eye, she pictured Mayor Woody's latest campaign to raise the population by those last twenty-two babies to reach ten thousand people. Here in Bloomfield, everyone knew he was serious, that it wasn't just a joke.

When she left town with her tail between her legs, that would make it twenty-three more people needed to reach Mayor Woody's goal.

Amber nearly banged her head against the desktop to knock some sense into herself. She hadn't left yet. For now she was still a member of the garden club, and for now the garden club members stopped at her store first when they wanted accessories for their garden, or for unique gifts. If she could get this figured out and find out who was doing this, and why, and get Gnorman and the trophy back where they belonged, one day she would look back at this and laugh, even though she certainly wasn't laughing now.

Her mind went back to the weeks before her store had been egged. Usually such an act was performed by bored teens, the same with dumping their soda all over her car. But the way someone taunted her, holding the trophy over her head, then running away with it again, even though they never actually showed it to her, was very adult. She didn't want to play this game, but she had no choice if she hoped to recover the cherished trophy. Whoever wanted to pay her back for something had made her punishment into a cat and mouse game that she couldn't win. She had to play the game until she either got the trophy back . . . or she didn't.

More depressed than ever, Amber shut down her computer program and returned to the store to clear some space for what hopefully would be fast-selling and profitable items.

Maybe, if she made some *Christmas in July* signs and decorations, she could reap the benefits of some early holiday shopping, which was of course her busiest time of the year.

All her decorations were at home in the attic. Stan could help her bring them down. He would probably even get a laugh out of putting up Christmas decorations when the temperature would soon be in the nineties. He'd complain about it being too hot for Christmas. Then she would remind him that in Australia it was indeed hot like that in December, even hotter.

Amber sighed. It wasn't like she was desperate.

Yet, actually, she was.

Instead of getting clinically depressed, Amber picked up the wholesaler's catalog and paged through it again. She stopped to check out the Thanksgiving section when the phone rang.

The caller ID showed Libby's name and number.

Her heart pounded in her chest. If little Tobie had sniffed out the Gnome-Gnapper-slash-Trophy-Taker, all her problems would be solved and life could go back to normal. Or as normal as could be until she paid off her loan shark uncle.

Before she could recite her greeting for the store, Libby interrupted her. "I'm so sorry, dear. Gnorman was here for four whole days, and this morning, when I got up to water my Forty-niners, he was gone. I don't know why Tobie didn't alert me, but this means only one thing."

Amber held her breath. "What?"

Libby's voice lowered. "It means Tobie knows the person who came into our yard and took your little Gnorman away."

Finally the list narrowed. Amber reached for a pen and paper, waiting, pen poised and ready. "Then who could it be?"

"Someone in the garden club, of course."

"Which means how many people? Who is familiar with Tobie?"

"Tobie comes with me to every meeting. He knows everyone. So if we count the two people who just joined, that means seventy-nine members."

Amber's heart sank. "Well. . . . That helps." Or not.

"There's more. Whoever took Gnorman left an envelope. I haven't opened it. I'm leaving the house now, so I can drop it off at your store for you to read. I'll see you soon. Bye, now." The dial tone sounded in her ear.

Amber nearly groaned out loud. Another note.

She pulled the handset away from her ear but didn't hang up. Instead, she stared at it so long that the tone changed to an annoying beep.

When she finally hung up, she did the only thing she could think to do.

She called Stan.

AS THE SHOP DOOR closed behind him, Stan could already feel his ears burning. He suspected the guys had started talking about him before he reached the parking lot.

He'd taken more breaks from work in the past few weeks than he had in the entire past year, and he knew the guys had started talking about him before he was out of the parking lot. But he didn't care. Amber needed him, and he wasn't going to let her down.

He made the short trip to Amber's house in record time, almost as if everyone got out of the way of his pickup. This might be true, if there were many cars on the road, which there weren't. Still, it didn't matter.

Something wasn't right. He couldn't put his finger on it, but today he heard something in Amber's voice that was different. Instead of talking to her about it on the phone, he needed to see her.

He found Amber sitting on the stool behind the counter, staring at the latest note. Her eyes didn't appear quite focused, just looking at it without actually reading it.

It unnerved him.

Before he could think of what to say, she turned to him with an expression almost like her dog had died, except she didn't have a dog. Her gnome was missing, but since Gnorman wasn't real, that wasn't the same.

He cleared his throat to clear his brain, but it didn't work. "What's up?" was the best he could think of.

She sighed and looked down at the note, giving him the impression that she deliberately avoided making direct eye contact. He didn't like that.

"I don't know," she mumbled with her lips barely moving.

He strode to the counter to see for himself. "I don't get it. This looks exactly the same as the last note."

"It is the last note. The new note from Libby's house only said to follow the clue from the last note. I don't see any clue here."

He read it again, hating clowns even more. "I don't either."

Without asking, she pushed what must have been the new note across the counter to him.

He picked up it. It was constructed exactly the same as the previous notes—words and letters cut out from the newspaper.

follow the clue from the last note.

"You're right. That's exactly what it says."

"So here's the last note. All it says is not to be a party pooper and bring out the balloons. There are no balloons here. I don't even own balloons. I hate balloons. They're not environmentally friendly."

What a somber pair they made. He hated clowns, and she hated balloons. If the clue was about them being party poopers, they both were certainly that. Although he didn't think that was going to help find Gnorman and the trophy.

Instead he put his finger on the note and looked at her face, even though she had turned away. "Maybe the clue is that

Gnorman is going back to Becky's garden, with the trophy inside a balloon."

She made a very unladylike snort. "That would be too easy. I don't suppose you have any balloons at your shop or your house?"

"Jordan's wife bought me one of those foil helium balloons for my last birthday and brought it to work. The guys all sang 'Happy Birthday,' badly, I might add, then Hank accidentally let the balloon go, and it's still stuck up in the ceiling rafters."

"I don't think that would count."

He waited for her to say something more, but she didn't.

With the last outfit, bad as it was, Stan had been starting to get into the mood to follow Gnorman around town until whoever was playing cat and mouse with them decided to give it up or decided they were worthy of the prize. He'd taken it as a challenge, and he'd never met a challenge he didn't follow.

The last challenge was when Amber told him that even though he was a decent cook, he could never make decent deviled eggs. He'd taken her up on that, then while he'd waited for the eggs to cook, he'd turned on the television and got distracted watching the last period of an NHL playoff game, and the eggs boiled dry. He hadn't known eggs could explode. He still found pieces of egg in the strangest places in his kitchen. But he'd met her challenge, and done it again without turning on the television, and made a very tasty batch.

But he didn't know what kind of challenge could involve balloons.

Amber sighed, poked the note with her finger, and then . . . nothing. She wasn't excited. She barely looked interested. Usually a stickler for details, she liked little mysteries. Today she seemed lost, discouraged, and even a little depressed.

Stan walked around the counter to stand beside her instead of having a barrier between them. "You're kind of quiet. Is something wrong? Not that Gnorman and the trophy going missing like this isn't wrong enough, but something else?"

She turned and stared out the window as she spoke. "No, not really. I'm just thinking about stuff."

Now he knew there was something else wrong. She wouldn't look at him.

He had to do something to fix this.

"I have an idea. Since we can't figure out what the clue is, how about if we blow up a balloon and tie it to your door? Even if it's wrong, at least whoever is doing this will know we're trying, and maybe they'll give us a better clue to follow."

He held his breath, waiting for a spark of excitement. Agreement. A better idea. Anything.

She blinked and sighed. "Sure. I guess. Why not . . ." Her voice trailed off and she sighed again.

All Stan could do was watch her as she continued to stare blankly out the window. He wasn't sure what to do, but the thought entered his head that maybe Amber could use a hug, except he wasn't a huggy kind of guy. Although, when he thought of holding Amber, more crossed his mind than a simple hug. She'd be soft and warm, and her hair would smell like fruity shampoo, and she'd fit against him in all the right places.

But this was Amber. His buddy who'd pretended to be beavers with him in primary school when they'd both lost their baby incisor teeth at the same time.

He shook his head and stepped away from her until his rear pressed against her counter. "I'm going to the five-and-dime across the street. I'll be right back."

Chapter Ten

Amber didn't know whether to laugh or cry. She really felt like both, but that might make people think she was going crazy. Maybe she was, but she didn't want to advertise it.

The balloon Stan had tied to the door of her store hadn't drawn in the Gnome Gnapper, but it had attracted the attention of many passersby, most of whom weren't members of the garden club. Because of the balloon, everyone who'd wandered in had asked if she was having a sale. She hadn't planned on it, but she quickly put a few featured items on special and called it an impulse rainy day sale, despite the clear skies. She hadn't sold so much in one day since the Christmas shopping season, and this time she hadn't spent a dime for advertising.

Unless she counted the dollar plus tax Stan spent on the bag of balloons.

The next step would be to replenish her stock, then expand her product list to include more of the type of items people had seemed interested in, but she didn't have the right color or some other small detail. Someone had asked her if she was going to have a similar sale next time it really rained and promised to return to catch a few items she'd been interested in but weren't on sale because it wasn't raining.

Amber had never prayed for bad weather, but rain wasn't really bad unless there was too much of it at once.

She'd had a great day, the best she'd had in a long time.

If only she could do this every day, without the balloon or promise of rain. Then she wouldn't have to worry about her ability to survive.

She'd almost finished the bank deposit when the phone rang.

"I hear your store was packed all day. Did the Gnome Gnapper come? Did you get another note?"

For the first time all day, Amber broke out into a spontaneous smile. "Hello, Stan. It's good to hear from you. I'm fine, how are you?"

If she'd ever heard a pregnant pause, this was one of them.

"Hi," he finally muttered, his voice an octave lower than usual. "How are you?" Another silence hung on the line, silent except for a frustrated sigh. "Are you going to leave me in suspense?"

"Would I do that to you?"

He mumbled something she couldn't quite hear or understand, which was probably not a bad thing. She told him all about her day, and while she talked, she absently twisted a scrap piece of leftover pink wire into a flamingo. "So even though we didn't get any further on finding Gnorman or the trophy, I had a great day. What about you?"

While Stan rambled on about another frustrating misadventure with Aunt Edna and her vintage Caddy, Amber made the figure of another flamingo. After she hung up with Stan, rather than going home or finishing her bank deposit, she glued on beads for eyes, added a few feathers for wings, and attached legs, making them into rather cute indoor plant ornaments. To add a dash of color to her display, she stuck them into one of the fake plants in her window, then finished the deposit and closed the store.

After she tested the door to be sure it was locked, she stood still and stared at the balloon, still stuck to the outside of the door. It hadn't brought the desired result, but the business it had brought was fantastic. Today she'd hopefully made a lot of new customers, which encouraged her to try new products that she'd never carried. It was time to sink or swim.

Tomorrow was another day.

AMBER SAT AT HER counter watching the door. Unlike yesterday, only a few people came in, none of them the Gnome Gnapper. Even though it was unrealistic to expect that the balloon on the door would bring in the same surprise results two days in a row, especially since today wasn't raining either, she couldn't help but feel discouraged. She'd even put a brand new balloon on the door because the other one had become somewhat deflated overnight.

In an effort to keep herself from sinking into a pit of disappointment, she kept her hands and mind occupied by making more wire flamingos since she couldn't leave the store unattended to go to her studio in the back of the building. Rather than making flamingoes out of scraps, she needed to go to her studio to re-create the elaborate projects sold in yesterday's rush.

By lunchtime she'd made over a dozen of the little flamingos. While very cute, they were a questionable use of her materials since she no longer used scraps, but instead used her regular stock.

Fortunately, before she started another one, the bell above the door jingled.

Caroline, who owned the B&B with her daughter, and whose roses were a close second to Libby's, walked in the door grinning from ear to ear. "I heard about your non-rainy day sale yesterday. I'm so sorry I missed it. Sherry showed me the ceramic rose she bought, and I just have to have one. Where are they?"

"The last one I have is in the window display. I'll get it for you." Amber searched for the base to the glue gun so she could put it down without dripping hot glue onto the counter.

"Never mind," Caroline said, turning. "I can get it myself. I hope you'll give it to me for the same price as Sherry's."

"Of course."

Caroline carefully picked through the other ceramic flowers, then plucked out the rose. Before she left the window, she picked up one of the little flamingos. "I have to have one of these too. They're so cute. There's no price tag. How much is it?"

Amber sunk her teeth into her bottom lip. While she always hoped to sell everything she made, she hadn't yet thought about the flamingos. She'd made them more out of frustration than with a profit in mind. The first few she'd made out of scraps, but even when she started using her stock materials, they were inexpensive to make, the bulk of them being constructed from wire that she bought by the spool.

She studied the mess on her table. She'd made about fifteen of them in one morning, without rushing, so her labor costs were also minimal. The ornaments she made every year for the First Bud celebration were more elaborate, composed mostly of ceramic materials, and she had to design molds to make the pieces and hand-paint them. No one in the club really knew how much work went into that yearly project, but it was always worth it when she did the bank deposit. For the flamingo, she'd twisted wire and added spare parts that were commercially available.

Caroline laid the rose and the flamingo on the only clear space on the counter. "I see you're gearing up for a promotion. I'm so excited to get the first little flamingo. Would you give me a promotional price on it, if I promise to tell the garden club how cute they are?"

If she sold them for the same price as the more difficult ornaments for the garden club, Amber would feel guilty. "I was thinking that I could put them on sale for—"

The electronic rendition of an old show tune blared from Caroline's purse. "Excuse me," she muttered as she pulled out her cell phone and hit a few buttons. Her brows knotted as she read a message. "I have to go. My daughter is having a hard time with a customer. If the flamingo costs more, put it on my tab."

Before Amber could calculate the cost of her labor for Caroline, in addition to the approximate cost of two dollars for materials, the money was on the counter, and Caroline was out the door and running down the sidewalk.

Amber couldn't help but smile at her good fortune as she finished the flamingo she'd started. But while she'd sold the first one, and even though they were cute, she didn't want to have too many on hand in case they didn't sell. She'd already made more than most of the new items she put out for a trial run.

Rather than make more, she unplugged her glue gun and had almost picked up all the loose feathers when the phone rang.

"Amber? It's me, Caroline. I hope I haven't ruined your plans for the flamingos, but my customer here that I had to run back for is a florist. I gave her the flamingo to apologize for the mix-up, so I hope you'll let me have another one for the same price."

"Of course I will," Amber said, the guilt at asking so much poking at her.

"But that's not all. I'm so sorry to take advantage of you, so you tell me if you can't do this. She loved the flamingo so much that she wants to buy some for her shop. I told her you'd probably honor the price you gave me, but if she ordered more, you might go for less. She was already interested, but now she's really interested. This is a custom design, right?"

"Yes, it is." Dollar signs floated through Amber's head. The price was already low, but they didn't take too long to make. "How many does she want?" She looked down at the drawer. If she could sell all that she'd made, nothing would be wasted after all.

"She said she'd start with a hundred. Is that okay?"

Amber was glad she was already sitting down. If she could make five in an hour, she'd be okay. "Uh . . . sure . . . I think I can go down a little bit."

"She also wants to see your catalog because every month she'd like to feature a different figure. If you can offer them at the same price. She's got to know for her budget." Caroline's voice lowered and a rustling noise echoed over the phone. "I don't know if you have a catalog," Caroline whispered. "Do you?"

"No, not really," Amber choked out. "But I can get a color printout of twelve unique designs." Once she figured out what else she could make. Pigs. They were one color. Squirrels were also cute animals and one color. Cows could still be considered trendy, but they were two colors, so she couldn't use that. Hippos were one color.

The phone rustled again, and Caroline's voice became normal as she talked to her customer, who still didn't have a name. "Amber says she doesn't have a formal catalog, but she can get her graphics people to get you a special printout of her unique designs. She says she can go down in price if you order at least one hundred. Is that okay? We should also discuss shipping."

Graphics people? She didn't have a graphics person, never mind people. Amber's heart pounded while the conversation on the other end of the phone continued.

Elephants. She could make elephants, but not back-to-back with hippos, because those would be the same color. Unless she made the elephants pink. Then she could use the same wire as the flamingos.

The phone rustled again. "She's going to come down right now to give you her deposit. Is that okay?"

Amber ran one hand down her faded T-shirt, then tried to pick a glue splotch off her jeans. She wasn't dressed for a business presentation. But she couldn't close the store to rush home and change. She'd left her car at home to save gas. "I guess so. Sure."

Her hand shook as she hung up the phone. She straightened and jumped to see Sherry and Pamela standing in front of her.

Amber pushed her hair off her face, and stood. "Sorry, ladies. I didn't hear the bell when you came in."

Sherry smiled. "That's okay. You were concentrating on that phone call. Is everything okay?"

Amber didn't know whether to nod or shake her head. "Yes. I just got a big corporate order for my new plant-pot flamingos. The woman is on the way to make a deposit." She held up one of the flamingos, both proud of her design and feeling caught in a whirlwind from which there was no return.

"He's adorable!" As Pamela took it from Amber and lifted it, the light from a sunbeam streamed through the window and caught the beads from its eyes, casting a sparkly rainbow on the wall. "I want one of these."

"Certainly."

"I want one, too," Sherry said, then she sighed when Amber removed one from the drawer and handed it to her. "Did you say these were a new design?"

"Yes. I've only made a few so far."

Pamela's eyebrows quirked. "You mean you've never sold these before?"

"That's right. I sold the first one to Caroline a few hours ago."

The two ladies nodded at each other, then stepped away for a short, whispered conversation, while poking at the flamingos and ruffling the feathered wings.

Amber's stomach churned. If Pamela and Sherry saw weakness in her design or construction, she didn't want to think that her new customer would do the same and change her mind and cancel the order before it was made.

After Pamela and Sherry returned to the counter, they exchanged a glance, letting Amber know there was some private message they'd probably never share with her.

Pamela spoke up first. "The garden club wants a special memento for everyone who attends the banquet party next month. You know, like when you go to a wedding and you get a small plastic champagne glass with a mint in it and a ribbon tied to it with a tag of the bride and groom's name. If you haven't sold any of these already except to Caroline, that means they're hot on the market, and they are a unique new item. We'll just say that Caroline is thrifty, and if Caroline bought one, that means the price is right." Pamela turned to Sherry, and she got a nod of agreement. "If you'll give us the same price you gave Caroline, we want to order one for everyone who attends the banquet."

Amber gulped. She'd been to all the banquets. They weren't small, and they were very exclusive. "How many is that?"

"Probably 250. But only if you give us the same price you gave to Caroline. Of course, since Sylvia is the treasurer she'd have to approve it, but we've already got money set aside for this much in our budget, so there won't be any problem. It would just be a technicality."

The bell above the door jingled. Amber had never seen the woman before and her stomach did a nervous flip.

"I'm Janice Sinclair. Which one of you is Amber Weathersby?"

Pamela and Sherry stepped back and pointed to Amber. Amber gulped, forced herself to smile, and held out one hand, hoping it wasn't shaking as much as her insides.

Janice loved the flamingos as much as Pamela and Sherry. What she didn't expect was for them to team up on her, which doubled their bargaining power. Amber's heart pounded while she gathered her strength and took a chance on insisting that her price was fixed, and that was the reason she could commit to giving both groups an exclusive on the flamingo. She wouldn't sell a single flamingo in her store for a year from the contract date and that sealed both deals.

She tried to make it look like she made this kind of negotiation all the time when she didn't know how no one heard her knees knocking under the table. After she signed the agreements for the flamingos, she made another tentative contract with Janice for eleven more exclusive animal plant-pot ornament designs for the following year, with the same terms and conditions. Amber honestly told Janice that she hadn't designed any of them yet, but assured her that she would soon produce a brochure showing the drafts for her approval.

By the time the three ladies left, Amber was exhausted and her head was spinning.

She'd just signed the biggest contract since she opened her store, and even more important, she'd collected a sizeable deposit. The only thing left to do was find a graphic artist to take pictures and make the promised brochure.

She didn't know anyone who could do something like that on short notice and make it look professional. But she knew who would.

She took a minute to say a short but heartfelt prayer of thanks for the much-needed income, then she called Stan.

CHAPTER Eleven

S tan arrived at Amber's store after it should have been closed, but the door opened. He pulled the balloon off the handle and went inside, flicking the lock behind him before he walked to the counter covered with piles of beads, pink feathers, and a jumble of cut pink wire.

"Amber? Where are you?" he called out toward the open door to her studio.

"I'll be right there. I need more glue."

He smiled. She'd told him about the windfall of two big orders, which happened indirectly because of the balloon he'd stuck to the door.

Best investment he'd ever made.

He held up the shrunken balloon as she appeared in the doorway. "It's a little deflated, but I think it served its purpose."

"Not really," Amber said as she plunked a box of glue sticks on the counter and inserted a new one into her glue gun. "Our purpose was to attract the Gnome Gnapper, and that didn't happen. I've got to find that trophy. After this big order for the next banquet, I'm more indebted to the garden club than ever. I've got to find it. What can we do?"

His inner balloon deflated, just like the one that had been outside. "I don't know. Since the balloon thing didn't work out, the note said not to be a party pooper. That has to be the clue. I guess that means we have to go to the banquet together."

Amber sighed. "We go to the banquet together every year. That can't be it. Besides, the banquet is a month away. Which is a good thing. I've got the flamingos down to ten minutes each, so it will take me forty hours to make all their flamingos, and that's if I don't eat or sleep or go to the bathroom."

He didn't want to comment on that last part. "That's not unreasonable. A normal workweek is forty hours. If you take time off for, uh, breaks and stuff, you'll have them done in a week and one day. Easy."

"Not including all the other things I do in a week to keep my business running smoothly. Or assist any customers who come in the door and need help, or just want to chat."

"Good point." He ran his fingers through his hair. That happened to him all the time. Most of the time he enjoyed chatting with his customers to maintain good client relationships. However, the more he chatted, the less work got done. His mind raced to recall the note. "One thing I do remember is that in the note, *balloons* was plural. Maybe that's what we're doing wrong. We need more than one."

In answer to his unasked question, Amber pulled the note out of the drawer. "Here's what it says. *Bring out the balloons. Should I be decorating my whole place with balloons?"

"I don't think so. It also said not to be a party pooper. Where is there going to be a party, with balloons?"

"Nowhere that I know. But . . ." Her eyes lit up and she smiled up at him.

Something in Stan's gut went AWOL. Like when he'd gone

up on the Ferris wheel with Amber, except this time nothing was moving. He couldn't speak.

"I can make my own party to celebrate the flamingos. I can show them off, but not sell any of them. It can be a promotion for the garden club's banquet. Then more people will buy tickets just to get one, since they'll be a special item where that's the only place you can get them except from that florist. But no one in the garden club would ever order flowers from a florist. They'd grow their own."

Stan snickered. "I don't think the garden club needs your help getting people to buy tickets for the big banquet."

She bowed her head, and the brightness disappeared from her face. "Probably not, but I need to get their loyalty." She gulped. "I need them to shop in my store. The flamingos help, but it's a one-time deal."

"Are you worried that everyone is going to go to that new store that opened up across town a few months ago, now that the owner also joined the garden club?"

Amber's eyes opened wide, and she gasped. "How did you know about that?"

"I heard one of my customers talking about it. He said everything they sell is cheap junk, so you don't need to worry."

As soon as the words left his mouth, he could tell that she was even more worried.

"Don't you get it? It's like the five-and-dime across the street from here. Full of cheap junk. Cheap junk is very popular. I can't survive if I sell cheap junk. I have to earn enough to live."

His mind whirred. "But how is that place going to survive then?"

"Because they buy cheap junk and sell it as cheap junk and everyone knows it's cheap junk and accept it as such. I buy good quality supplies and make most of what I sell. I have to figure my labor into the cost. I sell my stuff for what it's worth, covering materials and the time for my labor." She stopped and stared at the ground. "Except for the flamingoes. I would have sold them for less. I never count my time at the store because I'm already there with nothing else to do. But I never counted on so many, which changes the rules."

Stan grinned. "I guess God figured you needed that price then."

Her cheeks turned the cutest shade of pink, and she nibbled her lower lip without raising her head. "I guess so."

"If you're worried about it, how about if we go there one day, just to check out what they've got, so you know your competition."

That made her look up. "We can't do that."

"Sure we can. We can put on disguises, so they don't know we're scoping them out."

"Disguises? I hope you don't mean dark clothes and hats and sunglasses."

He did, but he couldn't admit that now. "We can do something so they don't recognize us. Just in case they've already been here, scoping you out."

Her eyes widened again, and he could almost see the wheels turning in her head. She closed her eyes and pinched the bridge of her nose. "Never mind that. For now, I've got to get Gnorman and the trophy back. I can get Helen at the bakery to make up some nice sugar cookies for me, I'll borrow the garden club's coffee urn, and I think that will be good. That will make it almost like a party, so I won't be a party pooper. I'll do it on Saturday so everyone can come, and say that in order to gain admission, everyone needs to bring . . ." Her voice trailed off and she extended one hand toward him.

"Some of their favorite seeds? Rose petals?" At each of his suggestions, she shook her head. Then a light bulb went on in Stan's head. Not the power-smart energy efficient type, but the old-fashioned incandescent kind that generated heat. He smiled ear to ear as he finished off her sentence—". . . a balloon."

AMBER HELD BACK A groan as the last garden club member finally left. The last, that was, except for Stan.

Every cookie had been eaten, most of the coffee had been consumed, and hundreds of people had oohed and aahed over her flamingos. Most of them had either bought a ceramic butterfly, or bought a kit to make one themselves. Many had gone home with rain checks.

She didn't know how word had spread, but more people had come than just the garden club. And every one of them had brought a balloon.

"I've never seen so many balloons in my life," Stan muttered from somewhere behind her.

At first they'd dutifully hung every balloon that arrived, but it hadn't taken long before every display, window, doorframe, and every wall, was covered. They'd piled them behind her counter, hung them from the metal cross bars on the ceiling, making sure not to cover the sprinklers or get too close to the light fixture to stay within safety regulations. When they ran out of empty space on the ceiling, they filled her studio.

It was amazing how much space a balloon occupied. She didn't know how many were there, but if every member of the garden club brought a balloon, that meant seventy-nine balloons. Since she'd seen many people who were not members, that amount had possibly doubled.

Stan planted his fists on his hips and eyed all the balloons in sight, then looked back to her studio. "There's enough balloons here to fill a delivery truck. Now what?"

She honestly had no idea. She didn't know what she'd expected, maybe that when she got enough balloons, the Gnome Gnapper would appear with Gnorman and the trophy. Of course that hadn't happened.

Now she was stuck with a truckload of balloons.

"We have to pop them," she said. "I have a business to run, and I need room to walk. I also need to get stock out of the studio."

"Wait. Before we start, I need to go to my shop. Sit down and have a coffee and take a break, I'll be right back."

Too tired to ask what he needed so badly, Amber flopped down on one of the rental chairs.

If Stan didn't hurry, she'd fall asleep before he got back.

Yet, she was too nervous to sleep. Being surrounded by so many balloons made her nearly claustrophobic. When the tape started to lose its stickiness, she would be buried, covered by a sea of balloons.

Stan got back in record time. He flicked a balloon with one finger. "I know the Gnome Gnapper was here. We had a party, we got the balloons. We met his or her conditions. Now we start looking for the next note."

Her head swam. She couldn't see any place a note would be left. "We'll never find a note. It would be covered by balloons."

Stan poked at another one. The tape gave way and the balloon drifted to the ground, landing beside other balloons already piling up on the floor. "No. They won't be covered. If you were going to sneak a note in here, think about it. It's going to be . . ."

Amber slapped one palm to her forehead. ". . . inside one of the balloons."

Together their gazes swept the sea of color.

She picked up the closest one and shook it. "That means we can't just pop them, we have to check every one first." She walked to the counter, pushed away enough balloons to open the drawer, pulled a couple of push-pins, and handed one to Stan. "We've got a lot of work to do. Let's get popping."

"Before we start, here's what I brought back from my shop." He held out his hand, displaying two sets of earplugs in his palm.

At first the thought of finding a note excited Amber, but as they popped more and more empty balloons, discouragement began to set in. Wearing earplugs made it pointless to attempt conversation, which made it even worse.

About halfway through the deluge, Stan tapped her on the shoulder. She pulled one earplug out and turned to him. He held up a small, note-sized piece of white paper that had been printed from a computer instead of words cut out of the newspaper.

The party was fun, and so it is said,
It's time to sit in the backyard with the gingerbread,
And to rock the night away.
That is all I've got to say.

Amber stared at the note until the words blurred. "This one is so different from all the others. I'm not sure if it's real."

"It has to be real. Who else could have known what we were expecting? This fits right in with the last note. Did anyone else know about the other note?"

"Just Libby."

They stared at each other, sharing the absurdity of that. They'd already ruled Libby out.

Amber reread the note. "This makes even less sense than the last note. Rock the night away? No one in the garden club is a rock 'n' roller. A lot of them are retired, some are middle-aged, and most are home owners. After all, you pretty much have to own a house or townhouse to have a garden."

Stan nodded. "Most people in the garden club are the relaxed mode kind of people. People who would sit in the backyard on an old-fashioned wooden swing and watch the flowers grow, not go to a rock concert."

Amber turned to him. "Maybe that's the reference. A rocking swing in the backyard. That's where people go to relax in the evening here in Bloomfield. That makes sense. But gingerbread?" She squeezed her eyes shut. While many of the garden club members were decent cooks, she could only think of Helen making gingerbread. But Helen didn't have a swing. "Who in the garden club has a swing in the backyard?"

Stan turned to her. "Libby does. Mostly everyone with a big backyard does."

She closed her eyes, trying to make a mental list of people who were at The Spring Fling who might have a backyard swing. But there were just too many.

"Maybe we should get a membership list and drive around." Although she was seriously trying to trim her budget, and the first thing she trimmed was spending money on gas by walking anyplace within half an hour of home.

"I have a better idea. We can cruise the Internet and use the satellite photos on Google Maps. You've got a membership list. We can take a look at everyone's house that way. A satellite view should show us most of the people who have a swing."

"Unless the swing is under a porch."

"But it's a start. We can begin with the As now, see how far we get, and finish up tomorrow after church."

"I suppose. We also have to finish popping the rest of the balloons tomorrow. I just can't do any more right now." They'd only done about half, and even with the earplugs, she had a buzzing in her head that wouldn't go away.

Stan tilted his head and whacked one ear with his palm, then shook his head. "I can't either. I have an idea, though. It seems wasteful to pop them all. Why don't I put as many as I can fit into the back of my truck, and I'll take a load to the children's wing of the hospital, and another load to the senior center? I'm sure they'd enjoy them."

"That's a great idea."

Stan made a few phone calls and reached a couple of people who would gladly take the balloons. After they finished loading up his truck and securing the balloons with a tarp, Stan drove away with the first load. Amber returned to her desk, turned on her computer, and pulled up the garden club's membership list. While looking at everyone's houses from the satellite view, she convinced herself that she wasn't violating anyone's privacy, even though she did feel invasive doing it this way. Driving down the street in front of everyone's homes would be just as bad, plus she'd be wasting gas.

Judging from the plant growth in each photo they pulled up, everything was a few months out of date, yet recent enough to see what she needed. She made a check mark beside everyone who had a swing in the backyard, then went on to the next on the list.

She'd gotten to the *E*s when Stan returned and peeked over her shoulder while she called up Sylvia Eddison's house.

Stan's breath caught and her fingers froze over the keyboard.

"Look at the house," she muttered.

"Gingerbread siding. You can't see it here, but I know Sylvia has a swing on her back porch."

She turned and their eyes met.

"We found Gnorman," they said in unison.

CHAPTER Twelve

Using the contact list, Amber dialed Sylvia's phone number, hoping it wasn't too late to phone. As a child, her mother never allowed her to make phone calls after 9:00 p.m., saying that the only times people called at that hour was when something bad had happened.

It was 8:55, so technically she was still within acceptable parameters. Sylvia answered with an edge of nervousness to her voice.

"Hi, Sylvia, it's Amber Weathersby. I'm sorry for calling so late, but I was wondering if you could do me a favor. Can you look outside and tell me if Gnorman is on or near the swing in your backyard?"

A pause hung on the line. "You mean your little gnome that went missing from Becky's? Why do you think he's here?"

Another thing Amber's mother always taught her. Never answer a question with another question. "Just a hunch, from a note I got at the flamingo party at my store today."

As Sylvia spoke, the background echoes and noises changed as Sylvia headed out back. "That was quite a crowd. I've been talking to people who said your store was crowded all day, and so many people brought balloons you didn't know what to do with them all." Shuffles and a creak, then the groan of old wood resonated through the phone, followed by the clunks of Sylvia's shoes on the deck. Amber held her breath and tried to shake the tension from her body as Sylvia's footsteps changed, indicating she was now going down the stairs to the backyard.

Sylvia's gasp came over the phone loud and clear. "You're right! Your little gnome is here."

"Does he have the trophy?" Although Amber had a feeling she knew the answer before she asked the question. As she spoke the words, Stan leaned closer to her.

"No." Amber waited for Sylvia to say more, but she didn't.

Amber turned to Stan and shook her head so he would know, then turned away, not wanting to look at Stan while she spoke to Sylvia. "Does he have a note with him?"

"Yes. Or at least an envelope. So I have to assume there's a note inside."

"Is he wearing a costume?"

"Yes. But I'm not sure what he's supposed to be. He's got a guitar."

"Does he look like a rock star?"

"Not really with his white beard. Although I know that a lot of the old bands are getting back together and going back on stage for older audiences. I suppose he could be an aging rock star who never quite made it big."

Amber sighed. "Thanks. Do you mind if I come over and get the note? I'll have to leave Gnorman in your yard for a few days, if that's okay with you."

"I don't mind at all. In fact, in a way, now that I'm getting used to him, he's kind of cute."

"Do you mind if I come over to get the note? We'll only be a few minutes."

"That would be fine. I can make some coffee for you and Stan, so please don't be in a rush."

Amber slumped. She didn't know if it was good or bad when people she didn't know tremendously well knew Stan would be with her. "Please, don't go to any trouble. See you soon."

Stan insisted on driving. On the way to Sylvia's house, instead of trying to start a conversation, Amber watched Stan.

He took everything in stride, including everyone's assumptions that he would be there to help her, because he always was. In expecting his help, she knew she took advantage of him. While she always appreciated everything he did for her, that didn't change the fact that she was doing it again. From Gnorman's first disappearance to his reappearances behind Naomi's townhouse at the Village . . . to being found at the cinema . . . then Libby's yard . . . and now Sylvia's, Stan had been there with her every time.

Even before the conundrum with Gnorman and the trophy, she couldn't count the things that Stan did for her, for no reason other than he was simply a nice guy. To make it worse, for all the things he did for her, he never let her do anything for him, not even cooking him a hot meal after a busy day. However, that could have been because he was a better cook than she was, which didn't say very much for her cooking talents, or lack thereof.

But that didn't matter. She couldn't take advantage of him any longer. As soon as she picked up the latest note, it was going to stop.

———— ◆ ————

STAN STOOD TO THE side and waited while Amber chatted with Sylvia and picked up the latest envelope with the new note.

Even though the sun had set over an hour ago, Sylvia's back-yard glowed. A line of floodlights illuminated a sea of colorful flowers and healthy green bushes. To the side, her swing hung in a dark corner on the porch. Between the darker area and the area flooded with light, stood Gnorman, who looked like an octogenarian rock star, if there could be such a thing.

This time, he'd hoped that since they were more on the heels of the Gnome Gnapper, they would have caught him or her in the act of moving Gnorman. However, after thinking about it, it made sense that Gnorman would have been placed in his new location while Sylvia was at Amber's store sometime that afternoon. Meaning, Gnorman could have been there for hours without anyone knowing.

He tried to remember what time Sylvia would have been at Amber's store. The Gnome Gnapper wouldn't have been there at the time Sylvia was. There had been hundreds of people at the store, and the Gnapper could have been there either before or after Sylvia to add their own balloon to the masses. The time that he or she arrived wouldn't have affected the time Gnorman was moved.

The easiest way to catch the window of opportunity would have been for the Gnapper to be at Amber's store watching for Sylvia to arrive, then to leave when Sylvia got there. But there were also other ways to know when Sylvia wasn't home.

Stan would have liked to ask if Sylvia had noticed anyone watching her house, keeping tabs on when she might leave, but nothing would have stuck out as unusual. Sylvia's neighborhood was by no means exclusive. He didn't know Sylvia well, but he did know she was a widow and that her husband had been a doctor, which was how she could afford a house like this and live alone. While her house was big and in a nice neighborhood, it wasn't a gated community, so anyone could drive up and down the street, even park their car in front of any of the nearby houses, and not look suspicious or out of place.

Whatever time, using whatever means, whoever this was, he or she planned their moves well. Like a serial killer keeping ahead of the police, the Gnapper always stayed one step, or even ten steps, ahead of Stan and Amber. But unlike a serial killer, no one had gotten hurt. Although, that wasn't quite true. One thing that might get hurt was Amber's reputation. If he could stand back and look at this like a disinterested third party, he might think the whole thing was amusing, even slightly funny. Or, at a minimum, entertaining. But this was no joke to Amber. Instead, she took it very personally, even a little on the obsessive side, which he didn't understand.

As the two ladies talked, he couldn't help but compare them. He guessed Sylvia to be about the same age as his mother, probably in her mid to late fifties. Since his mother's hair had begun to turn gray, he had to conclude that Sylvia's jet black hair stayed that way with a little help from Lady Clairol. Everything about her appeared well put together. She was neat and tidy, and her shirt was a perfect match with her pants. Even her shoes matched her clothes.

Amber, on the other hand, probably matched this morning, but she'd changed her shirt three times after getting coffee spilled on her and kids smearing icing from the cookies on her sleeves and down her legs. She now wore a T-shirt that had seen better days. She's started out the morning wearing nice pants, but changed to jeans dotted with splotches of glue. She'd given up on her pretty shoes by lunch time, saying her feet hurt from the pointy toes, and she changed into purple sneakers older than one of his mechanics' daughters.

Her hair started out nice as well with soft curls held up by some kind of barrette thing with shiny pink stones. That had come loose and, after multiple attempts to get it straight, she gave up on it and wore her hair loose most of the day, which he really liked. When he got back after getting the earplugs, she'd tied her hair up into a crooked ponytail with loose strands of hair sticking out all over the place.

Her makeup had been perfect that morning, but as the day wore on everything got smudged, her lipstick disappeared, and she had a black smear under one eye that she probably didn't know about, and he wasn't going to tell her.

Stan smiled. She looked adorable. Kind of like she did when they went on day-long treks in the forest that their parents didn't know about to pick wild berries. Except better somehow.

Instead of standing there staring like an idiot, Stan approached the two ladies. When Amber saw him coming, she ripped open the envelope, angled the paper toward the light, and started reading the note with Sylvia beside her.

He stood behind and read over her shoulder.

many seasons have lots of cheer
but christmas comes only once a year.
santa calls out ho ho ho.
that's where snowman will go go go.

Stan made a quick step back so he wouldn't get elbowed in the nose when Amber ran one hand through her hair, and she got her fingers caught in the elastic band of the ponytail.

"I don't get it. This makes even less sense than the rest of the notes."

"It's also pretty bad poetry," he mumbled.

She turned and looked up at him. "It's a long way from Christmas. We haven't even hit the hot part of the summer yet.

Nothing is decorated, none of the stores are selling Christmas stuff. I have no idea what they're using as a reference point."

"We need time to think about this. We'll figure it out, just like we did with the party and the balloons." Not that he thought that was what the Gnapper had in mind, but the bottom line was that it had worked. And thinking of things that didn't work, he turned to Sylvia. "We didn't mean to take up so much of your time. By the way, I saw your son the other day and he mentioned that your car was making a strange noise. How about if I take a look at it while I'm here."

"You don't have to do that. I don't want to be a bother."

He shrugged his shoulders. "It's no problem. I'm here." He looked down at his grease-streaked pants. "Besides, I'm already dirty."

"I won't say no. Thank you so much. I'll go get my keys. I'll be right back."

Upon her return, he followed Sylvia to the garage and hit the button to raise the door while she got in the car, flicked the hood release, and started the car.

This one was easy. "Turn it off now." He poked at the fan belt, which had too much slack. He could have tightened it in a few minutes, but Amber looked ready to fall down, and he didn't want to take the time to find what Sylvia had done with her husband's tools, if a doctor would even have tools in the garage. "It's just your fan belt. Bring it by the shop on Monday and I'll tighten it for you, no charge. We'll consider this returning a favor for keeping Gnorman in your yard for a few days."

She smiled. "That's not much of a favor, but I can accept it. Thank you very much."

He nodded and led Amber out of the yard, back to his pickup.

On the way back to Amber's house, she didn't say anything, but she kept looking at him rather strangely.

"What's up?" he asked when he couldn't stand it anymore.

He'd never understood the expression *doe eyes* before, but with Amber looking at him like that, he suddenly did.

"You're such a nice guy," she mumbled, making it so he barely understood.

He didn't know why, but even though she'd said it nicely, he wasn't sure it was a compliment. Instead it felt like the kiss of death at the end of a relationship. Except he didn't have a relationship with Amber. He waited for the inevitable *We can be just friends*, but it didn't come. They were just friends anyway.

"Here you are," he said as he stopped in her driveway.

"What are we doing here? I thought we were going back to my store, so I can get my car."

"You look like you're ready to drop. Just go to bed. I'll pick you up for church in the morning, then I'll drop you off at your store after the service to pick up your car."

He didn't know what he said that was so horrible, but her eyes got glassy, then kind of watery. He opened his mouth to ask, but she bolted out of the car so fast she left him sitting behind the wheel with his mouth hanging open. She unlocked her door and dashed inside, then waved at him before she closed the door. Stan waited for her to peek through the blinds and give him her signal that she'd remembered to lock the door, and drove off.

Tomorrow he would pick her up, they'd both be dressed up, and maybe after the service he'd make a detour and not go directly to her store to get her car. Maybe, since they'd both be wearing nice clothes, instead of grabbing a quick burger after church like they usually did, he'd take her someplace nice for lunch.

And hopefully she wouldn't fight with him and she'd let him pay for once.

CHAPTER Thirteen

I can't believe you talked me into this. What are we doing?"

"We're making sure no one will recognize us." Stan wiggled his fake mustache. "How do I look? Dashing? Like James Bond?"

"No. No James Bond I ever saw had a mustache." Although she had to admit, if she could push the thought of how ridiculous they were acting out of her mind, Stan didn't look half bad with a mustache, even if it didn't quite match his hair. Which was probably because he'd sprayed some kind of washout color on it, making his usually monotone dark brown hair an uneven blend of blond and brown because he hadn't sprayed it on evenly. If he'd gone to the salon, he would have spent a fortune on that look, and she doubted he'd used the whole can. He'd also brushed it back off his forehead, keeping it in place with hair gel, something else he never used.

"Since you wouldn't let me take you out for lunch, I figured we had a bunch of extra time, so this is a good idea."

Stan was the most innovative person she knew. He always had a wealth of great ideas. However, this wasn't one of them.

She adjusted the fake glasses and tucked a few stray strands of her hair back up under the blonde wig. "I feel like Boris and Natasha."

He stopped wiggling his mustache. "Who?"

"Ask your mother. Never mind. Natasha's hair was black." She reached up to pull off the wig, but Stan's fingers wrapped around her wrist.

"Don't. We have to arrive looking like this. No one around there can see us putting this stuff on, so we have to be already wearing it when we get into the neighborhood."

Amber's mouth opened, but no sound came out. Heat from Stan's grip seared her wrist. Not that he held her too tight—his grip was gentle, yet firm. But standing close enough to hold her wrist meant he was comfortably close. Except she didn't feel very comfortable.

They were still dressed in their church clothes. Today Stan had worn a suit. She didn't know why he'd dressed up a little better than usual, he just had. He'd even worn the tie that she'd given him for the last garden club banquet. The difference between Stan wearing his coveralls at work to the fitted suit was like comparing Fred Flintstone to Brad Pitt. Except Stan was better looking than Brad. Stan was distinguished and dashing, and very handsome and put together in his suit.

Amber knew she also looked better than usual. She'd selected a nice dress and shoes with heels that were a little too high for comfort, but they were a perfect match to her dress. Because she wore one of her best dresses, she'd taken extra care with her makeup as well. While she wasn't drop-dead gorgeous, with the right highlights and colors, she was by no means plain. Since she wore the good dress and shoes, and she'd even selected a matching purse, she'd wanted to stay put together, especially beside Stan in all his handsomeness.

For lunch they'd gone to the usual burger place and eaten in the car. After the carhop took the tray and empty wrappers away, it had dawned on her that her lipstick had wiped off. As Stan drove back to his house, she'd touched up her lipstick in the rearview mirror. Strangely, even though she'd fixed her lipstick many times in front of Stan, this time felt different, and he'd watched her so closely that he'd seemed distracted enough that she kept telling him to quit watching her and keep his eyes on the traffic.

Now here they were, all dressed up, adding the enhancements of disguises, like playing spy games when they were kids, except the dress-up clothes they had on now actually fit.

With the nuances of a spy mission bouncing around in her head, being so close and being held by a tall, dark, handsome, and mysterious stranger felt exciting. Energizing. Intriguing. Invigorating.

Romantic.

If they were characters in a movie, he'd use his other hand to tip her chin up, then his eyes would flutter shut as he leaned down to kiss her.

With that thought, she couldn't help herself. Her gaze flittered to Stan's mouth. She'd never really looked at it before, except for the time he'd fallen out of Aunt Edna's apple tree and split his lower lip in his final scramble to grab a branch as he crashed down through the branches. She'd had to clean him up and help him wipe up all the blood before his mother or Aunt Edna found out what they'd been doing.

He still had a scar that she could see if she looked close enough. A little scar, that made her want to stand on her tiptoes and kiss it to make it better.

Amber blinked, and her eyes lost focus. This was just Stan. What they were doing wasn't much different than playing *Spy vs Spy*, except they were bigger. Or rather, too big for games.

"What? Is my mustache crooked?" He reached up and touched it, pressing it down with his fingers.

Amber straightened her wig. "You're fine. I was just thinking that this is like playing out the characters from that spy thing we used to watch on television when we were younger." An exciting spy thing. With a suave and charming hero. Visions of a young Antonio Banderas flashed back and forth with images of Stan. She didn't know which one she liked better.

"Please don't tell me I look like Inspector Gadget. I was trying hard to make us look real."

"Inspector Gadget didn't have a mustache." Neither did Antonio Banderas, but that didn't matter.

He sighed and grasped one corner of the mustache, like he might pull it off.

She raised one hand to stop him, then whipped it back behind her before she actually touched him. "No. Keep the mustache. I like it." Too much. She fiddled with the wig once more and slipped on the fake glasses that Stan had bought for her. "Let's go."

Fortunately no one from Stan's neighborhood saw them, and by the time they arrived at her competition's store, most of the tension had eased and she felt almost normal, except that she couldn't see properly.

They walked into the store together and immediately started checking the place out.

"I can't focus with these fake glasses. Where did you get them?"

He leaned closer to whisper his answer, even though no one stood within hearing range if he spoke normally. "From the drugstore. They're reading glasses. I got the weakest ones I could find."

"You couldn't have gotten the wig from the same place, then."

"I got it from the consignment store. Tessa had a couple of Halloween costumes in the back. It was with one of them."

Suddenly she didn't feel so elegant anymore, but she couldn't take it off. "I shouldn't have asked. Is that where you got the fake mustache?"

"Yup."

She didn't want to ask what kind of costume the mustache came with right now, but one day she would.

Instead, she turned her attention to what they were there for and browsed through the store's gardening accessories. When she glanced over the price tags, she actually could read them quite well. Maybe it was time she got a vision test. "All this stuff is run-of-the-mill that can be bought at any store, including the lumber store."

"Then you're fine. The garden club likes the unique factor, that what you sell can't be found anywhere else."

"But the garden club also needs to watch their money. What if they want to buy something from this new person, now that she's a member?" She didn't want to tell Stan that the sales to the garden club were the final factor in whether or not she could make it or close the store. If he knew, she wouldn't put it past him to buy everything the garden club would have bought, and she wouldn't allow him to do that.

For now, the garden club still bought from her, and she would do anything to keep it that way.

A darling little white-haired lady with chubby cheeks and wearing a festive apron approached them, smiling. "Welcome. Is there something I can help you with?"

Even Amber had to look down at the sweet woman. Her heart sank at the thought that the owner hired such adorable and helpful sales staff.

As the woman smiled at her, Amber fought to keep her hands at her sides and not fiddle with the wig. "We're just browsing. Thanks for asking," she said, trying to manufacture a fake accent. She didn't know what kind of accent, and it didn't matter. As long as she didn't sound like herself.

"If there's anything you want, I can order it in for you. I haven't been open long, and I want to let everyone know that I'll do special orders."

Amber felt her heart turn to ice. This sweet little old lady was the owner. She didn't have a chance.

The lady, whose name tag read Florence, smiled even more sweetly. "I've just joined the Bloomfield Garden Club, so I've ordered a lot more garden accessories. If you don't see what you're looking for, I hope you'll come back next week when my new stock should be in."

She could see her status of being the sole supplier for the garden club's accessories evaporating in a puff of smoke.

She rested her hand on Stan's arm. "Thank you, but I think we've seen enough. Come on, Ssss . . ." She barely cut herself off in time not to say Stan's name. If she said his name in front of the woman, especially since she was a garden club member, she would recognize him at their next meeting, even without the mustache and altered hair. ". . . Sssweetheart. We should go."

Without waiting for his reply, she gave him a not-too-gentle tug, hoping he would take the hint.

His eyebrows quirked. "Sure. Sweetiepoo. We should go," he said in a voice about an octave deeper than his natural voice. He turned to the woman. "It was nice meeting you."

The car door had barely closed before she turned and glared

at him. "Sweetiepoo? Whoever calls their girlfriend *Sweetiepoo*? Couldn't you get any more original than that?"

Not looking at her, he inserted the key into the ignition switch and turned it. "My mind kind of went blank when you called me Sweetheart."

"What? Why?"

He twisted to watch as he backed out of the spot, then faced directly forward to drive away. "In addition to the really bad fake accent, you almost blew our cover."

"There wasn't anyone else in the store. Nothing could have blown our cover." Except them saying each other's real names. Or if his mustache fell off.

"Never mind. We should go over what we've learned. She's selling stuff anyone can buy anywhere."

Now that they were far enough away, Amber took off the glasses so she could see Stan properly, even though he wouldn't look at her. "That's true, but when people buy stuff for their gardens, unique isn't always the deciding factor. Sometimes the cheaper thing that everyone else can buy simply matches better. Since this lady is now a member of the garden club, a lot of members are going to want to support her too. The average garden can only have a certain number of ornaments before it starts to look like an overpriced tourist trap. So her new store means lost business for me."

"No. You're a long-standing member, and you do a lot for the club. You've got their loyalty."

Which didn't always extend to the pocketbook, something that Amber had learned the hard way when her uncle doubled the interest on her loan payments. Even though she had her favorite brands at the grocery store, she'd started buying the cheaper store-brand products. Yet, she did still go to the stores where members of the garden club worked. They did have her loyalty, just not as much of it.

"I hope so," she muttered, part of her wanting to tell Stan why she needed their loyalty so much, but at the same time knowing she couldn't.

Stan turned in the direction of Sylvia's house. "Let's pay Sylvia a visit and see if there are any new notes with Gnorman, and then I'm taking you out for supper. To the restaurant of my choice." He quickly glanced at her before he returned his attention to the road. "But first we have to go to my place. I've got to get this glop out of my hair. It probably looks pretty stupid."

Amber shook her head. "No, it looks good on you. It kind of goes with the mustache. I like it. We also have to go to my place so I can fix my hair after being mashed up under this wig for hours." She reached up to pull the wig off, but as her fingers twined through the strands, she stilled. "Unless you want me to leave this on. And you can leave the mustache on and don't take the color out of your hair. We can keep our disguises on and go somewhere we've never been before and see what happens, then go to Sylvia's later. This might be fun."

CHAPTER Fourteen

Where are we going? Why aren't we going to the Fancy Schmantzy?"

"Because." Stan grinned. Even though they'd never been to the Fancy Schmantzy together, it was still familiar to both of them because he drove by it every day on his way to work. Tonight they pretended not to be themselves, and part of the fantasy, at least his, was to go someplace totally unfamiliar to complete the illusion of mystery. It was going to be their special night, even though they weren't really themselves. "I thought we'd go to that place on Wren and Sidewinder for a big, fat, juicy steak. I've never been there, but I hear it's good."

"Why do men always do that? The first thing you think of when going out is expensive steak. There are other foods that are better for you, and just as elegant."

He turned to her as he stopped for a red light. "I don't want elegant. I want meat. I also want to pay. Going there is my idea, and it's my treat. So don't argue with me. Go big. Order whatever you want, without guilt. I don't care if you put on a

pound or two. That only proves I can afford to feed you right."
He didn't like that Amber had been losing weight lately. She
hadn't said she was on a diet, so the reason had to be something
unintentional. If worry about Gnorman and the trophy was
the cause, he would do his best tonight to make her forget her
troubles and simply have fun, like she said.

Besides, all of those really thin women in the magazines
were probably anemic from lack of good nutrition. Tonight he
was going to make sure that whatever Amber ate, it was good as
well as good for her.

"Are you sure about that? We didn't plan for this. Its only
spur of the moment."

"I had planned on taking you out for a nice lunch, then not
only did we just have burgers, you insisted on paying for your
own. If you think you're going to pay for your own meal tonight,
I'm going to turn around and take you home. In fact, I'm hoping
you're going to have steak and lobster." As soon as the words
left his mouth, Stan held his breath, hoping and praying that she
wouldn't call his bluff. He would take her home and do Chinese
takeout rather than have her pay for her own meal again.

"You want to feed me steak and lobster? Really? I've never
had lobster before."

He wasn't above using temptation. He turned and flashed
her a grin as the traffic started moving forward. "It's really
good. I mean really, really good."

She raised one hand and flicked the hair on the wig. He
noticed she'd been doing a lot of that today.

The power of suggestion made one hand leave the steering
wheel to brush the hair on the fake mustache with his fingertips.

Amber hadn't said the wig was uncomfortable. He imagined
it felt like a hat, except snugger. The mustache wasn't exactly
uncomfortable, but it felt strange. It came with a small bottle
of alcohol-based oily adhesive, flexible with his skin but sticky

enough so that the mustache wouldn't fall off. He would have taken it off, but for some reason Amber liked it.

He planned to take a closer look at himself in the mirror when he got home. When he'd put it on, he had only concentrated on getting it straight and making sure none of the hairs got in his mouth. He didn't know what it was made out of, but he didn't really want to know.

They chatted about nothing in particular as he drove, but every time he stopped at a red light, Amber used the time to touch up her eye makeup and reapply a dark red lipstick.

He pulled into a parking spot near the restaurant's entrance, then ran around to Amber's side and opened her door while she tugged at the wig again. "Do you think I should wear the glasses? They are part of the disguise."

Stan extended one hand to help her out. "Only if you want to. If you can't see properly, or if you think they'll give you a headache, don't."

She slipped them on. "I'd probably get a headache if I was looking at distances, but I think I'll be fine if I only look at you. Is that okay?"

He gulped. If she only looked at him, he didn't know if that made him happy or nervous. "Sure."

Since it was still early for supper, they were escorted to a table without waiting.

After the waiter handed them menus and left, Amber nudged the glasses halfway down her nose, lowered her head, and peered around the restaurant over top of them.

Stan would check the place out after they ordered. He picked up the menu and started looking for the steak section. Just as he found it, Amber's toes poked at his ankle.

"Look," she whispered. "To my left. There's a couple from the garden club. I don't remember their names, but I've spoken to them at the meetings."

Without moving his head, Stan looked at the couple in question. "His name is Blake. I don't remember his wife's name. And over there, a couple of tables down. There's Debbie and Ralph." He went back to the menu to read the choices to decide if he wanted filet mignon, rib eye, chateaubriand, or a good old-fashioned T-bone.

"I see them," she whispered back. "I heard Ralph was browsing inside the jewelry store." Her voice lowered even more. "Without Debbie."

His attention immediately left the selection of steaks, and he studied the young couple gazing at each other with stars in their eyes that had nothing to do with the golden glow of the candle flickering between them. "I heard that too."

He wondered what it would be like to be in love like that, with eyes only for each other, not caring about the rest of the world. His first thoughts went to Jordan at work. He and his wife were due to have a baby in a few weeks. He could tell whenever Jordan's wife phoned. Jordan's voice changed to a softer and more melodic tone, deeper, and he always spoke in complete sentences. Whenever Jordan's buddies phoned, the conversations were over quickly, with the repeated word *dude* having an assorted number of meanings with the changes in the tone of Jordan's voice.

Man-speak. Stan could understand that.

"Well? What do you think?"

Stan blinked and looked back to Amber, who was studying him through the glasses.

He felt his ears heat up. "Sorry. I was thinking about something else."

Her head tipped a little bit. "What? You can tell me."

On that, she was right. He could tell her everything, only he usually didn't. Most of the time, she guessed, and she was right.

"You were looking at Debbie and Ralph and comparing them to Jordan and Trish, weren't you?"

He grinned. "Dude."

"You are so busted." She rolled her eyes, and it seemed hypnotic with all the eye makeup she had on. All he could do was stare. And wish that she wasn't wearing those silly glasses.

The waiter appeared. "Are you ready to order? Or would you like to hear about our special? Tonight we have a romantic dinner combination of steak and lobster for two with asparagus and an assortment of our favorite appetizers."

Amber's eyes widened, which he took to mean they were ordering the special.

He closed his menu. The rib eye he wanted no longer mattered. An any-kind-of-steak and lobster dinner sounded exactly like the right thing for tonight. He could easily ignore the romantic part of the special, especially since he was with Amber, and just enjoy the combo.

The waiter took the details for their sides and how they wanted their steaks cooked, and left as quietly as he came.

Again Amber lowered the glasses and looked around the restaurant. "This is quite the romantic place. Every table has two people who are obviously a couple at it."

"Don't look now, but another couple just walked in." Stan held his breath, not knowing if he should crawl under the table, or stand and shake hands.

Amber gasped, and shrank in her seat. "Aunt Edna and Uncle Bill. What are they doing here? Everything this place serves is loaded with cholesterol."

"It looks like your aunt is helping your uncle break his diet."

"Look at the waiter. He knows them. I've heard Aunt Edna and Uncle Bill talking about date night. This must be it. They must come here once a week."

Stan snickered, making sure to remain quiet. "Maybe this is why they're still in love after all those years."

"We can't let them know we're here. Knowing we know would destroy a special secret they've managed to keep from everyone else for a lot of years."

"What about Blake and his wife, and Ralph and Debbie?"

Amber glanced at the other two couples over the top of the glasses. Neither couple moved or broke eye contact. "They don't seem to have noticed, they're so wrapped up in each other. The waiter led Aunt Edna and Uncle Bill to a small private table in the corner, and they've got their backs to the rest of the restaurant. Unless you saw them come in, you wouldn't know they were there. We can't let them know we saw them."

"Isn't that the purpose of our disguises? So no one knows it's us?" When they started the evening it had just been a game. Now failure was no longer an option. "All we have to do is blend in."

Again Amber's gaze swept the restaurant, and he was sure she had the same impression he did. This place was a romantic hideaway. He wasn't sure how to deal with it. He'd never been to a place like this before. He didn't know if she had either, except that if she had, the thought bothered him.

Suddenly she smiled a quirky little smile, leaned forward, and ran her fingers up the back of his hand.

His heart stopped, then picked up in double time at the intimate touch.

Her voice dropped to a husky drawl. "Is my wig on straight? I can't tell, but I think I pulled it to the right."

His heart continued to pound as he mentally calculated if both sides of the blonde wig were equidistant from each eye.

Wide, beautiful eyes. Eyes that were the windows to her soul.

"Well?"

"Yeah. Sure. It's fine."

As quietly as the previous time, the waiter returned, this time with their appetizers, which he placed in the middle of the table for them to share.

Stan thought there was never a better time for food. Even little snacks he couldn't identify.

They were in a public restaurant, so instead of saying grace aloud, he reached forward so they could hold hands across the table. He said his prayer in silence, and he knew Amber did too. He gave her hands a gentle squeeze when he finished, and she returned the squeeze so that he knew she was too.

Amber picked up one of the little morsels, blew on it, and wrapped her lips around it without having any food come in contact with the lipstick, and it disappeared. She closed her eyes and sighed. "Whatever that was, you've got to have one."

He didn't say a word while they shared the appetizers. All he could do was listen to whatever she said and watch her eat, mesmerized by her ruby red lips. When every piece was gone, he thought it amazing that her lipstick still looked just as perfect as when they sat down. He'd wondered how women did that, and now he knew.

She wasn't so successful when the steak and lobster came. By the time they were done, all traces of her lipstick were as gone as the food.

He had to smile. She'd eaten most of his lobster, and he'd eaten most of her steak. He couldn't say which one of them enjoyed the meal more.

Time was on their side. They finished eating before Bill and Edna, and the other two couples they knew from the garden club had already left. They chose to forgo the dessert and decided to get while the getting was good.

Stan still wanted to keep the romantic mood of the restaurant, so he reached out and rested his fingers at the small of

Amber's back to escort her as they left the restaurant, just like they were on a real date.

He'd never done something like this before. He'd touched her, but touching her this way seemed more personal, more intimate. Probably because they didn't have that kind of relationship.

But maybe it was about time to change that. He couldn't remember ever enjoying himself more while out on a date. Not that he'd been on many. But this one was different.

She smiled at him as he opened the car door and waited for her to be comfortably seated before closing it and jogging around to the driver's door and getting in.

This time she removed the glasses right away.

"Time to go home," she said as he started the engine.

Stan shook his head. "No, it's not. It's still early. I think we should go to Sylvia's house and check on Gnorman."

With the glasses already off, Amber stuck her fingers under the wig, pulled it off, shook her head like a wet dog, and ran her fingers through her hair until it hung reasonably normal. Lifting her purse, she reached inside, removed a brush, and started working her hair into its usual shape. "I'm fine, but we can't go anywhere with you looking like that."

For a moment he simply stared at her. Without the glasses and the wig, his Amber was back. Yet something had changed. He'd always thought she was pretty, but tonight she was downright beautiful, even though her makeup was a little worn off, the lipstick was gone, and her hair was a mess despite her best attempts with the brush.

Using the utmost care, he tried not to wince in front of Amber as he slowly pulled off the mustache like a bandage and rubbed the tender skin. When it felt like all remnants of the glue were gone, he leaned back, reached behind the seats, pulled out his favorite baseball cap, and plopped it on his head, effectively covering most of his hair. He removed the suit jacket and tie, unfastened the top two buttons of his shirt, rolled up his sleeves halfway up his forearms, and grinned at Amber. "I'm ready to be seen in public if you are. Let's go."

AMBER STOOD ON HER doorstep, fiddling with her keys while Stan waited behind her.

Their visit with Sylvia had been short. Gnorman was still in place as an aging rock star in Sylvia's backyard, and no additional notes had been left.

So now, here she was, back home, with Stan behind her waiting to bid her good night.

Only she didn't know what this particular good night involved. Tonight had been different than any other night she'd ever spent with him.

She wasn't quite sure, but despite the strange circumstances, it had felt like a date. Except this one had been with Stan, so it couldn't have been a date.

They'd been together at a romantic restaurant with soft music playing in the background, surrounded by couples, young and old, in various stages of a life of love.

Except she'd been with Stan. Her lifelong friend. Her buddy.

Now, here they were. If this had been a real date, it would be time for the traditional good-night kiss. She couldn't do that with Stan.

Stan's voice echoed behind her while she stood like a statue in front of the door, afraid to turn around and face him.

"I suppose we should decide what we're going to do."

She gulped. She really didn't know. She'd read enough romance novels and knew enough people to know that if they kissed—really kissed—that things would never be the same between them again. She didn't want that. Stan had always been her best friend in the whole world, and she wanted him to always be her best friend.

Except she wondered what it would be like if they did kiss, bumping their relationship up to the next level. Was she willing to take that risk? If it didn't work, there was no going back.

Amber tested the doorknob, opened the door just an inch then, and turned around in slow motion. Stan stepped closer to her. So close that he could kiss her. Which would have been a reasonable conclusion to the wonderful evening they'd shared. More than just the evening, like so often, they'd shared the entire day. He'd picked her up for church, they'd gone out for lunch, they'd been on an adventure and visited her competitor's store, and he'd taken her out for the best meal she'd had in her entire life. They'd been together, side by side, for nearly twelve hours.

He smiled and brushed her cheek with one finger. "I know this sounds lame, but I had a really nice time tonight. I hope you did too."

This was it. The set-up-to-kiss-you line. Her heart started pounding like her pottery wheel when a stone got stuck in the gear. She gulped. "Yeah. I did."

There was so much more she could have said, and should have said, but everything in her brain felt as mixed up as if she'd put all her thoughts into a paper bag and turned it upside down and shaken it. The evening had been so right, but yet so wrong. The tall, dark, handsome man standing kissing distance in front of her was Good Ol' Stan.

If she didn't do this now, she wouldn't be able to maintain her courage.

"Thank you," she whispered, rested her hands on his shoulders, stood on her tiptoes, brushed a quick kiss on his cheek, then spun around and dashed inside her townhouse and closed the door.

"I guess I'll see you tomorrow," he called gently through the door.

"Yeah. Tomorrow," she called back through the wood. Coward that she was.

Amber pressed her ear to the door. Stan's steps echoed, becoming quieter as he walked the length of her sidewalk.

His pickup started, and he drove way.

Amber pushed her hands to the door and squeezed her eyes shut.

Tomorrow would be another day.

She didn't know if that was good or bad.

CHAPTER Fifteen

Stan tilted his head back and let the hot water sluice through his hair, finally getting rid of the last of the temporary color after the third application of shampoo.

He didn't know why he thought playing dress-up and going out on a fake date would be a good idea.

All it did was show him how much he was missing.

Just like in a proverbial B-grade chick flick, love, in all its stages, surrounded him.

At work, whenever Jordan thought about the baby, his eyes lost focus and he made a goofy smile, then snuck away to phone his wife, Trish, and check on her.

Then there was Hayden, his best friend, who after a short and painful marriage, desperately searched for the right love.

Tonight they'd seen Ralph and Debbie from church with stars in their eyes, nearly swooning over each other, just about to become engaged.

Then Blake and his wife, whose name he still couldn't remember, from the garden club, who'd left the kids at home with a sitter and went to a nice-but-not-too-expensive place, just the two of them, for a night out.

And Amber's aunt and uncle. After more than forty years of marriage, they snuck out together to have some forbidden fruit, or rather, forbidden steak.

At first it had been fun acting the play couple. Until there was only one piece of lobster on the plate between them, and they'd both reached for it at the same time. They'd stopped and looked up at each other, and Amber had puckered up and blown him a kiss. By then, all of her lipstick was gone and he'd frozen up, and all he could think about was leaning over the table and kissing her for real. While he sat there staring at her like an idiot, she stabbed and popped the last piece of lobster into her mouth, then made a big drama about how much she enjoyed it as she chewed. He'd sat there in a trance, watching, considering ordering another lobster tail just to have it happen again, and then kiss her for real.

If there was ever a pivotal moment in his life, he'd had it tonight. Not like back in high school when Amber had whacked him up the back of the head with her math textbook and told him to stop fooling around so much and concentrate on his studies or he'd never graduate. Not when they'd both decided at the same time to go to college together. Not at graduation, not when he'd decided to hire staff after struggling with his business for a few years and prayed he could bring in enough income to cover their paychecks.

That lifetime pivotal moment came when Amber gave him a fleeting peck on the cheek and slammed the door in his face.

He'd had his chance to kiss her for real after their first real date, and he'd been too slow on the draw.

At that moment it had occurred to him that he was in love with Amber. Whom he'd been buddies with his whole life.

Together since they were in diapers. There had never been a time in his life when they hadn't known each other, bonded to each other, even if they were too young to know what bonding meant.

Just like Hayden searching for a soul mate, it hit Stan that, unlike Hayden, he already had one and hadn't realized it.

Amber.

He didn't know why it had taken so long to see it. He loved her. He couldn't remember a time in his life when he hadn't loved her.

But she wasn't in love with him. As friends, they were inseparable. He saw Amber more than he saw his best friend, Hayden.

He knew she liked him, but after tonight it was clear that she didn't want to kiss him.

Now he wanted to kiss her more than ever.

He wiped the fog off the mirror, looked at his reflection, stroked the stubble on his jaw, and ran a couple of fingers on the skin under his nose.

Amber had liked his look. He wasn't about to go to the salon and spend big money to put fancy colors in his hair that would just grow out anyway, but he could grow a mustache without an expensive stylist. He had a feeling that was what she liked more than the blond streaks anyway.

He'd heard that a mustache made a guy's nose look bigger, and that was something he really couldn't afford; but for Amber, he'd take the risk.

Stan swiped the towel over his hair, which was finally the right color, and squeezed some toothpaste onto his brush as he got ready for bed. Tomorrow was Monday, his most hectic day with all the weekend breakdowns and people who were desperate for their cars. But more than that, it was time to make a plan and put it into action.

———— ❦ ————

AMBER'S HEART MADE A little flip-flop as she approached her store. From down the street, as she'd walked closer she'd seen what appeared to be some kind of plant in a pot in front of the door. As she got closer, she spotted a new envelope wedged in the door.

Because it was easier, she searched the plant first, to see if the two were related. She didn't find a note or anything tucked into the leaves. All it had was the usual plastic tag with care and watering instructions. The tag promised this plant was easy to care for, and that it flowered for most of the summer when kept in a sunny location. In a black felt pen, looking suspiciously like Stan's sloppy handwriting, a note added, "Put beside your front door."

With the tag in her hand, she stared at the envelope wedged between the door and frame, afraid to open it; at the same time, afraid not to.

The last note had hinted about Christmas, but Bloomfield was too small to support a business that catered to Christmas all year long. Those kinds of places only existed in the large cities. The only thought that she and Stan had shared was that with Gnorman's white beard, he was a shoo-in for Santa. Which was no help in finding him, only that they had figured out what his next costume would probably be.

With trembling fingers, Amber tore the envelope open.

who is a cheery and jolly fellow with a heart of gold and a belly like a marshmallow?

with hair and beard
changing to white
he'll do what he can to put
up a good fight.

Amber stared at the words. She ignored the bad rhyme between *fellow* and *marshmallow* and concentrated on what was hopefully the important clue. Santa's hair was already white, so she could only think that the changing hair color was a clue as to where she would find Gnorman—dressed like Santa. The first person with changing hair color she thought of was Stan, even though that change had been artificial, and temporary, and hopefully still anonymous. By today it would all be washed out and back to his normal dark brown.

She smiled. Knowing Stan, he'd probably washed it all out last night. He didn't know that she knew, but because of his job, he always showered in the evening when he got home from work, then didn't shower in the morning in his mad rush to get out the door.

Tucking the note under her arm, she turned the key and carried her new plant inside, quickly turning off the alarm.

From across the room the red light on her phone flashed, telling her that she had a new message.

As soon as she heard Sylvia's recorded voice, she knew before listening what the news would be, and she was right. Gnorman was gone, and Sylvia didn't see anyone take him. There was no note.

The next new note, of course, was already in her possession. And if the pattern was going to be the same, someone would call her within an hour to say that they had found Gnorman in their backyard, not knowing how he got there, and that he was wearing a new costume. This time she suspected that person would find Santa Claus . . . along with a new note.

The phone didn't ring often, but every time it did Amber felt like her heart would leap out of her chest. Yet every time it rang, it was a real customer with a real question.

By the end of the day, not only had no one phoned to say they'd found Gnorman in their yard, but also, Stan hadn't phoned to say why he'd left her a plant.

At closing time, before she prepared to lock the door, Amber once again read the note. She didn't know any women in the garden club who had a belly like a marshmallow. The only person she knew of was the pregnant wife of one of Stan's mechanics. But that belly was nothing like a marshmallow.

No men she could think of had an expanded waistline like a marshmallow either. Although she did know a lot of people with hearts of gold.

Again she looked down at the plant.

Stan certainly had a heart of gold. But he wasn't old enough to have his hair starting to go gray like Santa.

She'd recently gone through the membership list in her hunt for a backyard swing, but she'd stopped at the Es, at Sylvia's name. So instead of leaving, she locked the door, turned on the light to say she had closed, booted her computer back up, and opened the garden club membership list.

This time, she skipped by all the female names, and concentrated on the men, assuming that no women in the club could grow a beard. She'd gotten all the way to the Ws without success, when off in the distance, her cell phone rang out from her purse.

By the time she made it across the room and found it in the bottom of the jumble, it had stopped ringing. She tried to get her fingers to stop shaking enough to hit the buttons to show the caller ID and find out who had called.

As soon as she hit the button, she stiffened from head to toe. Andy Barnhardt. The fire chief. And also the past president of the garden club.

She hoped and prayed he wasn't calling because her townhouse was on fire.

Instead of picturing the charred remains of her home, she pictured Andy. She figured he was close to fifty, and he did have a bit of gray at his temples, although he was always clean shaven. He certainly didn't have a belly like a marshmallow. But then again, being the fire chief, he was active in charity events, especially at Christmas time. If memory served her correctly, last year he had dressed up as Santa and had done something for the children's wing at the hospital. For that night Andy did indeed have a belly like a marshmallow, and he did have white hair and a beard.

She'd found Gnorman.

When Andy answered the phone, she smiled. She was right. Andy had been working a twelve-hour shift and just gotten home. When he opened his patio door, he'd seen the red of the Santa costume and called her.

Naturally, after she disconnected, she aimed her finger to autodial Stan, then stopped.

Every day she'd bugged Stan, obligating him to help her find Gnorman, and hopefully the trophy. The quest to recover her gnome from the Gnome Gnapper had turned into a wild goose chase.

It was time to give Stan his life back. He had better things to do. He'd been such a sweetie last night at the restaurant, she couldn't remember ever having more fun on a date, and with Stan of all people. She hadn't pictured Stan as a romantic kind of guy, but he was. He'd been charming and delightful, and, even though she'd never thought about him in that way before, he was hot. She always thought of all the things they'd done together when they were growing up and never gave him credit for the man he'd become. Living in the present, he was charming and handsome, and instead of taking up all his free time, she owed it to him to turn him loose.

Watching Ralph and Debbie at the restaurant, probably a day or two before Ralph proposed, was a reminder to her that even though they were older, both she and Stan were still painfully single.

For herself, she couldn't do anything about that until she settled her finances with her uncle. Her liabilities and heavy debt load were her problem, and she couldn't start a relationship with a man when she could possibly be dragged into bankruptcy. Nor could she start a relationship in Bloomfield if she failed before she got her loan paid off and had to move to Chicago.

But Stan could, and should, start a relationship. His business was successful and stable, and it was time to find that special someone before everyone was married except for him, and her. Which meant giving him the time he needed, without her pestering him every day.

Amber texted Stan with a nice thank-you for the plant, shut down her computer, locked up her store, and went to Andy's house alone.

CHAPTER Sixteen

Amber's stomach made a loud grumble as she pulled into Andy's driveway. It had taken her twenty minutes to walk home, which wasn't long, but added to the time she'd spent at the store trying to figure out where Gnorman had been moved to, and the ten-minute drive to Andy's house, it was an hour past her supper time. She'd skipped lunch, and she never ate breakfast; however, with all she'd had to eat yesterday at the restaurant with Stan, it wasn't like she was going to starve to death. She'd eaten enough calories in that one meal to sustain her for a week, and she didn't feel one iota of guilt.

Just as she put the car into Park, her cell phone buzzed with a text message from Stan. Short and sweet and to the point, as always.

where r u

Amber sighed and hit Reply.

Andy's. Gnorman is here.

She didn't bother putting her phone away. For a man with big fingers, he texted fast.

why didn't u call me

She sighed again, and in the middle of her sigh her breath caught as her stomach grumbled and a wave of pain shot through her. She wished she had an apple in her purse, but like her fridge, her purse was bare except for nonedible junk. She gritted her teeth as it passed, using the time to think of how to word her reply to Stan without hurting his feelings.

cuz I can't keep being a pest. c u tomrw

Instead of texting for half an hour from Andy's driveway, she turned the phone off and tucked it back into her purse. She would phone Stan when she got home, but this wasn't the time, nor the place. What she found would not be a surprise. She already knew what it would be, but some evil little bug on her shoulder told her she had to see for herself.

Amber stepped out of the car and onto Andy's driveway, and looked up at his house. The sun, ready to set, cast a golden aura around his home.

His perfectly manicured lawn, neatly trimmed around the edges, bordered his immaculately swept driveway. Instead of clumps of bushes like she'd seen at other garden club members' homes, Andy's flowers were set in neat rows with almost military precision. Like his lawn, all were in perfect condition with no hints of brown on any of the leaves or flowers.

Likewise, his home showed the same care. The shutters appeared freshly painted and new, a stately contrast to the old brick that made up the building. While it wasn't a huge house, it was certainly large for one person.

Suddenly she wished she hadn't tried to be noble and had asked Stan to join her. It hadn't been difficult to ask any of the ladies to escort her to their backyards to see Gnorman's new temporary home, but somehow having to ask Andy seemed . . . intimidating.

Gathering her courage, she knocked on the door. As it opened, instead of the gentle creak of an old hinge, an ear-shattering yowl pierced the silence.

Before her stood Andy, tall and still. On the floor beside him, Andy's brightly-colored parrot stretched out his wings and screeched like a stuck pig.

For a man old enough to be her father, Andy was quite a dashing and handsome fellow, even if a bit of a curmudgeon. She absolutely adored the little crow's feet that appeared around his eyes in the rare times that he smiled. She didn't adore the noisy parrot.

He tapped his watch. "What took you so long?"

When Amber opened her mouth to respond that she'd made it in good time considering she'd walked home instead of driven, the squawking parrot picked up his volume. Amber resisted the urge to cover her ears with her hands. "What's with him? I didn't do anything."

"Yes, you did. You banged on my door, and I opened it."

"But that's so annoying."

"I like it. Murray's better than a watchdog or one of them high-tech alarm systems."

"Are you saying he's a watch parrot?"

A harrumph escaped Andy's lips. "I suppose you could say that. How'd ya like to come in?" As Andy stepped away to give her room to enter, the parrot, still screeching, hopped backward.

Amber stepped in and shuffled away from the door quickly. "As long as you make sure he won't bite me in the ankle."

"He won't bite unless you try to take something away from him, and he'll stop hollering as soon as I close the door."

Amber quickly slipped past both of them to give Andy room to close the door. The second it clicked closed, the bird did exactly as he'd promised.

Her ears rang with the silence.

"See?"

She stared down at the parrot, who now looked almost friendly.

Almost.

"Do you think Murray might have noticed when Gnorman was placed in your backyard?"

"Probably, but it's not like he would fly outside and attack an intruder." He raised both of his bushy eyebrows as he looked down at Amber. "Most people ignore him. After all, he's not the least bit dangerous. He spends most of his days napping." Andy's face relaxed, and he bent down to touch the bird's head with one finger. "Your gnome arrived when I was out on duty. Come this way, and I'll show you where he is."

Amber tried not to be nosey, but she couldn't help making mental notes of Andy's house as he led her through to the back patio door. She tried not to cringe as the parrot half hopped and half flew behind them.

Everything in Andy's home was in balance as if he'd had a feng shui expert come in; although from her impression of him at the garden club meetings, he was probably a natural at it. All of his furniture was large and stately, in dark, masculine tones, and with no extras. There was nothing ornamental, only furniture that had a practical use, including a few sparse photographs depicting what appeared to be important events in his life.

The only other male-dominated house she'd ever been in was Stan's, and she couldn't exactly call that totally male-dominated because she'd helped him pick the furniture and accent colors. He hadn't let her do anything too girly, but it was far from blends of blacks, browns, and navy blue. Even though

Stan's house was never as clean as she would have liked, it was comfortable and well presented. While Andy's home was comfortable, everything about it yelled that a man did the decorating, and that a man lived there alone.

"There he is," Andy said as he reached for the door handle.

This time Amber prepared for the shrieking. She covered her ears with her hands and followed him outside. The parrot also went outside, where he flew up to a perch on the back porch, then flapped his wings and screeched at the open door. At the exact moment the door closed, the parrot silenced and folded his wings.

She looked up at the quirky bird. She could have sworn the bird winked at her. "Aren't you afraid he's going to fly away? Or are his wings clipped?"

Andy reached forward to tickle the bird's bright yellow belly, now at shoulder height, or at least shoulder height for her, even though it wasn't for Andy. She would never do that in fear of having her fingers nipped.

"Nope. None of the above. He's more than happy here, guarding the backyard. Maybe the colored flowers remind Murray of home."

She narrowed her eyes and glared at the bird. She didn't have any experiences with parrots or birds of any kind, and didn't figure this was the time to start. The only thing she knew was that birds liked to sit on anything that could serve as a perch.

She stared at Gnorman's raised hand—the hand that should have had the trophy strapped to it.

She didn't want bird poop on her gnome. "You're sure he won't leave his perch on the porch?"

"Absolutely not. When we go back to the house, he'll follow me in because he knows he's supposed to. Just like when I tell him to go into his cage, he will. Parrots are very smart."

She'd also heard pigs were smart, but she wouldn't put one to the test, or have one in her home.

But she wasn't here to learn about Andy's parrot. However, while she was here, she couldn't help but check out Andy's yard. Like the front, his backyard was set up nearly to the point of meticulous. He'd arranged all his plants and bushes by height, so the smallest stood at the edges, and everything grew taller toward the fence or the house. It was so organized that it was nearly perfect except for a spade and a fork leaning against the small garden shed that looked like he'd forgotten to put them away.

Gnorman had been placed on the grass, fortunately not in the flower bed, next to something with purple blooms that clashed horribly with the red Santa suit.

"I need to check and see if Gnorman's got a note somewhere. Every time he's moved, he gets a new note with a—"

Without warning, Murray screeched, again flapping his wings. This time, without Andy beside him, he extended his wings fully, which had to be a wingspan of nearly five feet. She'd never realized how big the bird was. Being so big and nasty, just as Andy said, Murray really could be considered a watch parrot. She certainly wouldn't want to tangle with him.

Amber ducked and covered her head with both hands, just in case he decided to launch and take whatever was annoying him out on her.

Just as suddenly as he started, the parrot silenced and folded his wings, once again sitting on his perch like nothing had happened.

"Murray hates the gate opening even worse than the door."

A different male voice echoed with the quick taps of footsteps. "What's going on? When did Gnorman get here?"

Amber lowered her arms to her sides, stood, and spun around. "Stan? What are you doing here?"

He stiffened at the mention of his name. "I came to see Gnorman and check out the new note." He paused, and his voice lowered. "And to find out why you didn't want me to come."

"It wasn't that I didn't want you to come, I just . . ." She let her voice trail off. She truly hadn't wanted him to come. But not for the reasons he thought. Not that she could know exactly what he was thinking, but judging from his expression, it wasn't good.

This was not a conversation she wanted to have in front of Andy.

Stan's eyes narrowed, and he crossed his arms over his chest.

Amber sucked in a deep breath and held it. Stan was angry. Really angry.

This was definitely not a conversation they were going to have in Andy's backyard, with Andy and his parrot watching and listening. She could trust Andy, but she didn't know much about parrots, except that they repeated words. She didn't want the parrot repeating anything discussed between her and Stan.

"How about if we get the new note, and talk about this later? I think—"

Her words caught in her throat as a wave of nausea washed over her. Past the point of pain from being overly hungry, she now felt like she might vomit.

"Amber? What's wrong?"

She pressed her hand into her stomach and forced herself to breathe deeply, hoping the feeling would pass. For a second her vision blurred, and the world started to spin. Even if she managed not to vomit this time, she would any minute, even though there was nothing to expel, if she didn't get something into her stomach right away. As she looked up at Stan, her vision started to narrow, like looking into a tunnel. The center went bright, her knees went weak, and the world began to fade to black.

Without knowing how she got there, she found herself seated on the ground with her knees up, her arms around her shins, and her head lowered between her knees.

A hand pressed firmly against her back, keeping her steady. "Breathe deeply. Slowly. Like that. Easy. In. Out."

Slowly, everything settled back into the right colors, and the world came back into focus. A cross between a buzzing and a ring pierced her ears.

Stan knelt to her right with one arm reaching behind her and his palm splayed on her back. Andy hunkered down to her left.

"Are you going to be okay?" Andy asked, while Stan continued to steady her. The ringing settled to a dull roar, then faded.

"I think so," she mumbled, unable to raise her head. "But I feel all shaky. I see stars."

Andy's fingers touched her throat. She knew he was feeling her pulse but couldn't move her arms to push him away. "Do you feel chest pains or numbness in your arms or legs?" he asked.

"No. I think I just need to eat something."

Andy stood. "I'll get her some juice. I'll be right back."

From down on the ground she saw his boots turn away, then more of him came into her field of vision as he jogged into the house. The parrot squawked as the door opened, so she knew she wasn't dead or hallucinating.

"What's wrong? Say something," Stan's voice came out a little shaky and scared. She hated to have done that to him.

"I'll be okay. I haven't eaten all day, and I think it just caught up with me."

"What do you mean? Have you been sick?"

"No." She shook her head, but as she did she knew she made a mistake. Her stomach rolled again, along with her head. She gulped and held herself stock-still until it started to pass. "I just got busy and didn't have time to eat. Then I thought I would come here before supper. That's all."

The momentary squawk sounded again, and she soon saw the boots beside her head. Andy hunkered down and handed her a glass of red juice. She used two hands to steady it while she drank. Andy kept one hand hovering close by, probably in case he had to grab the glass fast, and Stan's hand remained against her back.

She tried to keep her hand from shaking as she gave the glass back to Andy. "That was just what I needed. I'm going to be okay. Thank you. I'm so sorry."

Andy remained hunkered down. "You should stay down like that for ten to fifteen minutes, just to be safe. I'm also going to make sure you're okay before you leave, and you shouldn't be driving."

She may not have been back to her 100 percent fine self, but there was no way she was sitting like an invalid lump in Andy's yard for that long. Besides, her butt was getting cold, and she felt sure she now had a damp spot on the seat of her pants from sitting so long on the cooling evening grass. She put her hands down on the grass and pushed herself up. Before she got all the way to a standing position, Stan's hands wrapped around her waist, and he pulled her the rest of the way.

"She's not going home, and she's definitely not driving. I'll take her and get some good food into her. But first I'll move her car onto the street so you can get yours out of the garage in the morning, if it's okay that we leave it here on the street.

"That's fine with me. If you're going to be on your way, you'll probably want this." Andy handed the envelope to Stan, like she didn't exist. "Phone me when you get home, just so I know everything's okay."

Stan nodded. "We'll do that. Thanks."

Stan released her waist, but only for a millisecond. One hand went around her back at her shoulder blades, and he bent over, reaching for the back of her knees.

Even though she still felt shaky, she shuffled to the side. "No. Please don't pick me up. I feel embarrassed enough as it is. I'm going to walk, and then I'm going to get in my car and drive home."

"If you walk, you're walking to my pickup, and you're going to get inside and stay there while I move your car, and then I'm going to take you home. If you have any thoughts about moving your car yourself, or driving it, I'm going to pick you up, whether you like it or not, caveman-style, and plunk you in my truck and drive away, and let Andy move your car. Your choice."

That didn't sound like much of a choice at all. Amber opened her mouth to tell him exactly what she thought of his tyrannical behavior, but no words came out. His eyes narrowed, his cheeks tightened, and his brows knotted. She'd seen pictures of friendlier grizzly bears. She had no doubt he meant what he said and that he would carry out what he promised, or threatened. For now, she'd let him have his way. She still felt weak and shaky. But as soon as he left and she felt better, she would walk back to Andy's house, get her car and drive it home, and life would go on as normal.

Yet, even with the Neanderthal attitude, she couldn't be mad at him. He was obviously worried, no less than she'd been the time he'd got knocked over when a cyclist ran into him when they'd been walking through the park at college. In the end, just like this, it had been nothing, but at the time she'd been terrified, watching him hit the ground and bounce, then remain unmoving for those very long seconds, getting his breath back and waiting for his world to stop spinning as he lay face down in the dirt.

Truly, she felt better after drinking the juice. When she got home she would make herself some toast, and she'd be good.

Because she'd promised, once Stan made sure she was seated in his pickup with the seat belt fastened to his satisfaction,

Amber watched him move her car out of Andy's driveway and park it on the street. He pocketed her keys, got in, and drove away.

"Stan? Where are you going? You missed the turn to go to my house."

"I'm not going to your house. You're going to my house. Don't bother complaining, because this is nonnegotiable. So sit back and enjoy the ride."

CHAPTER Seventeen

It took all Stan's strength and concentration to hold on to the steering wheel, and to keep holding on, when he really wanted to hold Amber.

He'd never been so scared in his life as when all the color drained from her face, her eyes rolled back, she swayed, then collapsed.

Being a firefighter, Andy was trained as a first responder in an emergency, compared to Stan's rudimentary level first aid certificate, which, come to think of it, had expired. Fortunately, instead of his mind going blank with panic, Stan had kicked into autopilot as he helped Andy ease Amber to the ground and put her head between her knees.

Then, he'd felt terrified. Now that the crisis was over, he just felt angry.

But he had to hold it in. At work, he could bang a dozen things to get it out of his system. Here, he had Amber.

Soft, gentle, and for now, frail, little Amber.

Of course, once he got some food into her system and had her all fueled up, she'd again be a fighting machine, ready to take on her corner of the world. But for now she needed someone to take care of her, and that someone was him.

She remained silent the whole trip to his house, which was a good thing. He didn't want to start a conversation, because he didn't trust himself not to say something stupid.

And speaking of stupid, Amber wasn't. When they got to his house, she stayed in the seat and waited while he ran around the truck and opened the door for her and helped her down. Even though he didn't have to help her keep steady, he put his arm around her anyway, just because he wanted to, and walked with her like that to his door. And, not being stupid, Amber didn't say anything; she just let him have his way.

He knew her acquiescence wouldn't last, so he took advantage of it while he could.

He guided her to the couch and helped her to sit down. When she looked comfortable, he dragged the ottoman in front of her and sat on it to face her.

"We need to talk," he said, even though he wasn't good at that talking stuff. That's why he ran a business fixing cars instead of working in an office or doing a sales job. He wasn't a talker. He just liked to do things, especially when it didn't involve words.

He waited for a response. Something. Anything. Right now, his mind whirled a mile a minute. He'd been through so many ups and downs that he didn't know where to start. All day long his thoughts had returned to Amber, about how much fun they'd had the previous night, but not the usual way they had fun together. Last night he'd seen another side to her, the side of Amber that she didn't always show him, at least not on purpose—sweet, funny, smart, and even though she would never admit it to him, feminine. It truly had been a real date, even with the disguises. He didn't know why it had taken the disguises to make everything so obvious. It had been there all along—they were soul mates—and all these years, he'd missed it.

Most of the morning he'd waited like a besotted idiot for her to call, but she hadn't. He'd spent all day making sure he could hear his phone. He'd even checked it multiple times, just in case he'd missed her call and it had gone to voice mail. He'd wanted to hear her sweet, melodic voice, even in just a message, maybe saying she'd missed him too.

But that hadn't happened.

During the day she'd obviously received a note with another clue, figured out where Gnorman was, then gone to see Gnorman and get the new note. When he figured out what happened and the chain of events, he'd lost it.

He'd gone storming over to Andy's house, about to tell her what he thought of her ignoring him, and arrived just in time to see her crumple to the ground like a deflated balloon. Even though it felt so clichéd, he'd almost blurted out to Amber that he loved her as she tumbled into his arms.

She looked at him, and her eyes went wide, wider than he'd ever seen. "Did you want to ask me something?"

Stan swallowed. Hard. "Yeah. Now that we're here, what would you like for supper?"

AMBER STRUGGLED TO KEEP her relief from showing. A wide range of expressions flittered across Stan's face, but she couldn't tell what he was thinking. It would be a relief if he scolded her for fainting like a seventeenth-century lady-in-waiting with her girdle on too tight, but he didn't. Instead, Stan simply wanted to help her. Again. Still.

He was the best buddy a woman could ever have. Somewhere out there was a woman who would be perfect for him, someone who could love him the way he deserved to be loved, because he had what it took to love a woman back. One day he would meet such a woman. Amber might even like that woman. If she could stop herself from scratching the woman's eyes out.

She cleared her throat. "I don't know. Something light. What have you got?"

He glanced over his shoulder toward the kitchen, then back at her. "How about a grilled cheese sandwich, with three kinds of cheese and onions. On whole wheat bread."

Fried in lots of butter, no doubt. Her stomach lurched, just thinking about it.

"When I said light, I meant something like an apple."

"An apple isn't supper. How about leftover spaghetti?"

"That sounds great."

She followed him into the kitchen and sat at the table, watching as he spooned a massive portion onto a plate, drowned it with sauce, and sprinkled it liberally with grated parmesan cheese. "Here you go," he said as he put it in the microwave and pushed the button.

"I hope you're going to eat that with me. That's enough for three people."

He grinned, no doubt thinking she was kidding. "Don't worry. I'm going to make a plate for myself too."

The volume of his leftovers could feed her for three days while, for her, leftovers were a thing of the past. After contracting the orders for the flamingos for both the florist and the garden club's banquet, she had to buy the materials to make them. Her wholesaler had offered a discount if she paid for everything at the time she placed the order, and since she had to make every penny count, it was a deal she couldn't refuse. She couldn't take the money off her lease, she'd just paid her insurance, her car was running on fumes when she couldn't walk to where she needed to go, and she certainly had to make the current payment to Uncle Henry on time.

The only place left, the last place where she could get money, was her grocery budget. For the last few weeks she'd been living pretty much on macaroni and wieners, minus the wieners, or toast and peanut butter, and she'd gotten to the point of scraping the bottom of the jar.

When she'd gone out for lunch after church with Stan, she'd insisted on paying for her own burger and fries, and that had cut deeply into her grocery budget for the rest of the week.

She'd snuck a peek at the amount when Stan paid the bill for their extravagant dinner. The way she'd so carefully budgeted her groceries, she could have eaten for an entire week with what he spent on their one meal.

Still, she couldn't begrudge him that. He worked hard for his money, and he deserved to spend it however he wanted. It had been an honor that he'd spent it on her. However, if he had any idea of how she struggled, he would insist on paying for everything until she was back on her feet. That was just the kind of friend he was. It would be kind, but it would also be another loan she couldn't afford to pay back until she got a handle on repaying Uncle Henry. She could never accept money from Stan. He would refuse repayment, no matter what she did to try to persuade him. Taking money from Stan would start a downward spiral that began with kindness and ended their friendship. She couldn't live without Stan's friendship.

When he placed the heaping plate of spaghetti in front of her, she almost asked if she could have a doggie bag. Because she was so hungry, and because it had been so long since she'd eaten, if she ate even half of what he set before her, she'd be sick.

"I can't eat all this. It's too much."

"Then eat what you feel you can handle. But I'm warning you, it better be enough to sustain you. Now eat."

He sat down in front of her to lead a short and very sweet prayer of thanks for the food and that she was fine, and he watched her eat until the microwave dinged with his portion.

"You always tell me when you're on a diet, but you didn't say anything this time. If you ask me, you don't need to go on a diet."

Her fork froze in midair. "Diet?"

"I've seen that you've been losing weight lately. I hope you're not planning on losing any more. Your pants don't fit right anymore."

Her cheeks started to burn. "You've been watching the way my pants fit?"

He broke out into a playful grin. "Yeah. Us guys do that."

"What do you mean, 'us guys'? What other guys?"

The grin dropped. "No other guys. I'm just saying."

She wanted to ask him what it was, exactly, that he was just saying, but the concept that Stan paid such close attention to her figure made her too nervous.

"I liked the way you ate when we went out last night. We'll have to do that again."

"The way I ate?"

The grin returned. "Yeah. You, uh, looked like you were really enjoying it."

The lobster was great, but way beyond her budget. Especially now. "Yes. I enjoyed it. It was a very pleasant surprise."

"Why don't I take you someplace else next weekend, and we can see what other surprises you might like?"

"I guess so." Something about his eyes made Amber feel there was some hidden meaning behind his question, but then he grinned, and she lost all ability to think. When Stan could do that just by smiling at her, it was time to change the subject.

"I saw that Andy gave you the new envelope. I think we should see what it says."

Stan shifted in the chair and pulled the crumpled envelope out of his pocket. He made short work of tearing it open, and slid the new note to her across the table. Again, like most of the others, it was constructed from words cut out from the *Gazette*.

Since it would be upside down for Stan, sitting opposite from her, Amber read it out loud.

in winter we skate
on a rink.
in spring we have flowers
of pink.
Summer is hot.
autumn is not.
and Gnorman is gone in
a Blink.

Stan stared at the note in the center of the table. "Is it my imagination, or are they getting worse every time?"

"It's not your imagination."

"The clues are getting worse too. This doesn't make any sense."

Amber looked up at Stan as he read the note for himself, realizing he was reading upside down. Not that it would have made any more sense right side up. It was still just as meaningless.

She reached and turned it around for him.

His brows knotted as he read it again. "If we followed the time line of this one, that means Gnorman is going to stay in

Andy's yard until fall, then disappear. We know that's not likely to happen."

"I agree. It can't mean that. Maybe it just means as sure as the seasons are predictable in their pattern, the same with Gnorman disappearing."

"Which doesn't help us one bit."

She should have read the note again, but instead, Amber watched Stan while he concentrated on the alleged clue.

Usually she could figure out what he was thinking, but lately, she couldn't. Her thoughts returned to their earlier conversation. She didn't know what to make of his comment about watching the way her clothes fit. Contrary to his stated opinion, she did need to lose weight. She was always five to ten pounds more than what the books said she should weigh, but she'd never been able to lose it. She wasn't trying to lose weight now, only trying to make her food budget stretch until the garden club committee paid her for at least some of the flamingos.

Nor could she comprehend what Stan meant when he said he liked the way she ate. While she'd thoroughly enjoyed the meal, from the appetizers to the last bite of lobster she'd swiped out from under him, for most of the meal she'd put on an exaggerated show of how good everything was, closing her eyes and puckering her lips, hamming it up because of the disguise. Acting a role. Simply having fun.

Even Stan had acted different than usual. Instead of the usual good ol' Stan, he really had acted like they were on a date, which was ridiculous, but so much fun.

The whole night had been fun until she thought he was going to kiss her good night.

Stan pressed his index finger to the note and raised his head. "I don't think this thing about winter is a valid clue. I don't think this could mean any private rinks people make in their yards, so there's only one real noteworthy rink in town, at the community center, and it's long melted."

"Mayor Woody says he wants to put it in the budget to build an indoor rink in Bloomfield."

Stan snorted. "Ain't gonna happen. There aren't enough people here to use it often enough to make it pay for itself. Now back to this note. It skirts summer and fall, but it does mention flowers, which for a garden club is really important. But to just say flowers in general, for a garden club, is pretty nonspecific."

Amber tapped one finger to her lips. "But it is specific about the flowers being pink. Except that everyone has pink flowers somewhere in their garden."

"Except you." His cheeks tightened, like he was trying not to laugh.

Amber looked around for something to smack him with, but he pushed the chair back and laughed anyway when she reached behind her, pulled the dishtowel from the handle on the oven door, swung it at him, and missed.

"I have some flowers. They just haven't bloomed yet. When they do, maybe some of them will be pink."

"I don't want to ask why you don't know what color flowers you have in your garden. Everyone else knows what they've planted. My mother even has a specific color scheme every year. Except for the roses. But all the annuals are always one color. This year they're all . . ." his voice trailed off.

". . . pink . . ." they said in unison.

For the first time they figured out where Gnorman was going to be, before he got there.

Now to figure out what to do about it.

CHAPTER Eighteen

Amber always enjoyed going to Stan's parents' house. They were still together, still happily married, and seeing the two of them together, in the same house they'd owned since they were married, next door to the house where she'd grown up, always made her feel grounded.

Still, a huge degree of sadness always weighted her down when she visited, even though she hadn't lived there for seven years. She doubted she'd ever get over the loss. After she graduated from college her parents went to visit her mother's family when her grandmother's heath began to fail. Once there, they found they enjoyed the difference from tiny town to mega-metropolis and made the move permanent. Amber had been happy for them, even though she missed them terribly. The worst day of her life was when she got the call from her mother's brother, Uncle Henry, telling her that her parents had been killed in an automobile accident.

If it hadn't been for Stan and his parents, she didn't know how she could have made it through that.

Even still, nearly every time she came to visit Kathy and Frank, Kathy pointed out the old garden shed that the new owners never did tear down. Her mother had marked both her and Stan's height on it every year until they both stopped growing. As a child, it had been fun. As a teen, it got rather embarrassing.

Just like always, Kathy gave her a big hug when she walked in the door, which Amber often thought odd. Kathy didn't hug her son when they visited, but she hugged her ex-neighbor.

"What brings you two out here? Did you find your little gnome?"

Like everyone else, the first thing people asked about was the gnome. So far, no one had asked about the trophy, which really was the most important of the two missing items. Every time someone asked, she had to assume that everyone thought that Gnorman and the trophy naturally went along as a set. The garden club members never really saw one without the other. When the trophy wasn't in someone's garden strapped to Gnorman's hand, it was in a case at Pamela's home. As president, she kept all the club's archives. When Gnorman wasn't proudly displaying the trophy, he lived in Amber's backyard. Until he started running around town, of course.

Amber smiled politely. "We haven't found him yet, but Stan and I think we're close to finding out who's been doing this. I wonder if you could do us a favor?"

"Anything."

Stan stepped forward and held out the box he'd been carrying. "Amber made a special garden ornament shaped like a squirrel and some flowers, and she's hoping to attract butterflies with it. We're wondering if we can keep it in your yard for a few days to test it out."

Amber quickly turned away so Kathy wouldn't see her face. At first she had wanted to attract butterflies, but her creation hadn't looked like it did now. She had a live Butterfly Bush in a planter, with the squirrel on the side reaching into the bush while he climbed the planter. Stan had switched the real plant with a jumble of wires and ceramic flowers meant not to adorn, but to mask. In the conglomeration of fake flowers, he'd hidden a small surveillance camera that transmitted to the receiver that was now hidden under the mulch in the planter, which used to be filled with potting soil.

At first they had planned to tell his mother what they were doing, but at the same time they both realized how much Kathy liked to talk. Amber had learned at a young age not to trust her neighbor with a secret because Kathy never could keep one. The quickest way to spread news around Bloomfield wasn't to take out an ad in the *Gazette*, it was to tell Kathy.

They were pretty sure the Gnome Gnapper was a member of the garden club. If they told Kathy about the hidden camera, the Gnapper would know before sunset. Then, all their hard work would be for naught.

If Kathy didn't know about the hidden camera, all they had to do was wait.

Kathy made a strange face at the sculpture, but Frank walked up to it and touched the ceramic flowers and poked at the wire supports. "Why do you think this would attract butterflies? They don't look like real flowers, and they have no scent. I don't think it's going to work."

Amber gritted her teeth. She'd told Stan that no one would believe it. She didn't know much about flowers, but she did know about butterflies. However, Stan convinced her that only real wires would support the camera and keep it aimed where they needed it, and they needed a spot to hide the receiver if they couldn't keep it in the house. The arrangement had become uglier and uglier as Stan worked to get it how he needed it. Now if anyone besides his parents saw it, she would faint again, only this time from embarrassment.

"I'm hoping the color will do it. If it doesn't work, I'm going to change the colors until I get it just right."

This time Kathy took a poke at one of the flowers, then touched the ceramic squirrel. "I don't know about this."

Stan gave his mother a huge, wide-eyed smile, something no mother could say no to. "Please? This is really important to us."

Both his mother and father quirked an eyebrow at the same time, almost like they'd practiced, but Amber knew they hadn't. Most of the time they didn't have a clue that they both did the same thing at the same time, often finishing each other's sentences. Amber had to wonder if it was a casualty of living together for so many decades.

"Us?" his mother quipped.

"Yes. You know how I'm always trying to help Amber with her garden. We think butterflies would make her garden happier. Also, if this works, she can make more so other people can put them in their gardens too."

Amber tried not to choke. They'd rehearsed what they were going to say, but Stan was going way over the top with it. Especially since she'd seen better artwork at the garden club's summer preschool craft program. There was a reason Stan was a mechanic.

Frank looked down at the project. "I don't know. It really won't match Kathy's color scheme this year."

"It's really important to us." Despite his father's protests, Stan carried the statue into the backyard. Amber and Kathy watched while Frank disagreed with everywhere Stan tried to place it. She knew Stan was trying to aim the camera to take in the biggest scope of where the Gnapper could leave Gnorman, but she had a feeling that Frank wanted to get it as far out of sight as possible.

Rather than watch the father/son debacle, Amber followed Kathy back into the house to help make some tea.

"Please tell me that Stan put that arrangement together, and not you."

Amber sighed. She couldn't tell Kathy the complete truth, or they would never get to the bottom of the problem. "Let's just say that I started it, and Stan finished it."

"I don't understand. He's got much better taste than that. Look at his house. I have to admit I was surprised, but it proves he's got a sense of style."

Amber nibbled her lower lip. She didn't want to say too much, but she couldn't lie. "I might have helped him decorate his house."

"Of course you did. We knew you helped him, but we never knew how much." Kathy's hands froze on the teapot. "Just exactly how much of his house did you decorate?"

"I think I'd rather not say." Too late Amber realized that she'd said more with what she didn't say, than what she did.

A silence hung while Kathy digested her son's lack of artistic ability and failure to coordinate colors. Amber had helped him choose his furniture, and she'd coordinated the colors, both for his house and garden. The only thing she didn't do was dress him. It didn't take a lot of coordination to match jeans and a T-shirt and put coveralls on top.

Although, when they went to church on Sundays, and then on their non-date last weekend, he sure did look good, and he'd done that on his own.

Either he wasn't as bad as he led her to believe, or he'd asked for help from the sales staff. Or perhaps he bought his outfits from the sale flyers and bought exactly the outfit pictured so that his good clothes were put together by the professionals who dressed the models for the photo shoot.

Next time he went shopping, Amber planned to ask to see the flyer.

Kathy tilted her head and studied her. "What are you smiling about?"

Amber felt her cheeks warm up. "Sorry," she muttered. "I was thinking about something else. I think the kettle is boiling."

Kathy poured Frank's tea and added just the right amount of milk for Frank, while Amber poured Stan's tea, adding a spoon and a half of sugar, just the way he liked it.

Frank and Stan appeared to have finally agreed on the best location for the hidden camera, although Stan didn't appear to be quite satisfied.

They made small talk and caught up on the events of the past week, and as soon as the cups were empty, Amber and Stan left.

After being in Andy's yard for three days, Gnorman's time there was nearing an end. When Gnorman found his next new temporary home, they would be ready for him.

CHAPTER Nineteen

Stan rubbed his hands together in anticipation of what they would find.

Sure enough, Gnorman appeared in his parents' yard, as anticipated.

Normally Amber enjoyed visiting Stan's parents, but this time it had almost killed her to find some excuse to make them stay inside the house while Stan ran into the yard to switch the memory card in the receiver. Now that they were back at Stan's house, she could hardly wait to find out who had been taunting them with Gnorman's escapes.

"I can't believe your mother didn't notice when Gnorman appeared in the backyard. She said she was home for most of the day and didn't hear or see a thing."

Stan pushed the card into the slot. "It doesn't surprise me that Dad noticed Gnorman first."

"I know. I thought it was funny when he said how badly the hippie costume clashed with your mother's pink color-of-the-year scheme."

Stan couldn't stop his snicker. "It was funnier watching my mother. I really thought she was going to lose it. She said it had to be some kind of hint that they were getting old. But really, if you do the math, my parents would only have been kids in the hippie generation. It's hard to believe that the activists of that generation are now retired grandparents."

"Time marches on. Now march that video on. I want to see who's been playing games with us. I need to get that trophy back into Becky's yard before snowfall."

"It's a long way from winter. We haven't reached the hottest part of the summer yet." Before hitting the button, Stan ran his hand over his back pocket, which held the newest note. They'd been so excited about catching the Gnapper that neither of them felt the note was important. They were about to find out the Gnapper's identity, yet he wasn't as relieved as he should have been. Even though chasing the gnome had been a lot of gnonsense . . . nonsense . . . he'd thoroughly enjoyed all the time he spent with Amber. Except when she keeled over and nearly sent him into cardiac arrest. However, going on a wild goose, or rather, wild gnome chase, gave him the excuse to be with her nearly every day, which made him recognize that he wanted to see her every day. When life returned to normal he would no longer have an excuse to drop by unannounced or spend an evening together just to kill time. Even when they didn't talk, he enjoyed simply being with her, which didn't make sense, but that was how he felt.

With mixed feelings, he hit the button. "Here goes," he said, trying to sound cheerful.

He set it to fast-forward, but it was still boring. Since they didn't know exactly what time Gnorman showed up, they started at the beginning to watch eight hours worth of the yard in the dark of night. By morning the yard was still bare, which was what he'd expected.

Not long after sunup, his mother entered the yard wearing baggy sweatpants and rubber boots with her weeding tools in her hands, and proceeded to start weeding the flower beds.

"I don't feel right about watching this," Amber mumbled. "It feels wrong when she doesn't know she's being recorded. But it is kind of amusing watching it on fast forward. I wish I could get my weeding done in fast-action like this."

As his mother made her way along the length of the bed, soon they had a close-up view of her rear end. Right in front of the camera, she got on her hands and knees and stretched to reach behind the bushes with her hand-held hoe.

"I don't want to see this," Stan muttered, and covered his eyes with his hands. "Tell me when she's done."

"She's done."

Just as Amber spoke, his father walked into the picture. Judging from the light, it was first thing in the morning, and he was leaving for work. He walked up to Stan's mother and gave her a long kiss, with one hand making a journey down her back, pulling her close to him. She went willingly, and her shovel dropped to the ground.

Stan groaned and covered his face again. "This is something else I don't want to see."

He could feel Amber's glare through his hands. He widened his fingers, looking between them to see Amber staring at him, her eyes narrowed, giving him the same look he used to get from his teacher in grade school when she caught him passing notes in the classroom.

"How dare you. It's so sweet that they still do that after all these years together. They're so in love after all this time. I wish I could see my mother and father like this."

A wave of guilt washed through him. Not only were his parents still in love after more than thirty years of marriage, but they were both alive and active. Maybe when Gnorman and the trophy were recovered, he'd take both his parents and Amber out for a nice dinner to celebrate together.

He lowered his hands and turned back to the screen. "You're right. After seeing so many marriages fail, I do appreciate the relationship my parents have. I just don't want to watch it. After all, they're my parents."

"You'd watch if this was a movie, and two strangers were doing that."

Instead of picturing strangers doing the same thing, he pictured himself with Amber.

He shook the thought from his head and returned his attention to the screen. His father left for work, and his mother returned to her weeding.

With the weeding complete, she went back into the house, and they watched the empty yard. It was almost as boring as watching the blackness of night, but not quite. It would have been more interesting if he'd turned the camera a bit more skyward, so they could at least watch the clouds move.

"Can you make the fast-forward go any faster?"

"No. There's only one speed. I had to buy this thing without a lot of notice, and there was only one kind available. It was this or nothing. There isn't a huge demand for surveillance equipment in Bloomfield."

Suddenly the picture swayed. With it Stan's stomach lurched, like he was seasick. The picture moved, and suddenly they saw the grass, from up close.

"What happened?"

Amber turned and snapped at him. "So much for your plan. That rattletrap conglomeration must have been too top-heavy, and got knocked over in the wind."

He turned to her. "There's no wind today. I had all the shop doors open. I would have felt any wind. I think someone knocked it down. "

From his peripheral vision, he detected more movement and turned back to the screen. When he did, Amber did too. The same movement of the camera happened in reverse, and the camera once again encompassed his parents' yard, only this time Gnorman was there.

"This is just great," he sighed. "The Gnapper knocked the statue over on the way into the yard, then very graciously righted it on his or her way out."

Amber stared at the screen. "Don't you think that was a little convenient?"

"No. It was top-heavy and we knew it. It would be easy to knock over."

"I'm wondering if the Gnapper knew it had a camera hidden in it, and knocked it over on purpose."

"That's impossible. No one knew."

"One person knew. Where did you buy the camera? Was it someone you knew?"

"That's a difficult thing to answer. Lots of people bring their cars into my shop and they remember me as their mechanic, but to me, from behind the counter, most of the people I meet jumble into a sea of faces. I meet over a hundred people every week. Some I only see once, some come six months later for the next oil change, and some are regulars. Maybe it was someone I met before. I don't know. But if it wasn't someone I knew well, they wouldn't know about me helping you try to find Gnorman and recover the trophy." As he spoke, he tried to remember if he'd ever seen the woman who sold him the spy camera, and he honestly couldn't.

"That's not true. They could have seen your name in the *Gazette*."

"While this is a lot of excitement for the garden club, this isn't an event that's going to make the local news in the paper."

"But you said when this first started that the *Gazette* was running a contest, with prizes to see who could guess Gnorman's next costume."

"Right. I forgot about that." He'd even read the article and groaned at how the reporter had worded the story. He or she had put a funny spin on it and had made it quite entertaining. Stan would have enjoyed it more if the story had been about someone else, but it was impersonal enough that he'd not felt it too invasive. Until now. "I'm sure I'd remember if I'd seen the woman before at the garden club." Almost sure, anyway. Truth be told, he didn't watch the women at the garden club. The only woman he watched was Amber. He wasn't really interested in talking to other single women, but a lot approached him to ask about car trouble. To that, he always told them to bring their car to the shop so he could have a proper look, then he got one of his three employees to do it.

"In other words, you don't know for sure."

"Something like that. But I'd certainly know if it was someone who came in often. Anyone who didn't wouldn't care enough to be interested."

"Did you use your personal charge card or your company charge card?"

Automatically he covered his wallet in his back pocket with his palm. "How did you know I used my credit card?"

"Because if it was over $20, you never carry enough cash."

Busted. "So what? You don't either."

"That wasn't the point. The point was that the person who sold you the spy camera knew your name and your business. If they were following the contest, they probably would have recognized your name and made the connection."

At the time the article had come out, he'd convinced himself that since the reporter had also mentioned the name of his business, it had been good free advertising. Hayden had been the first to mention it, but after that a number of people who came into his shop in the week following the article had also talked to him about it. Some he knew, some he didn't. Then he'd dug the issue out of his recycle bin and read it.

"I concede. Maybe the woman who worked there figured it out. But I say it's a long shot." He stared blankly at Gnorman the hippie, and sighed. "We have no choice. We have to tell my mother about the camera. It's the only way we can be sure we're going to catch whoever this is when Gnorman is removed."

Amber groaned. "Then for sure we'll be chasing Gnorman until it snows."

He reached into his back pocket for the envelope, then froze.

Reading it now would be admitting defeat. He couldn't do that.

He imagined his mother's reaction when she found out that they had video of her backside. "This is something we should do in person. On the way we need to stop at the grocery store. This probably calls for chocolate cheesecake."

CHAPTER Twenty

Amber followed Stan and the cheesecake as they entered Kathy and Frank's home.

It felt odd walking in without knocking, but it probably would have felt even stranger if Stan had knocked. For Amber as well, since she'd spent considerable time here. For many years their mothers had traded day-care arrangements while both worked part-time jobs, coordinating their schedules. When her mother was working, Stan's mother cared for her and Stan, and when Kathy was working, Amber's mother cared for the two of them.

For all the time they'd spent together until they went their separate ways after college, they should have had a severe case of separation anxiety. They'd nearly been joined at the hip.

Kathy sat at one end of the couch knitting, while Frank sat in the recliner watching a basketball game. She smiled brightly at Stan as they entered the living room.

"This is a surprise." Her gaze dropped to the cheesecake, and her smile transformed into a deep frown. "What did you do?" she asked, her voice taking on an accusing edge.

Amber turned her head so Kathy wouldn't see her trying not to laugh. She'd told Stan his mother would know something was up, but he'd insisted on buying the cheesecake anyway.

Like a little boy who'd just been caught with his fingers in the cookie jar, he blushed. "We need your help, so I brought a peace offering."

She could see the juxtaposition of thought as Kathy tried to connect the concept of help with an apology.

"It's about Amber's squirrel statue."

Kathy's smile returned. "I know it's not her usual caliber, and the colors don't coordinate with my garden, but it certainly doesn't need a cheesecake to apologize. As long as no one sees it, I'm fine. But I'll take the cheesecake anyway." Kathy set her knitting down, stood, and extended her hands to take the cheesecake from Stan. Her eyes lit up when she saw the label and noted that it was her favorite kind.

As soon as she closed her fingers around the box, Stan said, "Mom, we have a hidden camera in the statue."

It was a good thing he didn't let it go. Kathy's hands went limp, and her arms dropped to her side. "What are you talking about?"

Stan looked down at the cheesecake, as if intently reading the label. "We saw you doing your gardening, and we saw you and Dad, well, you know. I'm sorry."

Kathy's eyes lost focus, and Amber could see the exact moment Kathy figured out what she and Stan had seen because her cheeks turned a deep red.

Stan chose that moment to look up. When he saw his mother's red face, he blushed as well. "What we wanted to see was the person who keeps moving Gnorman around, but they knocked the statue over when they came into the yard and set it right when they left. It didn't catch who is doing this. So we need your help."

"What do you want me to do? I can't make sure they don't knock it over again, but they probably won't. I would think whoever knocked it over was afraid they broke it and won't go near it the second time."

"I need to anchor it so it won't fall, and I need to make sure it's aimed right at Gnorman so we can catch them red-handed. Or red-gnomed."

"I don't see a problem with that. Do you, Frank?"

Frank shook his head without taking his attention off the game.

"We're pretty sure it's someone in the garden club, and you know how fast news travels around there."

Amber bit her lower lip. Kathy showed no sign of acknowledging that she was the largest perpetrator of spreading said news, otherwise known as gossip. All she did was nod.

Stan and Kathy walked into the backyard while Amber took the cheesecake into the kitchen and cut it into slices. It was already dark outside, but enough residual light from the house and the glow of the streetlights allowed her to watch as Stan showed his mother where the lens was hidden. She poked and prodded, nodding as Stan explained how it worked before stepping back inside.

Frank picked up one of the plates and returned to the television, while Amber stayed in the kitchen with Stan and Kathy making small talk only for as long as it took to eat the dessert without rushing.

On the way back to her townhouse, Stan was silent for so long that she began to get nervous.

"What's wrong?" she finally asked as they rounded the last corner to her house.

"Nothing. I'm just trying to figure out what we're going to say when we confront this person once we know the truth. Have you thought about the possibilities?"

"Yes, and I haven't a clue who it is. But we have a good start on who it isn't. It isn't Naomi; we found Gnorman behind her place first."

Stan pulled into her driveway and turned off the ignition, but he didn't exit the truck. "It's not Ronnie or her mother, Minnie. We found him dressed like a pirate at the theater."

Amber held out one hand and counted down the non-suspects on her fingers. "It's not Libby; we found him dressed like a clown at her place. And it's not Sylvia. That's where he was the octogenarian rock star."

She kept counting on her fingers while Stan continued. "It's not Andy; that's where we found him dressed as Santa. And it's not my mother."

"We also know it's not Becky because Gnorman was stolen from her yard in the first place." She held out both hands. "That's seven who it's not. And it's not you or me." Her whole body sagged as she did the mental math.

"Nine down, seventy to go."

She sighed, not feeling the least bit encouraged. The hidden camera had to work. "You don't have to see me to the door. I'm tired, I just want to go to bed. I'll see you tomorrow."

IT WAS SIX EXCRUCIATING days before Gnorman disappeared. Amber figured out that the Gnapper did the opposite of making up for lost time by taking extra time to compensate for moving Gnorman quickly out of some of the other yards. Either that, or besides having something against her, the Gnapper also had something against Kathy, because Gnorman's outlandish costume clashed so badly with Kathy's color scheme of the year.

Every day they diligently went into Kathy's backyard to

reset the recorder to erase the memory card and start again. That way they wouldn't have to watch as much nothingness when Gnorman finally disappeared again. Now, finally, they had the answer.

Kathy had phoned Stan to say that Gnorman vanished while she went to the mall. Even though the screen was smaller than his PC, Stan arrived with his laptop to pick Amber up, and they went straight to Kathy and Frank's, although Stan made a quick trip at the drive-thru to pick up burgers for everyone's supper.

Amber was in no rush to eat. She knew they would have to watch an entire night's worth of video, and into the afternoon, and she already knew how long it would take. While prepared to eat leisurely, she hadn't expected Stan to watch her like a hawk to make sure she ate every crumb.

"Doesn't this thing go any faster?" Kathy asked.

Amber rested one hand on Stan's forearm. "It only goes one speed. All we can do is wait it out."

To kill time, knowing they would have their answer soon, Amber thought she could make a game out of it. After all, if the *Gazette* was holding a contest, she could do the same, on a much smaller scale, of course. "Tell me, Kathy, who do you think it is?"

"I think Stan should guess. After all, you two are the ones who have been chasing Gnorman around Bloomfield."

Stan's expression surely was the same as her own. She'd been positive that Kathy would be anxious to share her opinion, with a full story of why she considered that person her prime suspect.

"I have no idea," Stan replied. "We've been trying to figure this out all season. All we know is that it's a member of the garden club."

Also, someone with a terrible pentameter.

Finally the image on the screen lightened, and the strip of visible sky showed the glorious colors of the sunrise. In a way, it was a shame that Stan hadn't gotten the whole sunrise, but then again, at this speed, it was over in under a minute. The sky was blue and the morning had begun.

This time, when Kathy came out to weed the garden, she was dressed in good jeans, her hair was combed, and she wore makeup. As she weeded her garden, she kept turning around and waving at the camera. Every time Kathy saw herself waving in fast-action, she blushed, but she kept watching. Then she picked up her tools and disappeared.

"That sure looks funny at this speed. If this had audio, I would have sounded like Alvin and the Chipmunks, wouldn't I?"

Stan nodded. "Yes. But the point here is to watch, not listen. The system with audio capabilities cost more, and I decided we didn't need to hear the person. It's even unlikely he or she would speak. We only need to see who it is. It should be soon."

They continued watching, and suddenly the screen went black.

"What?" Stan gasped, and blinked. "I've had this laptop barely a year. How could the monitor go like that?" He made a little grumble that Amber couldn't understand, which was probably not a bad thing. She did catch the gist that his laptop was no longer under warranty, and a few snide comments about tech support.

Stan ran his fingers through his hair. "This is frustrating, but we can still watch it at home. I installed the program on both my laptop and my PC. We can—"

The picture appeared again, as bright as day . . . without Gnorman.

All three of them sat there, staring at Kathy's pretty pink garden.

Stan's eyebrows lowered and he crossed his arms over his chest, turning to glare at his mother. "Who did you tell about the hidden camera, Mother? Wasn't there a garden club committee meeting a few days ago?"

Amber cringed. Stan calling Kathy "Mother" instead of "Mom" wasn't a good sign. Kathy was in deep, deep trouble.

Kathy raised both palms in front of her. "I think I might have told Libby. But you know Libby. She likes to play detective. I thought she might have some ideas about Gnorman's next location."

Stan gritted his teeth. "And?"

Kathy lowered her head marginally. "I might have mentioned it to Pamela. She's the president, you know."

Stan continued to glare at her. "And?"

Kathy looked away. "Possibly Sylvia. But it was Sylvia who told Victoria."

"And so on, and so on, and so on. Is there anyone on the board you didn't tell?"

"I just told you. I didn't tell Victoria. Sylvia did."

Amber turned to Stan. "If that was three days ago . . ."

He nodded. ". . . Then the entire garden club has to know by now."

Stan stood, folded his laptop without shutting it off properly, tucked it under one arm, and strode out the door.

"He's mad, isn't he? I'm so sorry. I only told the board members. I thought they'd want to know."

"It's okay. We'll figure it out." Amber scooped up her purse.

She didn't know how, but they would have to. She'd circled the day that her garden club membership came up for renewal, and when she'd flipped the calendar, it had jumped out at her like it was on fire.

"I have to talk to Stan. I'll see you on Sunday at church."

CHAPTER Twenty-one

Amber dusted off the displays, taking special care to replace everything just so.

All morning she'd felt distracted.

It disturbed her to see Stan so angry. Another incident to do with trying to find her gnome had flared his usually even temper.

He wasn't angry at her, but she could tell by his clenched jaw that he had barely held back from a long tirade, and she respected his self-control. There were things that talking about wouldn't help, and this was one of them. She could respect that, too, which was why she had to give him some space. He needed it.

Tonight she would stay home and make flamingos.

The day passed uneventfully, with no notes and only the occasional customer asking about Gnorman and his continuing adventure. Just before she started to do up the bank deposit so she could leave, her cell phone buzzed. Surprised that Stan was ready to talk already, she checked the caller ID. It didn't show Stan calling. It was Hayden.

Her stomach tightened. The only reason Hayden would call would be if something happened to Stan. She hadn't seen an ambulance go by, but that didn't mean he wasn't hurt. All sorts of things could happen when working with machinery and heavy parts.

With a trembling finger, she pushed the button to answer the call.

"Hi, Amber." Hayden's voice sounded cheerful over the phone. "How are you?"

"Fine," she answered, pausing for the news to drop.

"I was wondering, if you're not busy chasing your gnome with Stan, if you'd like to join me for coffee tonight."

"Coffee? Tonight?" That was it?

"Yeah. I feel like going out, and I thought of you."

"Me? That was nice." And unexpected.

"I thought we could go to the donut place on Main and Fifth. No big deal. Just a couple cups of java, and if we're lucky, some hot donuts."

Over the years she'd spent a fair amount of time with Hayden. Although really she'd initially gone out with Stan, Hayden, being Stan's best friend, often joined them. They'd gotten to know each other by third party default.

His invitation sounded like a date, except it didn't involve a meal or a movie, therefore it couldn't be a date. But so what if it was? She wasn't seeing anyone special. Since Gnorman's disappearance, she'd spent nearly every evening and most of the weekends with Stan. She couldn't remember the last time she'd been on a date, not counting the evening she and Stan dressed up to check out her new competition, and then he took her out for supper. That wasn't a real date because it was Stan and they were in disguise, so they weren't really themselves.

With the mood Stan had been in last night, and was probably still in, leaving him alone with his thoughts wasn't a bad idea. She'd already decided that she needed to give him some time without her so he could meet women instead of wasting most of his time with her. Having an evening out with Hayden seemed like a perfect distraction. Besides, she needed a change in her routine, and she'd always enjoyed Hayden's company. This would be the first time in all the time she'd known Hayden that it would be just the two of them.

It was time to broaden her horizons.

"Sure. What time? I haven't done my bank deposit yet, so I'm still at the store."

"I have an idea. How about if I pick you up when you're done, and we can go out for dinner. Nothing fancy. We both have to go to work tomorrow. I'm calling from my office right now, I had to work a bit late as well. What do you think?"

Amber pressed one hand into her stomach. Again she'd skipped lunch, although this time she'd had a banana with peanut butter on top for breakfast. Still, she wasn't going to take the chance that she might get too hungry and have a repeat performance of what was probably the most embarrassing day of her life. Not going home and not needing to change sounded wonderful. "I think that's a great idea. I can be ready in twenty minutes."

"Super. See you then."

STAN NEARLY WILTED AS he flicked the switch to illuminate the sign to read that he was finally closed. He hadn't been this exhausted or worked this late since the early days of his business, when he was alone and barely making enough to pay the bills while he built a solid client base. In addition to being dog-tired, he hadn't ordered the parts he needed for tomorrow, or finished all his paperwork, or compiled his bank deposit.

On top of that, he'd hardly slept last night, torn between being angry with his mother for blabbing about the hidden camera and angry with himself for letting his temper show in front of Amber. He wasn't moody, he didn't brood, and he didn't have a short fuse.

Except that he was still angry. He didn't know why it was so very important that Amber be a member of the garden club. He only knew the fear obsessed her that if she didn't get the trophy back soon, she would be kicked out. Since it was important to her, it was important to him. They had been close, so close, to catching the Gnapper, then the chance slipped between his fingers like fresh synthetic oil.

Bless her kind and gentle heart, Amber hadn't been angry with his mother. Amber graciously showed forgiveness and all the things he should have.

So far they hadn't received a call from anyone saying they had discovered Gnorman's newest location, and he still had the last note in his pocket, the envelope unopened.

He needed to call Amber.

He'd apologize for his surly behavior, and make it up to her and bring her over to his place and cook supper for her. He would have preferred to take her out, but even with the coveralls, today he was too dirty to go out anywhere except to grab a burger, and he needed a shower. This time he would make something that she wouldn't take over while he showered. Then, after he took Amber home, he would come back to work and finish up everything he hadn't yet done. He had until midnight to order the parts, which gave him plenty of time.

As he pulled his cell phone out of his pocket, he hesitated before he hit the speed dial button for Amber's number. It was later than usual, much later. By now she would be home. Hopefully she hadn't already started cooking.

Before she spoke, the murmur of a room filled with people echoed over the line. "Hi, Stan. We were just talking about you."

"We?" His stomach knotted, and not because of hunger. She wasn't alone. "Who are you with? Where are you?"

"Hayden took me out to the cutest little place. It's called Burger Heaven, and it really is heavenly. Do you know where it is? Would you like to join us? We're nearly done, but we could wait for you. Hayden says the dessert menu is really good." She giggled.

Giggled. Not like a little kid with a new toy, but like a woman with a man she was becoming enraptured with.

A man who was his best friend, and single again, and back in the dating arena.

She was obviously having a good time with Hayden, and there was no reason she wouldn't. Hayden was a nice guy; they'd been buds since high school.

"That's okay, don't wait. I'm not hungry." Anymore. "You two have a nice time." Nice. What a pansy word. With no reference to the garden club's token spring flower.

Stan hung up, got a couple of bags of potato chips out of the vending machine, and finished his paperwork. It didn't take him nearly as long as he'd expected. Absently he ran his hand over the envelope in his back pocket. He still had time to open it with Amber.

And to find out if she had a good time with his ex-best friend.

He made it to Amber's in record time.

Hayden's car was not in her driveway. He relaxed, just a little. He really didn't want to talk to Hayden right now.

Amber answered the door with a mug of tea in her hand and a book draped over her arm. All she did was stare up at him, like he was the last person on earth she expected at the door at this hour. For a second he let his mind wander to who else might be knocking on her door so late on a weeknight, but he shook the thought from his head.

"Can I come in?"

Her cheeks turned the cutest shade of pink, and she backed up a step. "Sorry. Of course. What brings you here at this hour?"

He pulled the envelope out of his back pocket. "We never did open this, and I figured it was about time. Maybe it will give us a better clue than the others." Even though their best lead had disappeared like Marvin the Martian's Illudium Q-36 Explosive Space Modulator, from an old favorite Bugs Bunny cartoon.

"Sure. I can't believe I forgot to—"

Her words were cut off by the ringing of her cell phone. She handed him the book and mug and ran around the living room until she found her purse. The ringing stopped the same moment she touched it. She dug the phone out of her purse and pressed the button for the caller ID. "It's Victoria Masters. There's no reason for her to call me, so I guess we know where Gnorman is. I'd better call her back."

During Amber's short phone conversation, guilt washed over Stan at keeping the envelope so long, not that reading another bad poem would have helped. "Before we go, let's read this first."

She shrugged her shoulders. "Sure. I just don't want to take too long. She's waiting for us."

He couldn't help the sweep of relief at her word "us." He didn't want anything to change. He almost didn't care if they found the evasive trophy.

Amber ripped the envelope open, pulling out the paper with glued words from the newspaper. Because they were in a hurry, they didn't sit down to decipher it; Stan shuffled beside her, still holding her tea and her book.

if you think Gnoman will
be easy to find
certainly you are out of
your mind.
you can plot and plan and
scheme in advance
but still all you have is a
ghost of a chance.

Amber visibly shuddered. "It sounds like whoever this is, he or she is rather angry about the hidden surveillance camera."

"Yes, but the rhyme is better."

She turned and gave him a scathing glare and didn't reply.

He'd been starting to feel hungry again, but his stomach suddenly felt like it dropped into his boots like a seized differential joint. He had hoped from the bottom of his heart that his aborted scheme hadn't put Amber's goal of rescuing the trophy in jeopardy, but this note told them nothing except that they had angered the Gnapper. Still, realistically, it didn't make sense that anyone in the garden club would want to damage or destroy the trophy. It was an icon for the garden club, going back to its humble beginnings. The only purpose he could see was that some prankster had a sick idea of fun, torturing poor Amber while she stressed about getting kicked out of the garden club.

Careful not to lose her place, Stan set the book and mug down on the coffee table. "I would never have guessed Gnorman would show up at Victoria and Barry's next. If anything, this note would have sent me to that creepy guy who lives at the edge of the cemetery. I wouldn't want to go there. I've only met the man once, and he's weird. It's a little chilly out. Grab a sweater, and let's go."

They could have walked to the Masters' house so they could talk, but because it was getting late he didn't want to waste any time.

When they arrived, despite the darkness, Victoria and Barry's home was daunting. The turn-of-the-century Craftsman style home was in immaculate condition, large and stately. He'd been to a few of their barbecues with the garden club and had been inside the beautiful home. Strangely, the thing that fascinated him the most about the house was the half-story attic, which could have been easily converted to a low-ceilinged den. Instead, they used it for storage.

He'd already been in their backyard, also impressive. Their garden was loaded with a huge variety of flowers including roses, Oriental lilies, and all sorts of things he couldn't name. Last year, Victoria had been the winner of The Spring Fling, and they deserved the honor.

Barry answered the door and led them to the backyard with a minimum of small talk. A perfectly straight and recently stained fence surrounded the huge yard with its splendid garden and large stone patio. In the barbecue pit, next to Barry's prized industrial-sized grill, lurked a draped white shape with cut-out circles showing big baby blue eyes.

Stan couldn't help but smile. "A *ghost* of a chance? This is hilarious!" All the tension he'd penned up inside broke to the surface, and he laughed from the bottom of his gut. He didn't even care that he was the only one laughing.

When he managed to get his laughter under control, Barry cleared his throat. "I don't know how long he's been there. The only reason I found him was that I couldn't find my best tongs, and I thought I left them on the barbecue and went to check."

Victoria nudged Barry's arm, then tucked her hands in the

crook of his elbow. "I'm the one who sent y'all to look." Stan smiled. He loved Victoria's Southern accent. It wasn't thick or heavy like some he'd heard, just enough of a drawl to make her sound like a displaced Southern belle. She turned to Amber. "I'm hopin' I haven't called y'all too late."

"No," Amber replied. "You called with just the right timing. I hadn't been home long."

Stan's inner mirth dissolved as he mentally counted on his fingers just how long she'd been with Hayden.

He stepped forward and removed the new envelope from Gnorman's raised hand. "I hope you don't mind him staying here for a few days."

Barry shrugged his shoulders. "Not at all. We've been following the story in the *Gazette*. This seems to be the pattern. It's kind of fun to have him here. I'm having a family barbecue tomorrow, I'm sure he's going to be quite the conversation starter."

Friday night. He would have to think of what to do with Amber tomorrow that would top where Hayden had taken her.

He held out one hand toward her. "Come on, Amber, I'll take you home now."

CHAPTER Twenty-two

Amber stared out the truck window while Stan drove, fingering the envelope containing the new clue, trying not to feel completely discouraged. If just one thing didn't go wrong, it would help, but so far, nothing had gone right.

Today she'd gotten a form letter in the mail warning her that her membership was coming due at the end of the month, and that the weekend before her renewal, someone would come and inspect her garden to make sure it was up to the club's standards. It was, but barely.

What wasn't up to standards was that the trophy was still missing. No one had assured her that it didn't matter. The opposite, whenever one of the operating board members came into her store, they asked if she and Stan had found it yet.

She'd also received a letter from the bank, denying her application for a loan to pay off Uncle Henry.

At least she'd finished more flamingos, and the florist lady paid for them. Finally she was in the black, and she could afford to eat properly again. Until she had to buy the supplies to make the next month's project, which was hippos. But she'd be a little more ahead progressively each month. For now it wasn't enough to make a big difference yet.

If she had to say one good thing had happened, the forced diet helped her to lose that last five pounds she'd been fighting with for all of her adult life. When she could afford it, she would start by buying one pair of high-end brand-name jeans to celebrate. For now, there was always Walmart.

Stan followed her to the door, then into the kitchen where, as usual, he reached up to get the mugs out of the cupboard while she put on the kettle to make tea.

While the kettle heated up, she sat at the table. Stan dragged the other chair next to hers while she tore open the envelope.

YOU CAN'T SEE GNOMMAN,
BUT HE CAN SEE YOU
WITH HIS GORGEOUS EYES
OF BLUE
FROM BENEATH BARRY'S
BARBEQUE
GNOMMAN HAS A MESSAGE,
AND IT IS BOO!

They groaned in unison.

Amber thunked her forehead down on the table. "This is the worst one yet. Why do we bother? What does this person want from me? Why don't they ever mention the trophy in these ridiculous notes?"

"I don't know. All we can do is keep at it, and at some point our paths have to cross. We can do this, Amber."

With her forehead pressed to the tabletop, she couldn't see him, but she jumped when Stan's fingertips brushed the back of her hand. He flattened his hand over hers and wrapped his fingers around it, giving it a gentle squeeze.

After all the pressure of the past few months, the tender gesture was more than she could handle. The backs of her eyes burned, and she feared she might start crying. As if she hadn't done enough embarrassing things in front of poor Stan lately.

She kept her forehead pressed to the table and shook her head. "No, I'm not so sure we can continue this anymore." As her head moved, she felt her hair flop down around her head. She hoped she'd wiped up the peanut butter she'd smudged on the table that morning.

She felt a slight bit of pressure on her hand at the same time as Stan's chair grated on the floor and he shuffled closer to her. He slowly raised her hand off the table, and his grip changed as he grasped it from underneath, palm to palm. For a few seconds she felt his hot breath on the back of her hand, then the gentle brush of his warm lips as he kissed her there and pressed it to his cheek.

She should have yanked her hand away, but she couldn't move. Earlier tonight Hayden had kissed her good night as they parted ways on her doorstep. It was just a light peck on the lips, but it was on the lips. She'd felt nothing except surprise that he'd done it.

All Stan had kissed was her hand, and her heart pounded like she was standing on the railway tracks with a train coming straight for her.

Amber rolled her head to the side, pressing her cheek to the table as she looked up at Stan. His eyes were closed and he sighed, her hand still pressed to his cheek. His lips moved to a small, satisfied smile as his thumb gently rubbed her wrist.

She didn't know what he was doing, but she didn't want him to stop, peanut butter in her hair or not. It was the most romantic thing Stan had ever done.

Actually it was the only romantic thing he'd ever done.

Romantic? Stan?

Using her free hand, she pressed her palm to the table to steady her as she righted herself.

At the movement Stan opened his eyes and released her hand, but he still wore the goofy grin. "I'd like to take you out for dinner tomorrow night. How would you like to go to the Fancy Schmantzy?"

Amber gulped. If she hadn't been sure about last weekend when he'd taken her out, there would be no doubt about tomorrow. The Fancy Schmantzy would definitely be a date, and she wasn't sure that was something she wanted to do with Stan. Her buddy. They'd seen each other in diapers. Not that she remembered that far back, but that didn't negate the fact that it had happened. The only thing they hadn't done together was play in the sandbox, because her mother wouldn't allow it, always reminding them what cats did in sandboxes.

She wasn't ready to go on a real date with Stan that weekend. She didn't know if she would ever be ready.

She cleared her throat. "I can't. I need to do some shopping. For new jeans." Her single-digit bank account danced before her eyes. "I was going to go to Walmart tomorrow."

"But—"

"Do you want to come with me?"

"...I—"

"They have a McDonalds in the front of the store. We can eat there."

"...want—"

She sucked in a deep breath. "Please?" Just like in a sappy chick flick, she tilted her head and fluttered her eyelashes at him.

Stan's mouth opened, but no words came out.

She folded her hands and pressed them up under her chin. "I'd really like that."

He sighed. "Sure. I'll pick you up after I close up the shop."

WITH AMBER BESIDE HIM, Stan flexed a fishing rod, testing it to determine the point of give. "I like this one. I think I'm going to buy it."

Amber made a sound suspiciously like a snort. "How many fishing rods do you need? You can only catch one fish at a time, and most of the time you throw them back."

"How many pairs of shoes do you need? You only wear one pair at a time, and most of the time you try on half a dozen, throw them all back in the closet, and wear the black ones."

When she whacked him in the back with her purse, Stan smiled. A trip to Walmart wasn't what he had envisioned for the evening, but he was having a great time.

He hadn't been looking forward to waiting while she tried on a dozen pairs of jeans, but when she walked out of the dressing room and modeled each pair for his opinion, he changed his mind. He'd very much enjoyed that.

Next, he was going to pay for the ones she selected and tell her that buying the jeans was cheaper than buying dinner at the Fancy Schmantzy, even though he still had every intention of taking her there. Just not today.

On the way to the checkout, they became distracted at an end cap display of yarn. While he waited for Amber to pick just the right color from a selection of fuzzy stuff, a tiny lady next to Amber stood on her tiptoes and stretched as far as she could, trying to reach a ball of yarn on the top shelf. No matter how much she wiggled and squirmed, she couldn't touch the one she wanted.

Stan reached forward, picked it up, and handed it to her. "Is this the one you want?"

"Yes, thank you," she said as she read the numbers on the label, tucked it under one arm, turned to him and smiled.

Stan started to smile back, but his smile froze.

This was the woman from the store that was Amber's competition. Florence was her name, as he recalled. But he couldn't let her know that he knew that.

As she looked up into his face, she smiled. "I know you from somewhere. Where have we met?"

When Amber realized the woman was talking to him, she turned around. Like he did, she started to smile a greeting before she made eye contact. Stan could tell the split second Amber recognized the woman. Her eyes went as wide as saucers, and the color drained from her cheeks.

Gathering his courage, Stan faced the woman. "Maybe. I own and operate Stan's Shop. I'm Stan Wilson. Have you ever brought your car in?" He already knew the answer. He hoped she would say no, then he'd grab Amber's arm and drag her out of there to come back later, after Florence left.

"I don't think that's it. I never forget a face."

Stan's brain went blank.

Florence turned to Amber. "I think something about you is familiar, too."

He recalled the fake accent Amber had used. The last thing they wanted to happen was for the woman to make the connection, go into Amber's store, and start stocking similar items now that they knew what Florence sold in her own store.

"I don't think so," Amber said flatly.

Florence turned again to Stan. Her eyes narrowed as she studied him. "You seem very familiar. Do you have a brother?"

"That must be it."

The woman tilted her head and continued to study him. "I'm fairly new in town. Are you members of the Bloomfield Garden Club?"

Stan lifted his wrist and made a big show out of checking his watch. "Look at the time. We have to get going. It was nice meeting you."

Amber needed no encouragement to take his cue. She grabbed two balls of yarn without reading the labels, and started walking away.

In two strides Stan caught up to her, and they didn't break speed until they reached the line for the checkout.

She looked at all the people surrounding them, peeked down the aisle, and turned to him with a huge grin on her face. "A brother?"

He grinned back. "Yeah. Remind me to tell my mother that I'm not an only child anymore."

She smacked him again, and her smiled widened. "Forget it. That secret baby stuff only happens in bad romance novels. I hope we have everything we came for, because as soon as we pay for this stuff, we're so outta here."

They placed their purchases on the checkout belt, and when it was their turn, Stan removed the divider and informed the cashier that he was paying for everything.

He raised one hand toward Amber to silence her when her mouth opened, then shuffled to the side so the clerk wouldn't hear. "Don't argue with me. This is cheaper than the supper you wouldn't let me buy for you, so if you don't let me pay, you'll hurt my male ego."

She rolled her eyes, telling him he'd won. This round, anyway. They'd already had the burger and fries he'd promised for dinner, maybe he would push his luck and stop for coffee and donuts on the way home.

Or maybe the Fancy Schmantzy was a possibility for next weekend.

CHAPTER Twenty-three

Just like what happened every other time, Gnorman stayed in Victoria and Barry's garden for four days. In the middle of the day, when Stan and Amber were at work, and Victoria and Barry weren't home, Gnorman disappeared. Again. Also like every other time, just before Stan was ready to close, Amber phoned to say that someone had called on her cell, telling her they'd found Gnorman in their backyard when they got home from wherever they had been.

This time Gnorman was at Pamela's house.

When they got there, he couldn't help but feel amazed. Pamela's house wasn't huge, but the design with the covered front porch protected by an overhanging roof supported by four pillars made it look bigger than it really was. The green clapboards were the same color but a little darker than Amber's eyes, which instantly made him like it. With the gray roof and white trim around the old wooden windows, it made him consider painting his own house, and Amber would have no idea why he'd chosen the same paint as Pamela, just a little lighter.

As expected for the president of the garden club, Pamela's front yard was loaded with flowers of every color under the rainbow, and then some.

He guided Amber up the stairs in the dark and knocked, surprised that the lightbulb above the front door was out. If burned out, since he was tall enough to reach it without a ladder, he would offer to change it for Pamela before they left.

Pamela came to the door, almost dancing. "This is so exciting. He's finally come to my house. His little costume is so cute, you're going to love it."

They followed Pamela through the house and into the backyard, which was small, but still loaded with a million colors of flowers.

There was Gnorman, posed as if peeking through a bush, spying on Pamela's yard. Probably because he was dressed like a spy.

"Just look at him!" Pamela joined her hands and pressed them to one cheek. "He's so dashing, just like James Bond."

Stan didn't think Gnorman looked like any James Bond he'd ever seen. Gnorman looked ridiculous with the glasses and trench coat, but this costume was certainly better made and put together with more thought than the ghost costume they found him wearing at Victoria and Barry's place.

He waited for Amber to take the newest envelope from Gnorman's hand, and while Amber and Pamela exchanged small talk, he changed Pamela's lightbulb. Announcing that he had completed the task provided a good excuse to interrupt the conversation, and they drove back to Amber's townhouse.

This time she didn't bother to make tea. They sat at the table side by side and read the new note.

Gnoman is more than a
gnome on a mission
he is a spy, and he ain't
gone fishin'.
his clandestine capers and
plans have a reason
because he's keeping the
trophy at least for the
season.

As she read the note, Amber squeezed her eyes shut and
stiffened. "At least this time they mentioned the trophy,
although I don't know if that's good or bad. My membership is
up for renewal in a couple of weeks, and maybe this is a warning
that they won't pass my renewal application."

"They'll let you renew. Everyone likes you."

She shook her head. "This isn't a popularity club, it's a garden club, and my garden is horrible. It barely meets the minimum requirement for membership. If only one person opposes
my membership, then I'm out. Do you remember last year, they
did turn someone down. I don't remember the reason, but they
did. The same thing is going to happen to me. Someone wants
me out of the garden club."

"Let me see that."

Amber pushed the note across the table, allowing him to
study it. "Somewhere, in all the notes and costumes, there has
to be a common thread, no pun intended. We know it isn't Zoe,
the seamstress. Some of the costumes have been really good, but
others have looked like throw-togethers, especially the ghost.

We've got to find something with the notes that will point us to one person. There's certainly been enough of them by now."

Stan tried to recall the other notes. A couple of them he nearly had memorized. A few were pretty funny, but most were pretty bad. Despite what had to be true, the notes they didn't show an obvious personality. In fact, they were very disjointed. They weren't even glued together in a uniform manner. Some were glued with the precision of a typesetter, and others splattered with glue as if pieced together by a child. One of the early notes had donut sprinkles mixed in with the glue. "I can't think of any common wording or style. I only know that whoever this is, not only is he or she a bad poet, but they can't spell."

Amber craned her neck to look at the note in front of Stan. "Can't spell?"

Stan pressed one finger to the note. "Right here. *Clandestine* is spelled with an *E*, not an *I*."

Amber's eyes widened. "Let me see that."

He slid the paper across the table. "*Clandestine* isn't a common word. See, it wasn't even cut out as a word from the newspaper. It's pasted together from a few other words. It's even different sized letters. Since it's not the newspaper making a typo, someone has spelled it wrong."

"I've seen this spelling before." Amber pressed her fingers to her temple. "I know someone who spells it that way."

She tapped one finger to her forehead, reminding Stan of a childhood image from Winnie the Pooh. He bit his tongue, stopping from blurting out, "Think, think, think." He wished he could think of who spelled it like that, but people didn't write him notes. They told him the troubles they were having with their cars, and he wrote the notes, trying to figure out where to start tinkering. "I know how to spell it, but *clandestine* isn't a word I'd use in conversation. Who would?"

Amber turned to him, her finger still moving. "No one I

know. Besides, it wouldn't be in a spoken sentence. I've seen it written down. Spelled this way. Wrong." She squeezed her eyes shut. "What kind of person would put a word like *clandestine* into a sentence?"

He knew the answer to that one. "That's easy. Mystery writers."

Amber shot him a scathing dirty look. "Like we know a mystery writer. Here in Bloomfield."

He shrugged his shoulders. "You never know. Mystery writers have to live somewhere. Why not here?"

"Do you know anyone who writes mystery novels for a living?"

He wondered what kind of person wrote mystery novels at all, never mind for a living. All he'd learned about writers was what he'd seen in movies or on television. Most of the time writers of any genre were portrayed as reclusive, a little strange, and a lot quirky. While he knew a lot of quirky people, he didn't think any of them were writers. His neighbor was a quirky guy. Matt worked from home testing video games all day, every day, even weekends, and had never been fishing in his life.

The quirkiest person he'd ever met, even though he'd only met the man once, was the guy who looked after the cemetery. That guy was more than quirky, he was creepy. Someone had to take care of the cemetery, but this guy enjoyed it just a little too much.

He shook his head. "No, I don't know anyone who writes mystery novels. I don't know anyone who writes any kind of novels."

Amber's eyes brightened. "Then maybe it's someone who reads mystery novels. Who reads that kind of thing?"

"I do. That's how I recognized the wrong spelling. I read mystery novels when I have time." Which he hadn't lately. Maybe if he picked up a few, that would get his brain in sync with following clues and solving the crime. In a way, this was a crime, since the trophy had sort of been stolen. Although he honestly believed it would be returned, when the Gnapper's purpose was finished. Whatever the purpose was.

"You're not helping. It's obviously not you. Who do you know that reads them? Do you swap books, or discuss the latest one you read with anyone?"

"No. I don't belong to the book club. Maybe that's what you should do. Join the book club. See who is in both clubs, and then you'll have the Gnome Gnapper red-handed."

"I think most of the people in the book club also belong to the garden club. I hear them talking about books at a lot of the meetings."

Another dead end. "Then we have no other choice than to follow the spy lead. Is anyone around here mysterious?" Besides the guy who lived at the cemetery. If Gnorman went to the cemetery at night, Stan would just wait until he came out in his own good time. Thinking back, now he felt relieved that they hadn't read the note about the *ghost of a chance* until after Victoria had phoned Amber. He would have gone to the cemetery, at night, and had nightmares for weeks when the creepy guy appeared out of nowhere to find out what he was doing there.

"Not that I can think of." Amber checked her watch. "I don't want to be rude, and we're not getting anywhere. You should go home, we both have to get up for work in the morning."

CHAPTER Twenty-four

A mber ran out of her studio and stopped dead in her tracks. She'd taken a few minutes to touch up the paint on a ceramic statue and thought she'd heard the jingle of the bell above the door, but she saw no one in her store.

After all the talk about mysteries and mystery novels with Stan, a chill ran up Amber's spine. She scanned up and down the aisles, just in case someone had come in and was hiding, but she saw nothing unusual. She didn't notice anything missing from the shelves, so it hadn't been a grab-and-dash thief. But if someone was trying to scare her, it was working. Visions of broken eggs splattered all over her the door and the glass window of her store ran through her mind. Also, the trophy was still missing, and someone continued to play cat and mouse with her.

Someone didn't like her, and if they were trying to scare her, they were doing a good job.

Just as she turned around, a white envelope on the ground caught her eye.

With trembling fingers, she picked it up. All of the notes from the Gnapper had been stuck on the outside of her door, waiting for her when she arrived in the morning. So far, the elusive mystery person had not been inside her store.

Until now.

Slowly she ripped open the envelope.

This time the note looked different. It wasn't cut-out words glued together on a white piece of bond paper. This was a piece of lined paper torn from a coil notebook, like the kind students used in high school, and the note was neatly printed.

Dear Miss Weathersby,

I am very sorry that a couple of months ago I made a mess on your door and big window. I was bringing home groceries for my mother and the wheel on my skateboard got stuck and I fell, and the eggs went flying on to your door and my coke spilled all over your car. I was skipping school so I was too scared to stay and clean it up and I have been feeling bad ever since then. I want to say that I am sorry that you had to clean up the mess, so I took some of my allowance and made a donation to the Cancer Society with your name on it.

Attached to the paper was a tax deduction receipt for $15.

A tear slid out of the corner of her eye. While it had been a nightmare to clean up the mess, and there were still sticky spots in the doorjamb of her car, she felt sorry for the boy, assuming it was a boy, and hoped he hadn't been hurt when he fell.

She looked up at the clean door. At least no one hated her that bad. She could live with an accident.

But that still didn't account for the exploits of the Gnapper.

As she stood there staring at the door, her cell phone sang its electronic ring from her purse.

For years, when the phone rang at this hour, half an hour before closing, it had always been Stan. But over the last week, now when she hunted for the last place she'd left her purse so she could find her phone before it stopped ringing, she didn't know if it was going to be Stan or Hayden. Hayden had called her pretty much every second day since she'd gone out with him.

This time it was Hayden.

"I had to work a bit late at the office again, so I was wondering if you'd like to join me for dinner. I just talked to Stan, it's a typical busy day for him. He's swamped and he let his mechanics go home on time so they can watch the game, so he's going to be really late. How about it?"

It was quite interesting that Hayden had already checked with Stan to determine if she was available. She didn't know whether the thought rankled that he checked her availability without asking her first, or if it was sweet that he'd also thought of Stan.

"Sure. We can do that. As long as it's nothing fancy." Or expensive. After the number of times Stan had suggested they go to the Fancy Schmantzy lately, she was starting to get nervous about what the men in her life thought reasonable. "I'll meet you there."

This time Hayden had chosen a cute little bistro where he made a reservation and got a cute little table for two in the corner.

More than that, it was kind of a romantic little table, away from the rest of the dinner crowd.

She wasn't sure how she felt about that. While she'd decided that Stan needed to have more time away from her to spend his time meeting other women, and she had decided to spend her time with more of the male species than Stan, now that it was happening, she had mixed feelings.

Word had it amongst the female population of the garden club that Hayden had mostly recovered from his divorce after Marissa cheated on him, then stomped his heart into the dirt.

He was now seriously looking for someone, with the ultimate goal of getting married again.

Hayden was a nice man and would probably make a good husband, but Amber couldn't think about taking that step in life right now. Before she could consider getting into a permanent relationship, she had to pay off Uncle Henry. Until she did, she couldn't take the chance that she wasn't going to be forced to move to Chicago. The legal contract had no out clause saying that if she got married she wouldn't have to honor the agreement. At the time she hadn't thought about such a condition because, before the recession, she hadn't considered the possibility. Now, she felt like she'd made a deal with the devil.

Rather than depressing herself with such thoughts, she turned back to Hayden. Hayden was interesting and fun to talk to, and she thoroughly enjoyed having dinner with him.

As she looked at him, she thought about her feelings toward him. Even if she could forget about her debts and get married, she wouldn't marry Hayden. As much as she liked him, she didn't like him that way.

When they were done, just so he wouldn't get the wrong idea, she reached for the bill so that she could calculate her half.

The second her fingers touched the bill, Hayden laid his hand over top of hers, preventing her from taking it. "I knew you would do this. You agreed that this would be my treat before we got here. I insist."

Amber looked up at him, making direct eye contact so he would understand her position. "I know, but I just realized what you're looking for, and I'm not it. We've been just friends, and we'll always be just friends, and that's not what you're looking for. I want to be fair to you." She really couldn't afford a restaurant meal, but at least now, not like a couple of weeks ago, she could still afford to eat if she paid for her half.

One corner of his mouth quirked up. "Ah. The old 'we can be friends' line. Don't worry. I already figured that out a few weeks ago. Tonight I didn't want a date; I just wanted to relax and go out with a friend after a busy day. That means ordinary friends, not friends like you and Stan."

She made one more attempt to wrap her fingers around the bill to pull it out from under Hayden's hand, then froze. "Like me and Stan? What do you mean?"

He rolled his eyes. "You know what I mean. Everyone thinks you two are so funny. There's a line. People are waiting for our table. We should go."

The entire trip home, all she could think of was Hayden's comment. Contrary to his claim, she had no idea what he meant. For starters, she and Stan had always been friends, and nothing more. They'd never kissed, not even when they went together to the senior prom. At the time, neither of them could figure out why no one else had asked her to go. Every time Stan had asked a girl to go with him, they always asked why Amber wasn't going with him. They'd both resigned themselves to the inevitable, gone together, and had the time of their lives, even though he'd teased her mercilessly about her frilly pink prom dress and matching pink shoes.

Actually he had kissed her once. But she was too frozen from fear from being at the top of the Ferris wheel to process it. Besides, it had only been a kiss of triumph that she hadn't died.

So they'd always been a little inseparable. That didn't mean anything. Life went on, and so did they.

Thinking of Stan, she felt a twinge of disappointment when his pickup wasn't parked in her driveway when she got home.

No matter. She'd see him tomorrow anyway.

Just because she was thinking of him, before she went in the house, she pulled her cell phone out of her purse and texted him

a quick message reminding him that he had a dentist appointment the next day, and went inside.

———————— ⚘ ————————

"THIS FEELS WRONG," STAN grumbled from the passenger seat
of Amber's car. "I should be driving, and we should be in my
car."

"You don't have a car. You have a pickup truck. I'm not getting in and out of a truck in these shoes. So hush up and enjoy
the ride."

Stan bit back a grin. "You are so bossy." But he loved it,
and he loved Amber. He didn't know why it had taken him so
long to realize it, but he'd been thinking about it ever since she
fainted into his arms. If Andy hadn't been there, he would have
broken all land-speed records to get her to the ER. Yet, as an
eye-opener, it made him realize that he'd waited too long to tell
her how much he loved her. Tonight, even if words failed him,
he planned to show it to her.

Starting with being a little gracious and a lot amused by her
bossy attitude. No shrinking wallflower, his Amber.

He stilled. That was the point he wanted to make tonight.
She was his, he was hers, and all that romantic nonsense. Then,
when the night was over, they would see where it took them.

She pulled into the parking lot of the Fancy Schmantzy.
Before she had the car turned off and her seat belt unfastened, he
was out of the car and around her side, waiting for her to unlock
the door so he could open it and help her out.

She gave him a dirty look, but then accepted his arm anyway.

"I've never been here before," she muttered as he reached for
the door of the restaurant. "This feels weird."

"Me neither. So let's consider it an adventure." He pulled

the door open for Amber to enter ahead of him, and he followed her inside.

The maître d' found their reservation, seated them quickly, and left them alone.

"Wow," Amber muttered under her breath. "Look at this place."

The place was fancy indeed, just like the name stated. Most of the furnishings and decorating bordered on vintage, but instead of looking old or retro, it shouted class and dignity. Tall wooden partitions divided the large restaurant into a number of smaller sections, each slightly different, and private from each other. Dark, rich wood paneled walls and a high ceiling with thick wooden beams created an atmosphere of protection and stability. Likewise, the tables were solid wood, heavy and secure, blending with the hues of the walls. Burgundy curtains of heavy fabric graced the windows, allowing in some light, but completely shutting them off from the outside world. Ambient light was at just the perfect level for everyone to talk to the people at their own table and ignore the other patrons.

He'd never seen such clean, white tablecloths.

The waitstaff's ties matched the curtains. The whole place was a blend of deep, mellow tones and dollar signs.

It was a world unto itself.

And he was here with Amber, with no possibility of the world intruding on this time they'd set aside to be with each other.

He turned to her and wiggled his tie—the tie she'd given him as a stocking stuffer last Christmas. Like most of the men seated at other tables, he had worn his suit, he'd polished his shoes, and he'd even gotten a haircut. By now, since it had been a few weeks, the mustache he'd been growing was full enough to trim, and he'd gotten used to the feeling of something on his upper lip.

She'd teased him about it as it grew, but not once had she told him to shave it off.

Tonight he was as dashing and handsome as he was ever going to be.

As well, he'd never seen Amber so beautiful. She didn't wear makeup often, and when she did it was never much, but tonight she'd gone the full route, including the same color lipstick she'd worn to the other place that nearly sent him over the edge. Tonight she looked even prettier than the models on the magazine covers. She'd done some kind of upswept thing with her hair, keeping it in place with an assortment of sparkly hair ornaments. Sitting down, he couldn't see her entire dress, but he'd gotten a good view of her at her house before they got into her car. She told him it wasn't too expensive, that she'd gotten it just for tonight from Tessa's consignment store, but it was obviously expensive for the original buyer. This was the kind of fancy dress that a woman would wear only once, with the silly thought that she couldn't be seen wearing the same thing twice by the same crowd of people.

He would never think of not wearing his suit just because his friends had already seen him in it.

Likewise, he hoped Amber wore this dress again. It was a deep sea green, which really brought out the green in her eyes. It had a nice fitted waist, which emphasized the rest of her figure, and really showed that she'd lost weight recently. He wasn't sure he liked that she'd lost weight, but she sure did look great in the dress.

Of course, she had on her favorite black high-heeled shoes. He loved it when she wore high heels.

Before he started drooling, a waiter appeared with menus and told them the special of the day.

If it wasn't his imagination, Amber didn't appear to be listening. As soon as the waiter left them alone to make their selections, she started flipping through the menu. "I don't want the special. I really want steak and lobster, but I can't find it, and I want to know how much it costs."

He'd found the steak and lobster combo right away, and he knew she wouldn't want to know how much it cost. "Never mind that. I told you this was my treat. Order what you want. If you want steak and lobster, it's yours."

She peeked at him over the menu. "Are you sure?"

Stan nearly forgot to breathe. He always thought Amber had pretty eyes, but with the under-stated makeup on, they were eyes a man could get lost in. "Yeah. I'm sure," he said, hoping his voice sounded close to normal.

She closed the menu, laid it flat, gave it a pat, and smiled at him. "Then that's what I want. Thank you."

All he could do was stare into her eyes and hope his mouth wasn't hanging open. She was the most beautiful woman he'd ever seen in his entire life. Why hadn't he realized that before?

The waiter returned to take their orders. He couldn't remember what he wanted, so he just ordered the special.

"Look," she whispered as she tapped his ankle with her toe. "Over there. It's Victoria and Barry. Is it okay to wave in a place like this?"

"I guess so. But they came here for the same reason we did, and that's to be alone."

"I know that. It's just kind of special to be here, and not care that anyone recognizes us." They both waved once and nodded across the room when Victoria and Barry noticed them. Then, like Victoria and Barry, they returned their attention to each other.

The food was even better than he'd heard, and Stan enjoyed his meal of chicken with pasta and some kind of white sauce so much that he didn't miss not having a steak.

This time, since they were in no rush and didn't care if anyone saw them, they lingered over a rich dessert that Amber claimed was too fattening, but she ate it anyway.

Caught up in the ambiance of the place and the mood of the evening, Stan took hold of Amber's hand as they walked back to Amber's car, twined his fingers with hers, and gave her hand a little squeeze.

He'd never held hands with Amber before.

That was going to change.

Very soon, when they got to her townhouse, there was something else they'd never done before that was going to change too.

CHAPTER Twenty-five

Amber tried not to fumble getting the key into the lock on her front door.

Tonight had been a night she would never forget. She'd seen Stan in his suit before, but tonight had somehow been different. She didn't know what it was, but it was more than just the mustache. A flock of butterflies did a square dance in her stomach at the thought of Stan's mustache. He was good-looking before, but with it, he looked absolutely handsome. And dashing. Just like the cliché went, he was simply tall, dark, and handsome. She'd already thought the handsome, but he was doubly handsome right now, so she was allowed to think it twice. She didn't know why she hadn't realized exactly how handsome he was before tonight.

Every other day, because he didn't work at a desk job and was quite toned, he looked buff in his coveralls, but tonight in the suit, he looked movie-star handsome.

She wondered if he knew it, because Amber knew she looked good in her new-to-her dress and her favorite high heels.

She'd taken extra care with her hair and makeup, and all the time had been worth it.

Finally the lock cooperated, and she pushed the door open. Still holding the keys and the doorknob, she looked over her shoulder and up at Stan. "Would you like to come in?"

His eyebrows rose, like he was trying to figure out why she asked. She never had before. She didn't know why she'd asked either. Tonight just felt . . . different.

"Yes, I would," he said very formally.

Amber gulped. They weren't playing dress-up tonight, but in a way they really were. This wasn't the church Christmas party or the fellowship banquet. Being dressed up and feeding each other nibbles and sharing their rich desserts across the table had been a real date, whether she wanted to admit it, or not.

After twenty-six years, she'd been on a date with Stan. Really, nearly twenty-seven, because it was her birthday next month.

Not that she wanted anything else to drink, but she had to do something so she went into the kitchen to make tea.

Just like he always did, Stan followed her. The new Stan. The handsome one in the suit. With the mustache and sexy eyes.

Amber nearly tripped out of her high-heeled shoes. Sexy eyes?

"Amber? Are you okay? Do you want to take those shoes off? You always complain that your ankles aren't used to walking like that."

With the fancy dress, she needed these shoes, not her pink bunny slippers. Slippers would destroy the image that she'd worked so hard to create. She wasn't ready for it to be over.

"They're okay. I'm fine."

Stan tilted his head back a little and reached up to tug the knot of his tie.

"No!" Amber cleared her throat, and lowered her voice to

a normal speaking level. "I mean, no. Leave it on. It looks . . ." *Breathtaking. Spectacular. Incredible.* ". . . nice."

He smiled. Her knees suddenly felt wobbly.

She turned and grabbed the kettle from the stovetop and filled it with water. "That was really fun," she said over her shoulder. "No. Fun wasn't the right word. I really enjoyed myself. I guess that's what I'm trying to say."

"I did too. We'll have to do this again."

"Go out for dinner, yes, but there, no. That place was way too expensive."

Amber placed the kettle on the counter and plugged it in. Behind her, she heard the tapping of Stan's leather shoes on the tile floor as he approached her. She felt the light touch of his hand on her shoulder, and he nudged her ever so gently to turn around to face him.

He shuffled forward until they were toe to toe. His fingertips brushed her cheek and then traveled down to her chin. His voice lowered to a husky whisper. "Maybe, but some things are worth it."

With one more gentle nudge, he tipped her chin up slightly. The hand on her shoulder lowered to the small of her back.

"Close your eyes, Amber, because I'm going to kiss you."

She didn't think he would, but if this were someone else, they were in the right stance, the right position to kiss each other. So she closed her eyes.

Stan really did kiss her.

First his lips lightly brushed hers, almost teasing. It was nice. Gentle. Tender.

She felt him smile against her mouth.

Then he tilted his head and kissed her for real.

Amber slipped her arms under his suit jacket and around his waist, holding Stan as firmly as he held her. Something in her brain short-circuited that they were doing this, but that didn't make her stop, or want his kiss any less. Just like in the books she read, her heart raced and her brain short-circuited.

When they separated, he didn't step away. He embraced her with one arm around her waist and brushed the loose strands at her temple. After a short sigh, he pulled her close into a tender embrace, and just held her in a timeless, special moment.

The haze in her brain dissipated, and the impact of what had just happened smacked her.

She'd kissed Stan. Not just a little peck, but a real kiss, like she'd seen on television but never experienced. She'd had boyfriends, but she'd never felt like this, been kissed like this, nor had she ever kissed a man back like this. It had been so right, yet so very wrong. This was Stan. Her friend. The man who fixed her leaky toilet.

She started to move away, but his grip tightened.

"Please," he whispered. "Not yet." Slowly she felt the slight press of his cheek to the top of her head. "Just a minute longer."

Pressed against him, she felt his sigh from her cheek to her knees.

"Why didn't we do this sooner?" he murmured into her hair as he brushed her temple with his thumb.

She couldn't answer him. She couldn't think.

What they had done had just changed the parameters of their relationship. All their lives, they'd been friends. What were they now?

She stiffened, afraid, knowing that no matter what happened next, they could never go back.

Every time she looked at him, she would remember this moment.

She wanted the moment to happen again.

No. No, she didn't. This was Stan. Good Ol' Stan. Or he used to be Good Ol' Stan. What was he now?

He must have felt her stiffen, because he slowly eased his hold on her and released her from his embrace, keeping one hand cupping her cheek. As she looked up at him and he looked down at her, for the first time ever she couldn't tell what he was thinking. She couldn't read his expression. Confusion? Regret? Indecision?

"I think I should go. If I don't see you after work tomorrow, I'll pick you up for church on Sunday."

Because he was still close, she couldn't tell what he was going to do, but he bent slightly and pressed a short and sweet kiss to her lips, turned, and walked out.

Amber's feet remained frozen to the floor. She heard the front door open and close, the jingle of his keys and the snick of the lock as it turned. A short pause, and the engine of his truck roared to life, then faded to nothing.

Amber flopped down on to the kitchen chair, crossed her arms on the table, and plunked her head into her arms.

Stan had kissed her. Not just a peck kiss, but a melt-your-bones, curl-your-toes kiss.

She'd never be able to look at him again and still think they could be friends. Instead of the warm fuzzies she felt when they were close to each other, she'd battle with other feelings. Deeper feelings she didn't know if she could handle.

Deep in her heart, she knew she would never look at him again, and not wish for more of the same.

She had to think, but no answers came.

Behind her, the kettle whistled.

Amber kept her face buried in her arms. She didn't care if it boiled dry. It would shut off automatically.

Eventually.

CHAPTER Twenty-six

Is it my imagination, or is everyone staring at us?"

Stan tried to look around them without moving his head as they walked through the church's foyer, which was difficult, but not impossible. "Maybe a few people, but not everyone." He had seen a few heads turn as he led Amber to their usual spot before the service, but not too many.

However, now that the service was over and everyone was leaving, he had the distinct impression that more people gave them a double take than when they entered.

He tried not to smile. Not only did he not care that they looked, he liked that they were looking.

The only people at the restaurant that they knew on Friday night had been Victoria and Barry. It had been more than obvious that he and Amber had been on a date. Apparently Victoria or Barry had noticed that they'd left holding hands, and this raised the bar. At the time, he'd been feeling a little mushy inside and wanted the connection that holding hands made, and he hadn't cared about anything else. He hadn't thought that holding hands in a restaurant would announce to the world that they were suddenly a couple, but it appeared that it did.

He might just as well have sent up flares or hired a plane with a banner to fly over the town.

Thankfully, being church, no one outright stared, but lots of people shot them sly little glances, poked each other, and grinned.

Friday night had been what he'd thought was a private moment, but at the time he hadn't considered the fact that nothing was private in Bloomfield. Now, Sunday morning, thirty-eight hours later, if he'd counted on his fingers correctly, not only had news circulated through the garden club, the news had worked its way into the church, and they were now an item.

The sanctuary was now empty, and everyone had moved to the foyer to mingle and talk.

Beside him, Amber nearly missed a step. "Oh, no. There's Winifred Simpson."

Stan tried not to flinch. While his mother couldn't keep a secret, she didn't have to know all the details of what went on. Winifred, or Winnie, as her friends called her—and everyone was her friend because no one wanted to be her enemy—was the biggest snoop in town. She had to know everyone's business down to the last nitty-gritty detail. She could spot something out of the ordinary as quick as a flash, and judging from the look on her face, whatever she'd heard or imagined about him and Amber wasn't enough. Winnie claimed she needed to know all the details so she could pray for someone properly, but the reality was that she wanted to be the first person to know everything so she could laud her knowledge over others when they found out.

Winnie grinned, turned directly toward them, and quickened her pace.

Amber grabbed his upper arm, her fingers dug into his skin, almost pinching. "She's coming straight for us."

Winnie's brown eyes held an almost feral gleam. The closer she got, the more bounce appeared in her step, making her hair flop. Today it was a shade of reddish-brown, different than last week, making him wonder what color it really was. Her large black purse draped over her shoulder made her even more imposing, like she was ready to do battle.

Stan pulled Amber's hand off his arm, grabbed it without caring how, only that he had her tight, made a U-turn, and nearly dragged her back into the sanctuary, closing the door behind him. It wasn't much of a hiding spot, but at least here they were safe from Winnie's prying questions. The sanctuary was hallowed ground.

Amber yanked her hand out of his. "What are you doing? Is there another door out of here?"

"No. We have to wait until she leaves. She can't stay there forever. Pastor and the deacons have scheduled a meeting, and I know they're ordering in lunch, so they're going to be in the building for a long time. We can stay here for as long as we want. But Winnie's not going to wait all day in the foyer, and she won't come in here to give us the personal inquisition."

Amber pointed to the heavy wooden door. "She may not come in here, but knowing Winnie, she's going to wait. All day." Amber sank into one of the wooden pews, lowered her head, and buried her face in her hands. "We're trapped," she moaned into her hands.

"So what? We're in the church sanctuary. I can't think of a better place to spend a lot of time."

She spread her fingers and stared at him between them, then dropped her hands, scowled, and her expression hardened into a glare. "In Winnie's eyes, here we are, all alone, and you closed the door behind us."

He shrugged his shoulders. "What can she think? This is the church sanctuary. All people do in here when it's quiet is pray. If she spreads gossip about us praying in here for hours, that's fine with me." Although, as the words came out of his mouth, there was something else he was thinking about doing with Amber, and it wasn't at all proper in the church sanctuary.

Her anger only made him want to kiss her more. She was absolutely adorable. Except if he told her the old standard line that he thought she was adorable when she was angry, she was sure to get more angry and smack him, which wasn't proper in the church sanctuary either, but she would do it.

He couldn't help but grin.

Amber's scowl deepened. "What's so funny?"

He turned away so he could control himself. "Nothing. I just think you're overreacting. She's got to have something better to do that stand there and wait. Besides, there aren't any chairs out there. Did you see those ridiculous shoes she was wearing, with the bows on them? She usually wears low stuff, but today, they're high for Winnie. They're not as bad as those black ones you like so much, the ones you can't walk in for more than a couple of blocks. Why do women wear shoes like that? I pick my shoes by how they fit, that are the most comfortable, then I pick the right color." He owned one pair of black shoes, one pair of brown, his sneakers, which once upon a time were white, and his steel-toed safety boots.

He turned to face Amber and looked down to her feet.

She wore the black shoes. The ones he loved so much.

He had his answer. She wore them because they looked great. They weren't made for walking, or standing. They were made to look good—they sure did look good, and they made Amber's legs look great.

Inwardly he cringed, almost waiting for a bolt of lightning to strike him. He probably wasn't supposed to be thinking of stuff like that in there.

He felt bad that she wore shoes that became uncomfortable

if she walked too far in them. In fact, they'd been walking or standing for a while, and she'd only just sat down.

It really wouldn't be appropriate to take off her shoes and massage her feet in the sanctuary.

He had to get out of there. He harbored way too many thoughts that were inappropriate for church. He'd again been thinking about hugging and kissing Amber.

But he wasn't ready to face Winifred Simpson, not when he didn't know what he'd say. He could only say the truth, that he finally realized he was in love with Amber, his old pal, but he couldn't say those words to Winifred first. He had to say them to Amber first.

He turned his attention away from Amber's hot shoes to her face. She sat on the pew, her eyes narrowed, her arms folded over her chest, and one toe tapping.

This was definitely not the right moment to tell her that he loved her.

Instead, he sank down to sit beside her. "We've got lots of time. I think the first thing we can do is pray."

She nodded, and they angled themselves toward each other. Amber reached out to join hands with him. First, they prayed for guidance for what to do about Winnie waiting, then they moved on to other prayer issues. At their closing "Amen," she pulled her hands out of his and looked up at him.

Of all the things they'd prayed for, praying about themselves hadn't come up.

One thing he'd wanted to pray for was their relationship. He didn't know how to start, so he'd waited for Amber, but she hadn't started either. With her sitting there, just looking at him, he didn't know what to say or do, but the nagging thought poked at him that the longer the silence went on, the worse the result was going to be.

Just as he thought all was lost, she shimmied toward him on the bench, leaned against him, nestled her head on his chest, and sighed—just like she always did when she worked through an issue. It was almost ironic, because this time, he was the issue. That she was snuggling up against him and not running for the hills screaming had to encourage him.

He wrapped his arms around her and rested his chin on the top of her head, and enjoyed the silence.

He wished he knew more about relationships. It wasn't that he'd never dated, but nothing ever went longer than three dates with the same woman. He was nearing thirty years old, and he still hadn't had what could be called a serious relationship, and his best friend had been married, divorced, and was dating again.

No woman had ever held his interest, but then he probably hadn't given any of them a chance. Already by a second date, he thought of what that woman would be like for the long term, and next to Amber, everyone came up short.

Stan smiled, knowing Amber couldn't see him. He had it bad.

"What's so funny up there?"

Because she busted him, he smiled wider. That was his Amber. "Nothing's funny, but I am smiling. How can you tell?"

"I can just tell. Going to tell me why?"

"Nope."

"Do you think she's gone?"

He checked his watch over Amber's head. "Probably."

"Wanna go home?"

"Nope. I want to take you out for lunch. I think a time like this calls for chocolate."

This time he could feel her smile against his chest, through his shirt. "An offer I can't refuse. Let's go."

CHAPTER Twenty-seven

Amber hit the speed dial on her phone. Stan picked it up within two rings. "Gnorman is at—"

"—Sherry Butler's."

Amber sagged. "Oh. You heard. But I also learned something. I learned that Sherry knows how to spell *clandestine*."

"I don't know if that's good or bad."

"I know what you mean. It doesn't make any sense that Sherry would be the Gnapper, since Gnorman just showed up at her house. I just want this to be over. Are we going to go to Sherry's after work?"

"Couldn't keep me away." Somehow she knew he would say that. Stan had been with her every time Gnorman turned up at a new location. The one time she hadn't called him to come, to Andy's, he'd shown up anyway. That time she'd been glad he had been there.

It seemed natural for Stan to go with her to try to solve the mystery of the Gnome Gnapper, but for some reason it felt different knowing that everyone who called automatically expected Stan to be there. It wasn't until she realized that everyone naturally assumed they would be there together that it started to bother her.

By the time Stan pulled into her parking area, a million thoughts had gone through her head, not all of them to do with Gnorman.

Over the course of the spring, and now that they were into summer, she'd seen Stan nearly every day. She didn't want to monopolize his time, but every time she tried to separate from him a little, he came back like the proverbial cat, and spent even more time with her. From his desire to suddenly start dating, she had to assume that Stan had come to a point in his life that he was seeking a more permanent relationship. Rather than date her, she had to encourage him to go on real dates, not with her.

Her friend Sarah, the veterinarian, was single, as well as Tessa, who owned the consignment store. Either of them were good, smart women who could potentially be a good mate for Stan. On second thought, not Sarah. She didn't know if she could remain friends with Sarah if Sarah hooked up with Stan.

Amber shook her head and looked up. She had to stop worrying about Stan's love life and venture out to make sense of the next clue.

Stan waited for her to click on her seat belt before he put the truck into gear and drove off. "I was thinking about our hunt to find out who spells *clandestine* wrong. It's such a strange word. When we ask people how to spell it, they're going to know why. After all, it's not a word found in everyday conversation."

"I was thinking of that too. Maybe we could tell people that we're starting to write a book together, and we're looking for mystery-type words."

"Do you think people are going to believe that?"

"Why not?" She turned to face him. "We certainly spend

enough time together. Maybe we should write a book. Like you said, writers have to live somewhere, why not in Bloomfield?"

He snickered. "I can barely write out my grocery list. No one will believe that."

"You're probably right. My talents lie in making patterns and putting things together, not writing words. I probably couldn't string a paragraph together that would make sense. It's just that I'm getting desperate. I can't see a pattern. Everything is so mixed up, nothing is consistent except that once a week, at different days every week, Gnorman gets moved."

They pulled up to Sherry's home.

As she walked down the sidewalk, Amber admired Sherry's house. It was exactly the same kind of house she wanted when she could afford to buy a home of her own—a simple white, one-story frame building with a comfortable wrap-around porch. Naturally Sherry had baskets of hanging plants all around, filled with all impatiens, and fuchsias, pansies, and a number of pretty flowers she couldn't identify.

Amber could grow hanging baskets. Too bad plants had to be planted in the ground before they could be considered a garden, according to the rules of the garden club. Amber could have had a whole garden's worth of plants in hanging baskets, and then her membership wouldn't be in jeopardy. Except for Gnorman missing with the trophy. But soon she and Stan would find it. She knew they would

They had to.

Amber knocked on the door and didn't have to wait more than a few seconds before Sherry answered the door. She didn't waste any time in leading them into the backyard where they found Gnorman dressed as a ninja.

Stan dragged his fingers through his hair. "This is wrong on so many levels. He's a fat little old guy. He made a great Santa, but not this."

"Never mind that," Amber grumbled as she pulled the note out of Gnorman's hand. Hopefully, it would be another good lead, as good as the lead they got from the Gnapper's spelling mistake. If only they could figure out how to make that work to their advantage.

Both Stan and Sherry read the latest note over Amber's shoulder.

he's not jackie chan or even
bruce lee
but gnorman will defend
himself, as you can see.
he moves like the wind,
and you will never know
the next garden where he
is going to show.

Amber nearly groaned but held back showing her disappointment. At least in her face, she hoped. However, she couldn't keep from voicing her frustration. "I can't say this is going to be much help. Thanks for calling us, Sherry."

Sherry rested one hand on Amber's shoulder. "No problem." She looked up at Stan, then back to Amber. "I heard you two had a nice time at the Fancy Schmantzy last weekend."

Stan grinned so widely that Amber wanted to smack him. "Yeah. We did. Right, Amber?"

She wanted to say something to dissuade him from falling into what was surely going to hit the rumor mill as soon as they stepped off of Sherry's property. While Sherry wasn't a gossip, she was in the operating committee of the garden club, and they all loved to talk; and from there, word spread. But she couldn't lie. She'd had a great time, even better because it had been so long since she'd been on a romantic date. "Yes, we did. Now if you'll excuse us, we have to get going so we can try to figure out what this means."

Stan didn't need an invitation. When he pulled into her driveway, he got out of the car and followed her to the front door. He waited for her to unlock it and trailed her inside.

"I don't know why you told Sherry that we were going to try to figure out what the new note means. As far as I can see, it doesn't say anything specific and doesn't give a clue to anything."

"I just didn't want her to ask questions. We avoided Winnie, I also wanted to avoid Sherry."

"Sherry is nothing like Winnie."

"No, but word still travels around the garden club."

Stan crossed his arms over his chest. "So what if it does? I'm not ashamed to have taken you to a nice place on Friday night. In fact, I'd like to do the same thing next Friday." He grinned and winked. "Anything to get you to wear that green dress again."

Amber felt her mouth drop open. "What are you talking about?"

"You looked really great in that dress, and I'd like to see you wear it more often. So how about if I take you someplace else on Friday, somewhere nice, where you can wear that green dress?"

She didn't want to start a habit, but she didn't want to have spent so much money on the dress just to wear it only once. Besides, Stan had looked great in his suit, and with his new mustache adding a touch of mystery, she couldn't say no.

"Sure."

"On a totally nonrelated subject, I've been meaning to ask you, why haven't you been taking your car to your store very much lately? If there's something wrong, I can have a look." Without asking, he turned and took a step toward the door leading to the carport.

Amber touched his forearm, stopping him in his tracks. "There's nothing wrong with my car. Even if there was, I can't have you fixing it for free all the time."

"I don't fix it for free. You insist on paying for the parts."

"Me paying for the parts doesn't earn you any income, and you know it. You always give me everything at cost, so you don't make any money on the parts either."

He raised one finger in the air. "You're wrong. At the end of the year, I get two percent cash back on my purchases with my wholesaler, so I am making money on the parts."

Like he could live on that. She didn't want to tell him that she'd seen him deduct two percent off the price, and she didn't know why. Now she did. That only made her feel worse because he didn't get that amount back until the end of the year, meaning he worked at below cost until he got his money back. Now for sure she would never ask him to work on her car again. Not that she could afford for anyone else to fix it.

She stiffened and cleared her throat. "I figure it's good exercise for me to walk. It's not far."

"Only if you don't wear your black shoes. You'll wear those shoes with your green dress on Friday night, won't you?"

She didn't know how the conversation went from the garden club to her favorite shoes, but such things weren't unusual with Stan. Never a dull moment with him.

"Let's get back to the topic, which is discovering who is moving Gnorman around, and finding the trophy. I have one week to get it back, or I'm going to get kicked out of the garden club."

"You don't know that."

"I'm not willing to take the risk. Let me boot up my computer."

He followed her into the den, where they waited for her computer to open the member list for the garden club.

"What now?"

"I'm going to start by crossing off the names of every place he's been so far."

"By process of elimination that's going to leave seventy-two more people. I don't think that's going to help."

She froze, with her hands over the keyboard. "Have you got a better idea?"

"You know I don't."

One at a time, Amber highlighted in yellow the names of people where Gnorman had been so far.

Again, her hands froze over her keyboard.

"Do you see what I'm seeing?"

"I think so. The names so far are the operating board of the garden club. You've got everyone who's an elected member, and two out of three of the appointed positions."

Even though she always scolded Stan for touching her monitor screen, Amber pressed her finger to the last unhighlighted name on the committee.

"Caroline," they said in unison.

"That's where he's going to be next." Amber forced herself not to jump up in the chair with glee. "We're going to catch this person at Caroline's."

Stan pressed his hand onto her shoulder. "Not so fast. We can't set up a surveillance camera like we did at my parents' place. Caroline runs a bed and breakfast. What we did was bad enough at my parents', but it would be a complete invasion of privacy at the B&B."

She pressed her fingers to her temples, as if that would help her think. "There's got to be a way."

"Maybe we can pitch a tent in the backyard. Then we'll catch him or her."

"Don't you think the rumor mill has enough fodder? Can you imagine what everyone will say if we do that?"

"Then we can set up a couple of lawn chairs in the back of her yard, and just sit there all night." He leaned forward in his chair and his eyebrows rose, like he seriously thought it was a good and practical idea. "What do you think?"

"If we sit up all night, how are we going to get up for work in the morning? Besides, up until now, whoever is doing this is doing it in the middle of the day. I don't know how no one sees someone carrying a gnome around. That isn't exactly subtle."

"Maybe it's Winnie. Did you see that thing she was carrying that she calls a purse? I bet Gnorman could fit in there."

"Winnie is around sixty years old. I'm not saying she's fragile or frail, but Gnorman weighs a little too much to get away with something like that."

"I could do that."

"You're about a foot taller than Winnie, and you lug around hunks of cars all day."

"But I could still do it. The Gnapper could be a man, you know."

"Yeah. A man who carries a big purse." Automatically she crossed Winnie's name off her list. "One more down," she mumbled as she hit Save.

"If you cross your name and my name off, that's two less."

Amber turned to Stan. "I wonder if I should do that. You seem to be having a little too much fun with this. I'd also like to see you carrying a man-purse."

His mouth opened, but he didn't speak. She knew if he said he wasn't having fun, that it would be a lie. In a way, she was having fun too. If it wasn't so frustrating, and her membership with the garden club wasn't at stake, and people weren't starting to gossip about her and Stan.

Or, maybe the fun was dwindling.

Next week, when Gnorman was moved to Caroline's, some-how they would figure it out.

But that was another day. Her next thing to worry about was her pending date with Stan. She probably should have told him no, but she couldn't waste the dress.

At least that's what she told herself.

"I'm going to go over this list and see if there's anyone else I can cross off. Do you want to stay and help?"

She didn't need him to say the answer, she knew he would.

Chapter Twenty-eight

O h! Strike three! He's out!" Stan hooted and raised one fist in the air while shoving more popcorn into his mouth with his other hand.

"Ball!" Hayden shouted at the television. "Ump, you're blind!"

They watched while the coach yelled the exact same thing at the ump, who ignored everyone except the batter, looking even more angry than Hayden.

Hayden reached into the bowl and shoved a handful of popcorn into his mouth as well while they sat and watched everyone argue. "This would be a better game if they had a decent umpire," he grumbled through his mouthful.

Stan grinned. Despite the questionable call, he was enjoying himself.

He turned and looked at his best friend, who continued to shovel more popcorn into his mouth. Amber also yelled at the television, but she would eat the popcorn one kernel at a time, leaving more for him. Then she'd complain that he was a pig when they were down to the last handful, and go make more.

"Gonna make another bowl?" Stan asked, without turning his head from the game. "This one's almost all gone."

"Nope. It's your house. You make more popcorn. I'm a guest."

"Not a very grateful one."

Hayden raised one buttery hand in the air. "Do *not* tell me what Amber would do, or that Amber would make you more popcorn."

"She would."

Hayden rolled his eyes. "You two are more married than most married people I know."

Suddenly the formerly delicious popcorn turned to a lump of lead in Stan's stomach. He no longer had the desire for more, so he leaned back into the couch and stared blankly at the television.

"Uh-oh," Hayden muttered. "I think I hit a nerve. Trouble in paradise?"

"There is no paradise. Except for one date, nothing's changed."

"I heard it was a great date, though."

Stan slumped forward, plunked his elbows on his knees, and leaned his face into his palms. "What did you hear, and who did you hear it from?"

"First Barry, then Andy, then Tucker, then my mother, then your mother."

Stan was beyond words. He groaned into his hands.

"I heard you were holding hands and making goo-goo eyes at each other all night, and there's been varying degrees of discussion on a good-night kiss at the door, and that it was about time."

Goo-goo eyes. Stan pressed his face more into his hands and groaned again.

"I know you're not the type to kiss and tell. So I won't ask. But I'll listen if you want to tell me."

Suddenly Stan felt like punching his friend in the nose. He didn't drop his hands, but he turned his head and glared at Hayden.

"Another raw nerve. I'm serious if you say you want to talk. On the other hand, I'm going to say something I've been dying to tell you."

All Stan did was glare at Hayden.

Hayden flinched and slid down the couch, a few inches away. "She told you that I took her out for dinner a few days before she went out on that big date with you, didn't she?"

"Yes. But she didn't say very much."

"That's because there was nothing to tell. It was the worst nowhere date I've ever been on. It's not that we were bored or didn't get along. We had a nice time and all that. At the end of the night we were still friends, just the way we were before. Nothing changed. There was no spark. Nothing. Nada. She wouldn't even let me pay for her meal."

"She does that to me all the time."

"Then I'd like to say I feel better about not paying for a lady's meal, but I don't, really."

Stan almost said that she also did that to him all the time, too, but he didn't want to make himself even more depressed.

"We didn't lack for conversation, but do you know what was the most interesting topic we covered?"

"What?" Not that he really wanted to know. As selfish and wrong as it felt, he didn't want Hayden to have a good time with Amber. Especially if they were out on a date.

"You. I couldn't believe it, but we talked a lot about you. I wish you could have seen her. Her eyes lit up, and she smiled a lot. I don't think she realized she was doing it either. Right then I saw that door closing, right in my face. I like Amber. A lot. I know she likes me too. But not that way. The one she likes that way is you."

"But she doesn't. I know she doesn't."

"She does. When I kissed her good night, she—"

Before Stan realized what he was doing, he had Hayden by the shirt collar and was glaring into his face, a few inches between their eyes. His heart was pounding, his breathing choppy, and he held his whole body as tight as a drumhead.

"Dude!" Hayden raised his hands in surrender but didn't touch Stan or push him away. "It was nothing. I get more response from my mother's cat, who hates everyone except my mother."

Stan let go like Hayden was on fire, sank down into the couch, and covered his face with his hands again. "I'm sorry," he muttered. "I don't know why I did that."

"I do. You couldn't stand the thought of me kissing your girl."

He shook his head with his face still buried in his hands. "But she's not my girl."

"She is. She just doesn't think of it that way. But she is. I had to listen to her sing your praises all night. Every time I see her, whenever your name comes up, I hear it all again. I'm surprised your feet even touch the ground."

"My feet touch the ground. Make no doubt of that."

"Not in her eyes. She's crazy about you. I don't know why you haven't asked her to marry you. If she were interested in me like that, I'd ask her in a New York minute."

With a swirling in his gut, Stan knew that was just what he wanted. He was crazy in love with Amber, he'd spent all of his life with her, and he wanted to spend the rest of his life with her—on a deeper level. They weren't just buddies, like she kept saying. They were soul mates. He doubted men usually thought like that, but he did. At least about Amber.

He turned to his friend. "Unfortunately I know what her answer would be, and it wouldn't be the one I want. She'd tell me it's not like that, that we're just good friends. Lifelong buddies."

Hayden's eyes lost their sparkle, and his whole body sagged. "I wish it had been like that when I married Marissa. We weren't friends. We didn't like the same things, we didn't do the same things. Most of the time we didn't know what to talk about when we were both home at the same time. We both knew we never should have gotten married. We barely knew each other, and we never worked at getting to know each other. She didn't even feel guilty when I caught her with her new boyfriend, six months after our wedding. When she served me with divorce papers and left town, I wasn't surprised. It was almost a relief, but it still really hurt."

Stan gritted his teeth. When he found out he'd wanted to deny it because he couldn't bear that it was his best friend that everyone was talking about. Except it was all true. "I tried to tell you, but you wouldn't listen."

"That's because I didn't want to believe it. Until I actually caught them together." Hayden shrugged. "I'm over it now. For the most part, anyway. But what I'm saying is that what I'm looking for is what you and Amber have. I don't know why you're too stupid to see it."

Stan saw it, but Amber didn't.

"You need to ask Amber to marry you, dude."

"I would, except I know what she'd say, and it won't be the answer I want."

"Then you have to do something to change her mind."

"What?"

"I don't know. You know her better than I do. Think of something."

Stan stared blankly at the television. The game was over, he didn't know the score, and he didn't care.

Hayden stood. "I'm going home. When you think of something, bounce it off me."

"I will."

He hoped.

AMBER'S PHONE RANG. AGAIN, she cringed. It was almost as if highlighting their names on her spreadsheet of the garden club's membership had somehow made them call her. Strangely, instead of asking about her garden or setting up an appointment for the annual inspection, they all asked about Stan.

As if she'd know.

She hadn't seen him since yesterday. As far as she knew he was at home, watching the ball game with Hayden. After the third call asking about him, she'd nearly panicked and asked if something was wrong that she didn't know about. Pamela had only laughed and said that she was curious after seeing them together on Sunday.

They hadn't been any more together on this last Sunday than they'd been any other Sunday. Unless Winnie had told someone how long they'd hidden in the sanctuary until she got fed up and left, informationless.

All they'd done was pray, which was what people were supposed to do in the sanctuary.

The caller ID showed that it was another member of the garden club, but this time the caller wasn't on the operating committee. This time the caller was her friend, Sarah.

Amber grinned and flipped the phone open.

"Stan's fine, thank you for asking," she said instead of *hello*.

"How did you know I was going to ask?"

Amber squeezed her eyes shut. "Not you too."

"I guess I'm not the first, second, or tenth caller?"

"Maybe the tenth."

She could hear the smile in Sarah's voice without seeing her. "Then you have to tell me. You know you two have been the talk of the garden club these last few days."

"Ever since Friday night, right?"

"You got it, girlfriend. Feed me the juicy details."

"You know I don't kiss and tell."

The second the words left her mouth, she realized she'd just told. Sarah's silence told her that her friend understood what she hadn't said.

"It wasn't like that . . ." Amber mumbled, her voice trailing off.

"So it finally happened. There was talk about a betting pool."

"There was not."

"The only reason there wasn't was because I told them I refused to ask for details. Unless you want to tell me."

"I just said—"

"—that you don't kiss and tell. Then intimate. Let me guess between the lines. I hear he was hot in his suit. He wore a tie. Don't you just love that mustache?"

Amber tried not to groan. She refused to let Sarah bait her. "What was I wearing?"

"A dress. With high heels. That's how I know it was serious."

"Those black ones are my favorite shoes."

"That you only wear on very special occasions. Come on, Amber, you two went to the Fancy Schmantzy, not McDonalds."

Figures from her budget ran like a ticker-tape through her head. "There's nothing wrong with McDonalds. I eat there all the time." When she had extra money. Which hadn't been often lately.

"Quit trying to change the subject. Talk is that you two were making goo-goo eyes at each other all night. It's been killing me not to ask, but I've waited long enough. I have to know."

"Goo-goo eyes?" She rolled her eyes, which were not goo-gooing.

"Details, my friend."

"We had a nice time." The whole time she'd had difficulty comparing her usual buddy Stan to the charming man across the table. Not that he was ever rude or crude, but he showed and demonstrated manners and behavior fitting the class and dignity of the suit. She'd felt like she'd been swept away on a magic carpet ride, while her butt remained stuck to the padded chair at the restaurant.

"And?"

"The food was good." Better than good, she'd never eaten so well in her life. Of course, she'd never eaten a meal that cost so much in her life either. Everything was top quality, seasoned and cooked to perfection, and served with style. Stan's meal was as excellent as her own, and the rich cheesecake they'd had for dessert had been a taste sensation.

"And?"

"Then we went home." Because he was being such a baby about being in her car and that she'd driven to the restaurant, she'd let him drive home. That had been a mistake, because she'd ended up admiring how good he looked and thinking about how different the evening had been than anything they'd ever done before. Going out with him had been wonderful.

"And?"

"Then yes, just like you heard, he kissed me good night." A spectacular kiss that had her nearly melting into a little puddle on the kitchen floor. She'd been kissed senseless by her most long-standing and best friend in the world. She'd felt his pulse many times before, mostly she'd had to check that he was still alive after landing on the ground after falling off of something. But this time she'd felt his heart beating against her cheek while he had his arms wrapped tight around her, and she'd had her arms wrapped tight around him. She'd been scared that he would, then terrified that he wouldn't. Her whole world fell off its axis. The most romantic date she'd ever been on in her whole life had been with her buddy, Stan.

"And?"

"He went home. I made tea." Except that, by the time she could get her head off the table, the kettle had boiled dry and she had to put on a second pot of water. Then she'd stared at the cup until the tea got cold, without having a single sip.

"That doesn't say very much for your romantic evening with Stan."

Amber's throat clogged up. "I don't know what to say. I don't know what to think. Do I want more? Just like in all the books I read, everything has changed. What if I'm no different? We'll never be able to go back to the way it was before. What if we start dating, and it doesn't work out?"

"You ask too many questions. I think it would work, but that's not really up to me to decide. It's up to you. There's one question that you didn't ask, and that's the one you need to think about. If you continue on with Stan, it will either work or it won't. There won't be any middle ground. There never is. Is it worth the risk? I think I'll leave it at that. I have to go. I'll see you in a few days."

Amber flipped the phone closed and slipped it into her pocket.

She didn't have to think about her friend's question. She already knew the answer.

While the prize would be wonderful, the expense was too high. It was a risk she wasn't willing to take.

CHAPTER Twenty-nine

Just as Amber expected, a couple of days after nearly everyone in the garden club phoned her to ask about Stan, she got a call from Caroline in the middle of the afternoon, stating that Gnorman was in her garden, holding an envelope.

Just like everyone in the garden club would expect, Amber called Stan, and he immediately agreed to accompany her to Caroline's to get said envelope.

He picked her up after they both closed, and they arrived at Caroline's in good time. Instead of getting out of the truck, they both stared at the huge home.

Caroline's mansion was as opposite from Sherry's modest dwelling as the sun from the moon. Caroline's home was huge, a two-story Victorian built in the late nineteenth century by Caroline's great-grandparents, who were among the founders of the town of Bloomfield.

"Wow," Stan said with a whoosh of air. "How many bedrooms does this place have?"

"I don't know. Lots. All I know is that Caroline and her daughter live in the back, and the guest bedrooms are on the top floor. That big section in the front is the tearoom."

"I've never been here before, I've only driven past. What about you?"

"I've been to the tearoom, but it's been years. I've heard her garden is spectacular and she's won prizes for her azaleas, but she's never won one of the big contests."

"If the house is this huge, I can only imagine how big her garden is. I guess being so busy with the B&B, she probably can't spend as much time as a garden that size needs, and that's why she's never won The Spring Fling."

"Probably. Let's go talk to her."

When Caroline answered the door, Amber could tell that she and her daughter were just about ready to start eating supper. Being the friendly hostess that she was, Caroline smiled widely and invited them in, not acting like she was in a hurry to get rid of them. Amber refused to take advantage of the nice woman. In many ways Caroline reminded Amber of her own mother.

Since the tearoom was now closed, this was Caroline's personal time. All day long, as well as at the garden club meetings, Caroline kept her salt and pepper hair tied back, but this time it was loose, hanging to shoulder length. Amber liked it that way,

"I'll take you back to the garden. Let's cut through the tearoom, it's quicker than going outside and all the way around. Please don't mind the mess. I haven't cleaned it up from this afternoon yet."

The tearoom wasn't as much of a mess as Caroline had claimed. Amber thought the room seemed as charming as the name, The Pink Geranium. All the tables had antique white tablecloths, and the tables that hadn't been used that day were still set with pretty pink and pastel green napkins, which matched the baskets of pink geraniums hanging on the walls.

As they followed Caroline between the tables, Stan nudged her and leaned so he could speak softly to her as they walked. "How long is geranium season? Does she grow them all year long to go with the name of this place?"

Amber didn't know whether to laugh or cry that, once again, she and Stan were thinking of the same thing at the same time.

She waited for Stan to comment that the pastel green walls were the same color as the green napkins on the tables, but he didn't.

She let Caroline get a little ahead of her as she slowed to check out the centerpieces on the tables, which were small hurricane lamps with candles in the middle, surrounded by a ring of pastel-colored flowers.

The Pink Geranium Tearoom was the epitome of charming, making Amber almost consider closing her store for an hour and coming back for lunch. Caroline's Three Cheese Chicken Penne was to die for, and her specialty peach cobbler rivaled the cheesecake from the Fancy Schmantzy, at half the price for a dessert serving. She hadn't been here in years; the last time was with her mother, before her parents moved to Chicago. In all those years, not much had changed, and being inside once again made her realize how much she wanted to come back.

She slowed her pace even more, so she could get closer to Stan. "Do you want to come here for lunch one day?" she whispered, hoping Caroline couldn't hear, in case his answer was no.

His nose crinkled and his brows knotted. "I think this place is a little girly for me. If I came here, I'd damage the place's reputation. Did you see the pretty little cups and saucers? I would be afraid to touch that stuff. I'll pass."

"Fine. I'll ask Sarah. I know she'll come with me." When she got the next payment from the florist, Amber would consider tea and dessert at The Pink Geranium a treat, and if she didn't order lunch, it was one she could afford.

"You do that."

Amber quickened her pace to catch up to Caroline, who already opened the door leading to her garden.

Caroline's garden was as expansive as the house, but even as a marginal gardener, Amber could see that the bushes needed pruning, and the flowers needed to be deadheaded. However, unlike the rest of the garden, Caroline's azaleas were perfectly groomed, trimmed, and arranged. That section of the garden was obviously Caroline's pride and joy.

And there, in the middle of Caroline's pride and joy, stood Gnorman. Dressed as a thief with a little black mask, he had shown up in the middle of the day like a cat burglar when Caroline was out at the wholesale grocery depot, shopping for the tearoom.

Amber turned to Caroline. "I know you and your daughter were about to eat, and you need more time off your feet. You go have supper. Stan and I will take the note and see ourselves out through the gate."

Caroline smiled and nodded. "Thanks. I appreciate that. I hope you find the trophy soon." She smiled again, turned, and headed back toward her house.

The second the door closed behind Caroline, Stan crossed his arms and turned to Amber. "Do you realize she's the first person to mention the trophy?"

"What do you mean?"

"Every time we've arrived someplace else to find Gnorman, most people have commented on his costume, or that they didn't see how he got there. Not a single person has mentioned what's really missing, and that isn't Gnorman because he keeps showing up. The real purpose of this is ultimately to regain the trophy. Caroline is the first person to mention that."

Amber didn't open the envelope. She only stared at the closed door through which Caroline had disappeared. "You're right. Do you think that's significant?" Her brain spun in circles, trying to make the connection, but she came up with nothing.

"I have no idea. It's just that this time is different than what we've encountered so far."

"Caroline is running a multilayered business between the B&B and the tearoom, so she naturally needs to have more of a mind for the big picture."

"Are we looking at the right picture though? Your goal is to get the trophy back. What is it this person thinks they're gaining by making us run all over town, chasing a garden gnome? Other than making us look like idiots?"

Amber sank down onto one of the wooden benches in Caroline's yard. "Is that what everyone thinks? That we look like idiots jumping every time Gnorman shows up someplace else with another note that doesn't bring us any closer to finding the trophy?"

Stan sat beside her, plucked the envelope from her hand, laid it in his lap, and cupped both her hands with his. "No. It's really not that extreme. Actually, I've heard the garden club is greatly amused by watching us run around chasing him. It's just that knowing they're watching makes me feel stupid because whoever is doing this, leaving all these clues, there's something we're not getting."

Amber smiled weakly. "I feel the same way. But I'm so afraid that soon the entertainment factor will wear off, and the committee members will say they want the trophy back where it should be, and I won't be any farther in producing it." She tipped her head up, looking at Stan. He'd taken off his coveralls and come straight from work. Even though his clothes were relatively clean, the scents of his shop permeated his clothes and his hair. Being downwind from him, she reaped the benefits of his day at work right now. It wasn't a bad smell. In a strange way, this was the way she liked him best—less than perfect so she couldn't be too attracted to him. Especially when he shared what was on his heart.

He gave her hands a gentle squeeze and looked down at their joined hands.

"I know my mother is getting a real charge out of the whole thing. I was there checking out my dad's car yesterday and I heard my mom on the phone. I don't know who she was talking to, but since I heard her digging for details on our trip to the Fancy Schmantzy, it had to be Victoria. As soon as she saw me, she ended the conversation pretty quick."

"I know why. I was talking to Sarah, and she said someone tried to start a betting pool about us."

"A betting pool? What about us would be fodder for that?"

"I'm not sure of the exact details, but it was about last Friday." She refused to say the word *date* because she still struggled with the concept of dating her best buddy. She preferred to think that two friends enjoyed a nice evening out, with no particular event in mind, dressed in their good clothes, looking their best, just because they felt like it.

Stan looked up, his eyes narrowed. "This is making more sense. One thing my mother said to Victoria was, 'How should I know? I'm his mother. He would never tell me stuff like that.' I know exactly what I would and wouldn't tell my mother about when I go out with a lady." When he stopped talking, it was almost like she could see the gears whirring in his head.

"Sarah was trying to get me to spill details, but I didn't. She told me not to worry, that the pool didn't happen because she refused to be the reliable source of information they needed to confirm the exact details. In not so many words."

Stan stiffened, and she felt it all the way down to his hands that still held hers. "I can only think of one detail from Friday that those nosy busy-bodies would want to know."

Memories of Winnie standing in the foyer on Sunday danced through her mind.

A movement of the curtains from Caroline's house caught Amber's eye. "Settle down. I think Caroline is watching us from inside the house."

He stiffened even more. "Then let them put this in their betting pool," he said between his teeth. He dropped her hands, cupped her face, bent toward her, planted a quick kiss right on her mouth, and backed up.

Amber didn't have time to close her eyes. She didn't even have time to blink, it was done and over so fast.

Stan didn't drop his hands, but his expression softened as he continued to look at her. "I'm sorry. It shouldn't have been like that. It should be like this." His eyes drifted shut, he tilted his head, and bent slowly.

This time Amber closed her eyes.

He kissed her softly, lingering just a few seconds with a kiss that was very sweet, but chaste.

This time, when he pulled away, he released her face, grabbed one hand with one of his, grabbed the envelope with his other, and stood, pulling her up with him. "I don't want an audience for this. Let's get out of here."

Chapter Thirty

The closer they got to Amber's house, the higher the wall he felt go up between them. By the time he pulled into her driveway, the wall was up to the ceiling of the truck. Since it was a big truck, it was a high wall.

As he turned off the ignition and reached to open his door, Amber snapped at him. "What was that all about? What were you thinking?"

The trouble was, he hadn't been thinking. Or, he'd been thinking too much. All thought processes stalled when he learned that everyone was sticking their noses where they didn't belong, with the end result being a betting pool. He'd noticed Caroline watching them, making him remember Winnie waiting like a turkey vulture outside the sanctuary on Sunday.

It was like all the thoughts got tumbled into a paper sack and shaken. His brain backfired, something snapped, and all he could think to do was kiss Amber. Of course, he'd been thinking of kissing Amber multiple times a day since last Friday, and that had been the spark that broke the camel's back, or something like that. Because it was a spark. A spark that had ignited him into action.

Hayden was right, added to the fact that the garden club execs had made his love life, or lack thereof, their latest point of interest. It was time to make it clear to Amber that they needed to stop coasting through life, get serious, and get married.

He ran his fingers through his hair instead of opening the door. "I don't know what I was thinking. Do I owe you an apology?"

While he waited for her to say something, anything, his stomach flopped like a fish on dry land, and he had to tell himself to breathe because, like that fish, he couldn't find air.

First her stiff posture relaxed, just a little, then her brows unknotted, the tight glare in her eyes went to normal, and she sighed. "No. You don't owe me an apology."

If it wasn't his imagination, the sunset just turned prettier.

He grinned, hoping he didn't look like an eager puppy, then not caring if he did. "Then will you kiss me again? Nobody's watching, this time." Hoping she wouldn't smack him in the head with the map that was scrunched between the seats, he closed his eyes, leaned toward her, puckered up, and waited for the best. Or worst.

Not opening his eyes, he heard her sigh like she was annoyed, so he waited for the smack.

Time lingered, but he didn't move. He heard the rustle of the map getting pulled out from between the seats and tried not to cringe, but he remained motionless, eyes closed, puckered up, still waiting for the best.

He was as bad as a dumb dog about to be beaten, but unrealistically hoping for a pat.

At the same time, he felt a very light tap on the top of his head, and Amber's warm lips pressed into his with a comical smacking sound, then it was over.

He grinned and opened his eyes.

She grinned back at him. "Gotcha," she said at the same time as she tapped him on the head again.

His heart did a stupid little dance in his chest. There was hope.

They both straightened at the same time, and sat back in their seats.

This time, it was Amber who reached for the door handle. "I'm going in. Do not follow me. I mean it."

His optimism faded. "But we need to talk."

"About what?"

"I think I might have an idea, and talking is best done over coffee and donuts."

"I don't have any donuts."

He reached behind the seat and pulled the box of donuts he'd bought at Dunkin' Donuts on his way to pick her up. "I do," he said, unable to hold back his grin. "Now you can't say no."

She sighed. He knew the way to Amber's heart was through donuts. The ones with the multicolored candy sprinkles on top. Just in case, he popped the box open to show her that he had three of her favorite kind, and three of his. While holding the box with one hand, he reached behind the seat for the second box. "I bought Munchkins too. The chocolate ones." He shook the box slightly, so she could hear them rolling.

She sighed again, but he knew he'd won.

Boxes in hand, he followed her to the door and waited for her to unlock it, even though he had his own key to her place, just in case she lost her own. Not that she had, and come to think of it, the only time he'd ever used it was last Friday, when he locked her door on his way out. She had a key to his house that she'd never used either.

She also had a key to his truck. He should have realized then, the day he bought the truck, his pride and joy, that when he gave her the spare key, he'd also given her the key to his heart.

That was two years ago. What a sap he was.

Fortunately she didn't see him smiling as he followed her inside.

While she started making the coffee, he got out the cups, put out plates for the donuts, and pulled the new envelope out of his back pocket.

"I don't know why we should even bother with the new note. It's not going to tell us anything," she said.

"No, but I know what might tell us something."

He could see her interest perked. "What?"

"Not what. Who. My mother."

"Do you think she knows who is doing this?"

"No, but I think she can help flush him or her out. You know how she loves to talk. I told you how I caught her talking to Victoria. We know the garden club is talking about us, so let's also get them talking about how we're trying to find who's dressing up Gnorman and moving him around. If we tell my mother what we think, then she'll tell someone else, and soon the whole garden club will talk about it. Whoever is doing this is bound to mess up, and then the whole garden club will be talking about that, it will come back to my mother, and she'll tell me."

"In a skewed way, that almost sounds like a good idea. Give me one of those donuts and I'll think about it some more."

"The coffee isn't ready yet."

She sent him a dirty look cold enough to freeze steel. He caved and pushed the whole box to her. "I think it's a brilliant idea."

She bit into the donut, closed her eyes, and chewed slowly. "It's getting better. Pass me the Munchkins."

He'd give her the whole box if that made her agree. Actually, he'd planned to give her the whole box anyway.

"Okay. Let's tell your mother. She told everyone about the hidden camera, and the Gnapper obviously heard about it soon enough to cover the camera when he or she moved Gnorman out of your parents' yard. Let's see if it works. I suppose we don't have anything to lose."

While she enjoyed her second donut, Stan poured the coffee, added cream and sugar to his, double cream to hers, brought both cups to the table, and picked up the envelope. "Time to open it?"

"Sure. You can do it. My fingers are full of icing."

He tore open the envelope and spread the new note on the table. Just like all previous ones, it was made of cutout letters and words from the *Gazette*.

i have come like a thief in
the night
But i don't mean to give you
a fight
i may be sneaky
and even cheeky
don't you love the notes
i write?

They both stared at the note, unable to come up with a single comment.

As far as Stan saw, this was the worst one yet. It didn't mention the trophy, it didn't give a hint or clue, nor did it use any identifiable wording or phrases. The only thing it did was match the costume, which was no help at all.

Amber turned her head and faced him, both cheeks bulging like a squirrel. She lost focus on him for a second as she glanced at something over his shoulder, then her eyes widened, the color faded in her face, and she stopped chewing.

He turned and looked to see what was behind him and saw her calendar on the wall, with the date a week from today circled in red.

He turned back to her. "What's the matter?"

She swallowed hard, and her eyes went glassy. "I guess I pushed it out of my mind. We have exactly one week to find the trophy. That day I circled is the day that my membership comes up for renewal. What if telling your mother doesn't work?"

"Then we'll find another way. I wish you wouldn't worry about this so much. They're not going to kick you out of the garden club."

"But they kicked a lady out last year whose garden was better than mine. Even if they don't kick me out, I have to be in their good books. I need their loyalty so they'll keep buying the First Bud ornaments from me, and so that all the members will come into my store first when they want something different for their gardens. I really need their business. I don't want to give anyone any reason to check out that new lady's store."

"So what if they do? Your stuff is better. It's got character. You also honor a guarantee, not like all that cheap stuff made overseas." He closed the box to the donuts and stood. "I think there's no time like the present. Since you're so stressed about all this, and you're worried that we're getting short on time, let's go visit my mother right now. I know she'll help. Besides, she loves to talk to people, and this will give her more inside information to talk about."

Amber stood. "Okay."

The drive to his parents' home was pretty much in silence, but that gave Stan time to think about what he was going to say to his mother. He didn't want to call her a gossip; after all, he didn't want to hurt her feelings. Not that she really gossiped. She just found it hard not to share information. So he'd give her so much information she couldn't *not* share.

Since it was so late and he didn't want to scare his parents by barging in unexpected, Stan stood at the door with Amber and knocked. While he waited, because he thought Amber could use something to boost her sagging spirits, he slipped one arm around her shoulders and gave her a gentle squeeze. "It'll be okay. This will work. You just see. You know my mother. She loves to talk."

Just as he gave her another squeeze, his mother opened the door. Her gaze zoomed in on his arm around Amber's shoulders. Her mouth nearly dropped open, she closed it, cleared her throat, and backed up. "Frank!" she called over her shoulder. "Stan's here! With Amber!"

Stan stepped in with Amber and closed the door behind them.

"Not that I'm not happy to see you, but what are you doing here at this hour?"

Stan tried to smile, but Amber's somberness seemed to be rubbing off on him. "We need to talk to you about something."

His mother backed up even more. "Come in, come in." She guided them into the living room and pointed to the couch, obvious about expecting them to sit together, which Stan didn't mind at all.

His parents sat on the loveseat, kitty-corner from them, with his mother on the edge of her seat leaning forward, her hands clasped on her knees, smiling ear to ear, which Stan thought odd. "Yes?"

"We need your help."

Her smile quivered a little. "With what?"

"Amber's really worried about The Spring Fling trophy. We really thought that the Gnapper would have given up and returned it by now, but he or she hasn't. We need your help trying to find out who it is."

His mother's smile faltered, and she leaned back in the seat. "Gnapper?"

"That's what we've been calling the person who's been moving Gnorman around. The Gnome Gnapper. We'd like your help catching him or her."

"Oh."

Beside him, he felt Amber stiffen. Since the conversation wasn't quite as encouraging as he'd hoped, and she was feeling it, too, he reached out and grasped her hand, gave it a gentle squeeze, and didn't let go. "This is really important to us."

At his word *us*, his mother quirked one eyebrow. "I suppose I could, but what can I do?"

"It's got to be someone in the garden club, and we've got a couple of good clues. The best one is that the Gnapper can't spell *clandestine*. It was in one of the notes spelled with an *I* instead of an *E* in the middle. We were wondering if you could ask around the garden club and find out who spells it wrong. It's not something either of us can bring up in a normal conversation."

"*Clandestine*? What kind of word is that to use?"

"When Gnorman was moved to Pamela's yard, he was dressed as a spy. Every note he comes with seems to reflect the newest costume."

"Really? Where did he come from before that, and what was he wearing?"

Stan turned to Amber. "I'm not sure, do you remember?"

Amber nodded. "Yes. Before that, he came from Victoria and Barry's place. That time he was dressed as a ghost. The poem for that one was probably the worst of all of them." Amber made a weak smile, and turned to his mother. "All the notes have been pretty awful, so we know the Gnapper can't be Lynn because she's a teacher and would never write like that."

"Let me get this straight. You want me to ask people in the garden club how to spell *clandestine*, and see who spells it wrong?"

"Pretty much."

"I have no idea how to work that into a conversation, but I guess I'll think of a way."

Stan grinned. "If anyone can do it, I know you can. I think—" His sentence was cut off from the vibration of his cell phone in his pocket. He pulled it out to see that Hayden had texted him. Just as he hit the button to read it, the phone went dead.

He turned to Amber. "I have no idea what Hayden wants, but it must be important if he's texting me now. Do you have your charger in your purse?"

Amber rolled her eyes. "Of course I do. You know that."

He grinned wider. "It was a redundant question."

He waited for her to dig through her purse. When she handed the charger to him, he plugged it in and connected his phone.

His mother tilted her head and stared at him while he called up Hayden's message. "Do you two have the same kind of cell phone?"

"Yeah. They had a sale if you bought two, so we took advantage of it. Hayden wants to know if he forgot his sunglasses at my house, but he wasn't wearing his sunglasses. It was dark by the time he got to my place." He turned to Amber. "You didn't see Hayden's sunglasses at my house, did you?"

She shook her head.

Stan punched in a reply for Hayden to check behind the visor in his car, hit Send, and put the phone down on the coffee table to let it charge for a bit.

His mother stood. "Would you two like a cup of tea? I still have some left."

He didn't want to, but he would stay if Amber did. Although he doubted she would because there was still one of the donuts with sprinkles on top that she hadn't eaten.

"I'd love a cup of tea. Thank you."

So much for that. He released her hand, and she followed his mother into the kitchen.

When they were gone from the room and he couldn't see them anymore, his father spoke. "How's things going between you and Amber? A few people have been asking."

Stan gritted his teeth. "Sorry, Dad, but I hate being fodder for the rumor mill in the garden club."

His father leaned forward, resting his elbows on his knees. "They're not gossiping. They're concerned. Those people in the garden club, they're your friends. I know some are closer than others, but they only want to see you and Amber happy. Besides, this isn't them asking, it's me."

Stan only saw sincerity in his father's face. "Things are going better, but not where I want them to be. Let's just say I have to work on a few more things."

"That's good. Your mother and I only want to see you happy."

"Yeah. And have grandchildren."

His father grinned. "That, too."

Fortunately his mother and Amber returned, closing the door on that topic. The conversation drifted to easier and less personal subjects until the phone rang, giving Stan a cue to leave.

Amber gulped down the last sip of her tea, he waved a good-bye to his mother, and he hustled Amber out the door. The longer they stayed, the more chances there were that his mother would ask the same question as his father, and his mother wasn't as subtle as his father. Mostly, that wasn't something he wanted to address in front of Amber. At least not yet.

Just as he started the truck, Amber tapped him on the arm. "I need the charger for my cell phone back."

Stan smacked his palm to his forehead. "I forgot it inside, as well as my cell phone. It's still charging. Wait just a minute, I'll be right back."

Looking through the window, he saw that his mother was still on the phone, so he didn't knock, he just went straight in. His father was no longer in the living room, and his mother's back was to him, giving him a good opportunity to just grab his phone and the charger and get out of there before she saw him. If she did, then she'd ask the same questions as his father, only worse, since Amber was no longer with him. He didn't want to go through that again, not today, not ever.

He glanced at his mother. Since he was nearly six feet tall, even if he took off his boots and tiptoed across the room, she would still see him out of her peripheral vision. If not, he'd still cast a shadow, and she'd see that, even if she didn't see him.

He looked across the room to the coffee table, where his phone glowed with the charging icon flashing.

He needed his phone, and Amber needed her charger. He also needed to do this fast, because Amber was waiting in the truck.

Not caring that he felt as foolish as he probably looked, he lowered himself to his hands and knees and crawled across the living room without taking his boots off. The closer he got to his phone, the closer he got to his mother, so close that he could actually hear her conversation. He didn't want to listen in, but when her words hit him, he froze with his hand in midair above his phone.

". . . is spelled with an *E*, not an *I*. How could you use a word like that and not check how it's spelled? And another thing, they came in here to talk to me with his arm around her shoulder. Sylvia just called to tell me that about an hour ago she was driving by Amber's house and saw them smooching in his truck in her driveway. Earlier Caroline called to say Stan kissed Amber in the backyard when they came to get the new note. Our plan is working!"

A rush of adrenaline flooded Stan, filling him with the urge to either roar out loud or hit something really hard. Instead, he grabbed his phone, yanked the charger out of the wall and hightailed it back across the floor, his temper flaring with every step, or whatever it was when a person crawled instead of walked. It took all his mental strength to click the door shut rather than slam it, and he stormed back to his truck, struggling even more not to slam the truck door.

"What's wrong? What happened?"

"I'll tell you when we get back to your place," he snapped between his teeth, and the pickup roared off down the street.

CHAPTER Thirty-one

I've never seen you like this. Please tell me."

"I refuse to talk about it while I'm driving." He gripped the steering wheel so hard that his hands shook.

Amber gulped and said a prayer for their safety. Not only had she never seen Stan this angry, she'd never seen him drive so fast.

She almost prayed for Tucker or Bubba to come after them, in or out of uniform. Unless Stan was driving so fast that they'd have to throw him in jail. She couldn't pay his bail.

They made it home in record time, unescorted.

He stomped his way to her door, used his own key to unlock it, and was inside before she was halfway down the sidewalk.

Somebody had done something really, really bad. Since they'd just come from his parents' place, she had a sinking feeling it was his mother.

By the time Amber made it to the living room, Stan sat on the couch, leaning back, his arms crossed over his chest, his knees pressed tight together, his whole body as stiff as a board. She could almost see steam coming out of his ears.

The mental image almost made her laugh, telling her that she was nearly at the edge, herself. She didn't know whether she should try to lighten the moment by offering to get a fire extinguisher, or give him a hug to try to make his pain go away.

Instead, she sat beside him, not touching him, and waited for him to talk when he was ready.

"You don't have to worry about getting kicked out of the garden club," he snapped, his tone harsher than she'd ever heard out of Stan. "I think I know where the trophy is. You'll probably find it safe and sound in Pamela's den, in the same case where it's stored all winter."

"Do you mean the Gnapper is Pamela? That's not possible."

"It's not just Pamela. It's all of them."

"All of who?"

"All of them, every place where Gnorman's been. I heard my mother on the phone, scolding someone for spelling *clandestine* wrong. Then she told the bad speller that both Caroline and Sylvia called, and that their plan was working." He turned to Amber. "She didn't say 'my' plan, or 'your' plan, or 'their' plan. She said 'our' plan. That tells me there are at least four people involved, but the more I think about it, I think that everyone who has had Gnorman in their yard is somehow involved. That would explain how Gnorman so strategically disappeared from every single yard without being seen. They're all in on it."

The membership spreadsheet flashed before her eyes, with the operating board members highlighted in yellow. She counted on her fingers. "That means Pamela, Sherry, Libby, Sylvia, Victoria, Andy, Minnie, Caroline, Naomi, and your mother."

"Yup. All of them."

"Why? You said I'm not going to get kicked out of the garden club. I don't understand."

He gritted his teeth, sighed, ran one hand through his hair, then looked away. She'd never seen anyone working harder to avoid saying something.

"Come on. Just say it."

"It had nothing to do with your membership, or your garden, or even the garden club. It's a matchmaking scheme to get us together," he said, not facing her as he spoke.

"What?"

"You heard me. Caroline reported back to my mother that I kissed you in the backyard at the B&B, and Sylvia reported back to my mother that we were smooching in my truck in your driveway." He turned back to her, his expression looking like he was ready to blow a gasket or something. "Smooching! What kind of description is that? That's almost as dumb a word as *clandestine*!"

"You're yelling."

"Sorry," he snapped.

He didn't sound very sorry, but she wasn't about to tell him that. Besides, this whole thing wasn't his fault.

Amber turned away from him so she could think. She couldn't think with him glaring at her like that.

She tried to piece together the information he'd given her, but one phrase kept ringing through her head. *Matchmaking scheme.*

She turned back to him. "I don't understand at all. A matchmaking scheme would be something to throw together two people who don't know each other. We don't need to be matched. We already see each other nearly every day."

"I know."

"If Caroline and Sylvia were reporting back to your mother, does that mean that everyone is watching for us, spying on us?"

"I hope not."

"I haven't noticed anyone following me." But then, she'd never have a reason to look. From now on, though, she would. "Have you noticed anyone following you?"

"No."

"What are we going to do?"

"I don't know."

"You're sure full of answers. No sarcasm intended." Contrary to her words, she let her voice drip with sarcasm.

Again, he turned to glare at her. "I heard very little of the conversation. I was only in there for what, two minutes? Then I had to get out as fast as I could, before she saw me."

"You're right. I'm sorry. This is just such a . . . a shock. What were they thinking?"

"I don't know."

She looked at him, waiting for answers, but he had as many as she did, which at the time, was zero.

He opened his arms toward her. "Come here," he mumbled.

She didn't need any more invitation. Amber leaned against his chest, sliding one arm around his back, the other across the front of him, planting her open palm at his shoulder. When she was settled, Stan's arms wrapped around her and he held her tight.

She didn't talk. She didn't need to. Besides, she had nothing to say.

Apparently neither did Stan. The silence dragged so long she felt a compelling urge to turn on the television, but she couldn't reach the remote without pulling herself away from Stan, and she didn't want to do that.

She should have been overjoyed. Her membership with the garden club was safe. The steady income she earned with the garden club membership would remain unchanged, so unless something bad happened, her business was probably safe too.

The trophy was in the hands of someone on the operating board, probably the president of the club, so the trophy was safe.

Here she was, nestled in the arms of her lifetime buddy, driven there by the matchmaking schemes of the operating committee.

Her heart was definitely not safe. Being wrapped in Stan's embrace felt good . . . too good, even though she could still feel the tension of his anger in his body.

For her, to be caught up in a matchmaking plot was almost funny, except she wasn't laughing. Even though she no longer felt quite on the edge of going bankrupt, she still didn't feel secure that sometime in the next four years that she wouldn't. Then she'd still have to leave everything she knew and pack up and move to Chicago. Chicago wasn't a bad city, it just wasn't Bloomfield. She was in no position to be matched. Fortunately for her, no one knew how close she still was to the red. Often when that happened, people didn't feel secure, and they took their business elsewhere. That only worked to drive the struggling business all the way into the hole instead of just tottering on the edge. So if she counted herself safe, for now, she was, but she didn't know if it was only temporary.

Stan, on the other hand, was in a great position to be matched. Over the past few months he'd shown signs of being ready to settle down. She wanted him to be happy and to do whatever it took to find that happiness. Stan deserved it. For a man his size, he had a kind and gentle heart, even if he didn't want to admit it. Amber knew it, and so did many of the other women her age. She should have been the one trying to match him to someone suitable, not the operating committee of the garden club, and especially not his mother. However, now that he—or rather, they—were caught in the middle of a plan that had not yet been seen to conclusion by the conspirators, there was nothing she could do. Worse than that, no one could know they knew because then she'd be asked questions she didn't want to answer. Careless words or a retreat would make things even more complicated than they already had become. Even without their help, she had to be careful not to fall for Stan. She didn't need any help from interfering but well-meaning friends, if it wasn't too late already.

With her ear pressed to Stan's chest, his voice echoed with a deep rumble when he spoke. "You're thinking about something."

"So are you."

He grunted. "You first."

Even though she wanted the best for Stan, she couldn't share her current train of thought. "My mind is spinning with all this. My first thought is that we can't let anyone know we found out what they're doing, and especially not why."

"I was thinking the same thing. In fact, they'll be off our backs sooner if we let them think they got what they wanted. My mother's words to the bad speller were that their plan was working. If they feel confident enough that it worked, then we'll be free and clear."

"Are you saying what I think you're saying?"

"Yes. Word is that we've already been caught twice, and we've been seen on a date before that. My mother is telling everyone else that their plan is working, so if we go the whole way and start holding hands in public and stuff like that, they'll think it's a natural progression, give themselves a pat on the back for putting us through the wringer, and leave us alone and let nature take its course."

She wasn't very happy with faking public displays of affection, but she did like the part about everyone leaving them alone. "I suppose we could do that."

He sighed, and it wasn't a very happy sound. "I can't believe my mother would do this to me. I wonder if my father knows."

"I doubt it."

"I'm not so sure. He asked about you when you went into the kitchen with Mom to get your tea. So either they are thinking the same thing at the same time because they've been married so long, or he's in on it, or he's been listening to her schemes and dreams."

"Then that could go either way."

"Yup. No ally in my dad." He sighed. "Is this what it feels like to be a pawn in a chess game?"

"Probably."

He sighed again. "I should go home. I'm not feeling very sociable right now."

They shuffled apart, and she immediately missed his warmth.

She saw him to the door and had started to close it when his fingers appeared, grabbing the door, halting its movement. He pulled it back open, released the door, grasped her hands with his, and gently pulled her outside until they both stood on the mat.

"I'm sorry," he muttered. "It wasn't supposed to be like this." Then, right there, standing outside her front door, for all the neighborhood to see, he leaned down and kissed her. Not the bone-melting kiss of Friday night, but not the chaste peck like earlier that same day. Just as it felt like he was going to settle in for more, he yanked himself away, spun around, and stomped toward his truck.

Amber watched him drive away, then went inside and turned on the television.

It was already past her usual bedtime, but she knew it was going to be a sleepless night.

CHAPTER Thirty-two

Y ou're going to break something, boss."
Stan straightened, set the crowbar down, pulled a rag out of his pocket to wipe his hands, and then stared at Jordan.

Part of him wanted to reprimand Jordan for insubordination, part of him wanted to tell Jordan that if he did break something, he would fix it; but the smarter part of him needed to tell Jordan that he was right. The workplace was no place to exorcise his frustration. If one of his employees did what he had just done, Stan would probably have written him up.

"You're right. Thanks for pointing that out. Unless you just want me to be quiet so you can have a nap."

Jordan grinned, and his eyes lost focus. Stan mentally kicked himself. If Jordan was going to bring out more baby pictures and tell more baby stories, it was time to get out.

"She's sleeping better, and so are we." Jordan's smile widened, and he reached into his pocket for his cell phone. "Look at her little smile," he muttered as he turned the phone to camera mode and started scrolling through his photos.

Stan's phone picked that moment to ring. He checked the caller ID to see who it was, but he would have answered it even if it was his garbage collector.

It was Amber. "Sorry, dude. I have to take this." He walked through the open bay door and into the middle of the parking lot to get away from the noise of Hank using the impact wrench. "Hey. What's up?"

"I'm sorry to bother you, but I was wondering, what if someone calls and tells me they've got Gnorman in their yard? What do I say? What are we going to do?"

He honestly hadn't thought that far in advance. "Go with the flow, I suppose, and do the same thing. We'll go wherever he is and get the new note, but we'll have to do a little convincing while we're there." He didn't want to think that more people would be involved now that they'd pretty much figured out that it was the committee members. It would be interesting to see if Gnorman's next journey would be to the yard of someone who was just a regular member. If so, then the scheme was much more far-reaching than he feared, and he didn't know how he'd deal with that. He already had a hard enough time dealing with it. He'd simply assumed that Gnorman would go back to one of the same yards, and the circle would start again, not necessarily in the same order, just to keep them guessing.

"Okay. Just so we're on the same page. I'll call you the next time someone calls me, just the same as I did before. Thanks."

Stan hit the End Call button and shoved the phone back in his pocket.

They weren't on the same page at all.

He wanted exactly the same thing the committee wanted, and he had been getting there without their help, just not at the speed he wanted. He didn't know why Amber was so slow to respond, or why she seemed to be fighting the changes in their relationship, but he had been making progress. It may have been three steps forward and two steps back, but it was still forward. He'd taken her on two dates, and he'd kissed her a few times, and she'd responded. Now, with the interference of his mother and her cohorts, when he kept on his current trajectory, he wouldn't know if Amber's responses were sincere or just playing the part.

He looked inside the shop, where everyone once again worked diligently.

Again, he wanted to go back in and hit something.

This might kill him, but he didn't know what else to do, short of getting down on one knee, blurting out that he loved her, and asking her to marry him. He would do it in an instant if he thought she would realize he was serious and say yes. But knowing Amber, she wouldn't just say no. She'd retreat. Not only did she have a nearly terminal fear of heights, she also had an intense fear of making the wrong decision. He'd never known someone who hated to take chances more than Amber. He didn't know how she started up her business with a mind-set like that because many start-up businesses did fail. Yet she went with it, she worked seriously and diligently, and she still went with it, even in a tough economy.

He wished there was some way he could find out how to make her see things as he did.

He pulled out his phone and hit the speed dial for Amber's number. "I have an idea, but I don't want to talk about it over the phone. How about if I take you out for lunch? Jordan wouldn't mind sitting in your store for an hour. It will give him a chance to sort the 200 baby pictures on his phone."

"I don't know . . ."

Stan gritted his teeth. He didn't know why he was going to do this because it only showed how desperate he was. "I'll take you to Caroline's tearoom, The Pink Geranium." Even the name of the place made him itch.

Amber gasped. "Really? You told me recently you'd never go there. Are you sure about this?"

Stan turned and watched Jordan, who had just cornered Mark with his latest new batch of photos. "Yeah, I'm sure. I'll be there in twenty minutes."

As expected, Jordan welcomed the chance to once again have an hour of paid time to sit in Amber's store and play with his photos.

They arrived at the tearoom just before noon, just before the lunch rush, but the place was still fairly crowded, and most of the guests had gray hair.

Caroline was shocked at first to see them, then went all gushy and seated them at a cramped little table for two against the wall, right under a basket of pink geraniums. After they were seated, he switched napkins with Amber so she would have the pink one, and he could have the green one.

Caroline came back with menus and stood above them with her pencil poised over her notepad. "What kind of tea would you like? I just got a beautiful new fragrant Indian blend that's just magnificent." She turned to Stan. "I've got a peppermint tea that you'll probably like."

Stan looked down at the fragile little cup, painted with flowers and trimmed with swirls of gold. Amber's cup had pictures of chickens and other farm animals on it.

He should have traded cups too.

He looked up at Caroline. "Just normal tea is good."

Amber didn't look at the menu, she knew what she wanted, and Stan said he'd have the same.

Surrounded by fine china and flowers and candles and delicate pretty things, he felt like an elephant in a gift store. It didn't help that he was the only man in the place.

"Isn't this lovely?" Amber said when Caroline left, nearly gushing.

"Yeah," he mumbled, not quite sure why he thought this was such a great idea. One thing, though, the cuteness of the decor took the edge off his mood; he couldn't stay angry in a place like this. Everything was breakable.

He also couldn't concentrate. A few tables to the right were Libby and Pamela and Naomi, holding their teacups up in the air not using all their fingers, giggling at each other while they talked.

There was no way he could tell Amber what he wanted to with the troublesome trio so close to them, watching everything they did.

Just to rub it in, the three of them smiled and waved at them, so he and Amber smiled and waved back.

"Don't look so glum," Amber said to him. "Smile. This place is meant to lift the spirits."

"I'm not glum." He looked down into his teacup. Even the bottom of the cup had pictures of flowers. On the inside. "I guess you can't put these in the dishwasher, can you?"

"Absolutely not."

He couldn't imagine a restaurant that would hand-wash this many dishes a day, but he guessed Caroline's prices had to account for the extra labor. He didn't know, since he hadn't looked at the menu.

Amber managed to make him forget about Libby and Pamela and Naomi in the immediate vicinity by talking about the last ball game, although it was hard to get excited about sports surrounded by pink.

The food was as good as Amber told him it would be, which did a lot to soothe his savage stomach. The peach cobbler was also good, even better than his mother's, and he made Amber promise never to tell his mother he'd said that.

In the time it took to eat a full lunch, including a salad, plus dessert and a second cup of tea each, Libby and Pamela and

Naomi were still sitting there, giggling and yakking. Since both he and Amber had to get back to work, Stan didn't stop to chat with the ladies; he only gave them a polite smile and kept walking. But he did make sure that when he walked by them, he held Amber's hand.

As he walked by, he snuck a peek at them, all three of them staring back, poking each other and nodding their heads. And that made the whole embarrassing trip worthwhile.

He grinned at Amber as he tucked his wallet back into his pocket. "Jordan has probably used up the battery on his cell phone by now. I'm sure he's anxious for us to get back."

CHAPTER Thirty-three

"I ripped a hole in my pants. I need to go to Walmart on the way home. Want to grab something for supper at the McDonalds at the front of the store while we're there?"

Amber cringed, not sure if she wanted to hear the details. "Is there a reason you need me to go?"

"Yeah. I want to buy a T-shirt too. You're better at picking colors than me."

That made so much sense, especially remembering what he'd almost done to his house until he allowed her to decorate in colors that actually matched and weren't all shades of black, gray, and brown. "Sure. We can do that. I also need to buy another ball of yarn. I ran short on a project."

As they walked into the store, Stan grabbed her hand and led her to the men's clothing department. When she flinched, he only grinned, and didn't let go.

"Necessities first." He swept his free hand downward, drawing her attention to the slash in the leg of his jeans from his knee all the way down his leg, exposing the front of one work boot, with gray wool work socks sticking out, and his hairy shin.

"That looks nasty. But I don't see a cut on your leg, so I guess that's good."

"I suppose. It sliced through my coveralls too. On the way home I need to stop and drop them off at my parents' house. Mom said she'd patch them for me. I'll wear patched coveralls, but I won't wear patched jeans."

Once they arrived at the rack of jeans, without releasing her hand, Stan picked up a pair of his favorite jeans, read the label with the size, tucked it under his arm, and guided her toward the T-shirts. Using her free hand, Amber picked a nice blue that set off his skin tone in size Large and handed it to him. "How's this?"

"Great. Thanks." Still not letting go, he tucked the T-shirt under his arm with the jeans and started walking toward Domestics.

"Aren't you going to try those on?"

"Why? I know my size. The jeans are the same as what I've got on."

"But you still have to try them on."

"Why?"

She'd tried on eight pairs of jeans before she got just the right ones, and she didn't buy the same brand as what she'd been wearing. "Never mind," she grumbled as she walked with him.

They'd almost made it to the yarn display when he lowered his head and spoke in a stage whisper. "Don't look now, but you won't believe who's coming."

"I have to look, or else I won't see who it is."

"Don't say I didn't warn you."

"Amber! Stan! Over here!"

Amber turned her head and smiled. "Sherry, Sylvia, how nice to see you."

The ladies smiled, looked at their joined hands, both smiles widened as they looked up. "What fun to see you both here," Sylvia said, not losing her grin. "Isn't it a good night to shop?"

Sherry pointed her thumb over her shoulder, in the direction of the center aisle. "Did you see the new display with the new towels and pillows? All the new colors."

Amber didn't really want to go, and she certainly didn't need any more towels, but she did want to be polite. "I suppose we will later. We were just on our way to pick up some yarn, so we'll probably go look after we've paid for everything. It might be a while. Maybe we'll see you there?"

Sylvia nodded while Sherry shook her head, they looked at each other and laughed.

"Maybe," Sherry said, and then her face turned serious. "This year I was chosen to inspect your garden for your membership renewal. You close your store at 5:30 on Saturday, don't you? Would it work for me to take a quick look on Saturday after you get home?"

A mental picture of her pathetic garden flashed before her eyes. It was nothing spectacular, but thanks to Stan's automatic sprinklers, she at least had a garden. If she got out a flashlight and did her weeding Friday night, she could make it passable. "Yes, that would work for me. I'll expect you on Saturday."

The two ladies once again looked at their joined hands, smiled, nodded, and continued on their way to wherever they were originally headed.

Stan also watched them walk away. "This wasn't what I had in mind, but it will work in our favor. Do you realize that out of ten committee members, we've already seen five of them, just today? Soon we'll see my mother. That's six. Word will spread to the rest of them before we finish paying for our stuff."

The reminder of the matchmaking scheme effectively killed her good mood for the evening, but she forced herself not to let it show.

After having been seen by half of the committee in the space of half a day, the chances of coming across more weren't high, yet Stan didn't release her hand as they walked toward the checkout.

Even though they'd been coerced, what they were doing was a deception. She supposed they were succeeding in the small picture, but in the big picture they solved nothing. She also didn't know how long they needed to keep it up to satisfy the committee that they were sufficiently match-made so they would leave them alone.

She looked up at Stan as they walked. "This thing that we're doing. Is this really what you want to happen?"

He continued facing forward, not looking at her as he replied. "No, not really."

"What do you want to happen? In the big picture."

"I want to settle down. Get married. The white picket fence, the dog, the whole nine yards. What about you?"

Amber's heart sank. She wanted those same things. But they weren't going to happen until she paid off Uncle Henry, which, if she managed to make all her payments and didn't need to move to Chicago to work off an unpaid balance, would be in four more years.

Her lower lip quivered. Judging from Stan's comment, he didn't want to wait four years. He was ready now. Just as she'd felt over the last few months, she'd been correct. He truly was ready to settle down, and she couldn't make him wait for her. He was a sweet and decent and wonderful man—and hot with his mustache. Just like Santa at Christmas, she had to make sure he got what he desired.

She cleared her throat, hoping her voice came out even. "I want—"

"Stan! Amber! Yoo-hoo!"

Amber cringed as Kathy ran toward them, one arm loaded down with bags, the other waving wildly in the air.

"Mom? What are you doing here?"

"I was at the mall down the block and Sylvia phoned to tell me she saw you here. I know you're coming over for me to fix your coveralls tonight, so I sent your father home. He was just getting bored. I can keep shopping with you two, and you can take me home." She turned to Amber. "Isn't that a fun idea?"

"Sure," Stan replied, but his tone lacked sincerity. "But Amber and I were talking."

Kathy waved her hand in the air. "So go ahead and talk. Just pretend I'm not here."

Like that was realistically going to happen. Although maybe this wasn't such a bad thing. Stan had already dropped the bomb on her about wanting to settle down. Now she could take more time to adjust to it before it exploded in her face.

They continued walking, her on one side of him, because he wasn't releasing her hand, and his mother on his other side.

His relaxed expression was gone. There was a tightness in his jaw, like he was clenching his teeth.

Amber hadn't been aware that Stan had met someone because, with all the time he'd spent with her lately, he hadn't had time to pursue a relationship. But he had to have met someone, somewhere, because he told her his projection into the future for marriage.

She wondered how far along the relationship could be; after all, he'd kissed her a number of times. It couldn't be serious because Stan was not the type to cheat, especially after seeing how unfaithfulness devastated his best friend. This meant that even though the relationship wasn't far along, the woman was special enough that he saw what he ultimately wanted, and that he was prepared to do what it took to see if it could work. One day she also wanted long term, but she couldn't allow herself to think it could happen for her for a few more years.

For someone who wanted to shop, Kathy didn't do much browsing. They picked up a set of glasses to replace a set that had one missing from years ago, and a bottle of nail polish. After that, they paid for their purchases and went home.

Amber gave Kathy the front seat and climbed into the back. Strangely, even though Stan owned this big truck, a crew-cab with bucket seats, she'd never been in it with a third person, so she'd never been in the back seat. The back was littered with bags, wrappers, dried leaves, an empty donut box, and a few small tools. In a way, it was kind of funny. The outside was immaculate, including the back bed, but the inside behind the driver's area was a pig sty. This was a side of Stan she'd never seen.

She made a few pig grunts to give him the hint, but either he didn't hear her over his mother's chattering, or he ignored her.

As soon as they arrived at his parents' house, Stan slipped into his new jeans, which fit exactly the same as the ones he took off.

Instead of disappearing into Stan's old bedroom, which was now converted into a sewing room with both a regular sewing machine and a serger, Kathy joined Stan, Frank, and Amber in the living room, holding Stan's torn coveralls but not actually doing anything with them.

"I was wondering if you two have any plans for the weekend," she said, gazing expectantly at them, idly picking at a loose thread.

Both of them always worked Saturdays, so that didn't leave either of them with a lot of options. The weekend consisted of one day, Sunday, and they went to church in the morning.

"Not really," she replied.

"Yes," Stan said. "I was thinking of going to the museum."

"What?" Amber and Kathy asked in unison.

"One of my customers said they're having a dominoes competition, and his son is competing with his team. A team is four people, they have twenty minutes to set up, then one domino is flipped and they're judged. He gave me free tickets. Everyone who has a ticket gets to vote."

Amber blinked and stared at him. "Dominoes?"

Stan's ears turned red. "It sounded more interesting at the time. These are high school kids, and it seems like a wholesome project that requires a bit of thought and a lot of teamwork to put it together."

"I guess we can go."

Stan stood. "Speaking of going, I just realized that you probably can't fix those until they're washed. I'll take them back and throw them in the laundry, and bring them back next time I come. Sorry about that."

Kathy pressed her hands down on the coveralls. "It's true, I can't run my sewing machine through the grease spots, but I can wash them just as well here. Don't worry about it. You have another pair, I would think."

"I have a few more, yes." He extended one hand toward Amber. "Come on, Honey, let's go. I'll take you home."

Amber choked, and then coughed.

Kathy handed her a tissue. "Are you coming down with something? I have some cough suppressant. There's nothing worse than a summer cold, is there?"

"I'm fine," she gasped, finally managing to control herself, then followed Stan to the door.

She said her good-byes to Kathy and Frank, then climbed into Stan's truck—into the front seat, where it was clean.

"*Honey?*" she blurted out the second she closed the door. "What are you trying to do, kill me?"

"It's a term of endearment," he grumbled as he backed out of his parents' driveway and turned toward her townhouse.

"The Bloomfield Museum? A dominoes competition?"

"I was going to tell you, but we kept getting interrupted. If you don't want to go, we can do something else. I didn't make any promises. I said I had to ask you first."

"You did?"

"Of course. I wouldn't want to do anything you didn't want to do."

She thought of him earlier, at The Pink Geranium. He'd looked so out of place in the fussy tearoom, but the huge contrast between the burly mechanic and the delicate gray-haired ladies just made it even more special that he'd taken her there. He'd done something very special for her. Going to the dominoes competition to cheer on his customer's son was the least she could do for him.

He really deserved to find that someone special, someone who could be guaranteed to be there for him. She couldn't be the person he needed, so she needed to help him find that woman, even if it killed her to do it.

She couldn't be that person, but she would always be his friend, and that was more important than anything.

CHAPTER Thirty-four

Stan's cell phone rang at exactly the day and time when he knew who was calling, and why.

He flipped it open and spoke without looking at the caller ID. "Let me guess. Gnorman has been found in someone's garden, and he's got another note."

Amber's gleeful squeal pierced right through his head. "Yes! But you won't guess! He's in Becky's garden, he's got a note, and he's got the trophy!"

Stan should have smiled, but it wouldn't happen.

He should have been happy that it was finally over and life could get back to normal, but he didn't want normal. He was tired of normal.

As angry as he'd been about the committee's scheme, after he'd resigned himself to go with the flow for Amber's sake, he'd actually enjoyed the foray of chasing the gnome all over town—because he'd been doing the chasing with Amber. Being the target of the matchmaking scheme had brought his relationship with Amber to a deeper level with all the holding hands, cuddling, and the hugging. He'd especially enjoyed kissing her. She'd been distant the night he'd bought his new jeans, but after that, every time he'd kissed her, it only got better and better. One time, when he dropped her off at her townhouse and she told him not to bother coming in, she'd kissed him in the truck in such a way that he'd sat behind the wheel long after she'd gone inside, grinning like a besotted idiot until he remembered to start the engine and drive home.

It couldn't end. He wanted it all, and he wanted it with Amber.

A week ago he'd tried to get Amber to open up and talk to him about the possibility of marrying him. He'd almost got her to start talking when his mother had interrupted them, and after that every time he tried to work toward the topic of marriage, Amber steered the conversation away. It was almost like she was doing it on purpose.

Finding the trophy and having Gnorman back where he should be would make what was happening between them plummet to normal.

He couldn't go back.

Today he had to close the book on the saga of the Gnome Gnapper and open the book for the story of the rest of their lives. He didn't know how he could make that happen, but he had to think of something.

This time he didn't rush to beat any speed records on the way to Amber's store. He couldn't believe how slowly he made the trip, for the first time praying for red lights.

Still, he couldn't think of a thing to say.

All the way from Amber's store to Becky's house, he remained silent. Beside him, Amber nearly bounced in the seat. Conversation would have been useless.

It was almost poetic justice that when they found Gnorman in Becky's garden, the costume of the day was a tuxedo. Stan almost checked around the yard for wedding bells, but he knew that would have been more than Amber could handle right now.

Becky grinned from ear to ear, surrounded by a crowd of people taking pictures of her with Gnorman and the trophy, something she should have been able to do on the first day of spring, and now it was nearly fall.

Amber ran to Gnorman. "Excuse me," she said without waiting for an obvious pause in the picture taking, and pulled the envelope, the last envelope, from Gnorman's hand.

She ran back to him and tore it open with shaking hands.

She looked up at him with the biggest smile Stan had ever seen, her eyes sparkling so brightly that he wanted to grab her and kiss her and not care who was watching.

"This is it! The last note!"

Stan stood and read it beside Amber, her hands shaking so much he could barely make out the words.

with the trophy Becky's
delighted
with love, all are excited
gnorman will cheer
when the wedding is near
so we hope everyone's
invited

Amber gasped. "Wedding? Oh . . . no . . ."

Stan's stomach dropped. All the notes until now had been almost nonsense, even fun. A blatant statement saying that now everyone anticipated their wedding wasn't what he'd expected.

He wasn't ready. They hadn't talked about it. They hadn't exchanged words of love and devotion. He hadn't told her how much he loved her. There'd been no workup, no buildup.

This would be the time to propose, but he wasn't prepared.

He wore old jeans, so worn out that parts of them were threadbare. His T-shirt had a hole over his stomach. He still wore his steel-toed work boots. He had oil in his hair. After working in the grease pit in this heat, he needed a shower, really bad. He also didn't have time to shave this morning.

The romantic park-like setting of Becky's yard beckoned him, calling for the right moment, and this wasn't it. All the color had drained out of Amber's face, and she started to back away from him.

He cleared his throat. "We have to talk," he said, trying to keep the escalating panic out of his voice as he nudged Amber away from the crowd, toward the gazebo. Away from the crowd of people standing there staring at them, they sat side by side on the wooden bench inside.

"About that note, and the wedding reference . . ." His voice skipped while he struggled to find the right words.

Amber shook her head and rested her fingers on his arm. "It's okay. I know what you're going to say. I understand."

His heart leapt. "You do? That's great." He wanted to jump up and cheer, like the time at the last ball game when his team scored the winning run. They were getting married!

Amber nodded. "It's okay, I don't know her name, but when the day comes when the time is right, I'm sure you'll be very happy together."

His breath caught. "What are you talking about?"

"When we were shopping, and you said you wanted to get married, and that's okay. I'm sure you'll find your Miss Right really soon, and I'll be very happy for you." Her eyes started to go glassy. "I really will." She sucked in a breath and turned away.

Stan's stomach bottomed out. She didn't look very happy. In fact, she started to cry.

He reached up to brush his fingers against her chin, then nudged her cheek just enough to make her turn and look at him.

A tear rolled down her face.

Stan thought he might throw up.

"I have found my Miss Right, Amber. It's you. It's you I want to get married to."

"Me? But you can't. It won't work."

"Of course it will work. Please don't tell me we have to get to know each other better because we don't. It will be perfect."

"No, you don't understand. I can't. I might have to leave. I can't."

"That's okay. We can plan around it."

She shook her head. "You don't understand. I might have to leave Bloomfield. Permanently. At least permanently for four years."

"I don't understand. Are you in some kind of trouble? Why didn't you tell me?" The only thing he could think of that a person would have to leave for, suddenly with no notice, was witness protection, and nothing ever happened in Bloomfield that would warrant the need for that.

"Do you remember when I first started my business, instead of getting a loan from the bank like you did, I got a lower interest loan from a relative?"

"Yes. Some uncle. In . . ." He struggled to remember. It was a big city, really far away. ". . . Chicago. What's wrong? Is your uncle in trouble?"

"No. He's doing really well. So well that everything has gone to his head, and he's gone power crazy. When my parents died, he changed the terms on my loan, and when the bank wouldn't give me a loan to pay him off, I had to agree to his terms. Then about a year ago, he raised the interest rates and made it so I couldn't default in any way, not even bankruptcy. I don't know how legal it is, but if I can't afford to make the payments, I certainly can't afford a lawyer. When I first took out the loan, I foolishly signed a contract that if for any reason I can't pay off the loan, with no late payments being acceptable, the terms are that I'll go work for him at a wage agreed acceptable for the position he gives me until the loan is completely paid off."

"Why did you agree to something like that?"

"Because he's family—my mother's only brother—so I didn't get a lawyer. I just trusted him and signed it. At first it was easy to pay him back. But when my mother died, everything changed."

"But you're doing okay now, aren't you?"

"Barely. I have no safety zone. I'm considering giving up my townhouse and using my studio at the store to live in, except I'm caught up in the zoning bylaws."

"Would you be okay if you didn't have to pay rent?"

"I'm not letting you pay my rent."

He smiled. "No, but if we got married, you'd live at my house, and you wouldn't have to pay rent anymore."

She stiffened and backed away from his touch. "Free rent is not a reason to get married."

Stan squeezed his eyes shut. He'd done that wrong. "I didn't mean it like that." He opened his eyes and moved closer to her. "Then what about the loan? If we got married, it would be my loan too. I'd help you pay for it."

She stood and stared down at him. "I won't be a liability to you, Stan. You do so much for me, I can't let you do that too. That's way too much money. I won't start a marriage to you, or to anyone, in the red."

His stomach flip-flopped. He'd done that wrong too. "Then how about if we go to the bank, and I'll cosign a loan to pay off your uncle. If you're making the payments now, you'll still be making them. It won't cost me anything."

"That's just as much a liability. Why are you doing this? You should be asking for a prenup to keep your own business safe, not willingly bury yourself in my troubles and debts."

He cleared his throat. "Because I love you, Amber. Like a friend I've grown up with, and the woman I want to spend the rest of my life with. I love you, and I want to marry you."

"No . . . you can't. . . ."

"But I do."

She jumped to her feet. "You can't. It won't work."

Before he could tell her it could if she'd only give it a chance, she turned and ran out of the gazebo.

Without thinking, Stan followed his reflexes and ran after her. If he didn't stop her, she would keep going, right out the gate and walk all the way home, because he'd driven her there. It was about six miles to her house, but she was stubborn enough to do it. Even if he embarrassed them both and drove beside her, once she started walking, he'd never convince her to listen to him.

Even with his steel-toed work boots, he still ran faster than Amber. It didn't take long to run in front of her and extend his arms so she couldn't go around him, and he forced her to stop.

Just as she did, a voice came from beside Gnorman.

"Stan? Amber? What are you two doing?"

"Mother . . ." he ground out between his teeth. With his arms still extended, he turned to see his mother, camera in hand, with Becky, Sherry, and Pamela standing behind Gnorman and the trophy.

Just the people he didn't want to see this.

"What's going on?" his mother snapped at him.

He opened his mouth, trying to sort all the thoughts in his head, when Amber turned around to face the other ladies.

"I want to go home," she sniffled. "Would someone mind driving me?"

Pamela smiled at Amber, turned to glare at Stan, and then smiled back at Amber. "I'll take you home, dear."

Stan let his arms drop to his sides as Pamela and Amber left.

He crossed his arms over his chest, stiffened to his full height, and glared at his mother. "This is all your fault."

"My fault? It looks like you're the one who upset her."

He pointed to Gnorman and the miniature tuxedo.

"This is the fault of you and your crazy matchmaking scheme. Don't give me that look. We found out about it."

"It wasn't my scheme. It was Sylvia's idea. I only helped."

"Along with the entire garden club operating committee."

His mother gasped. "How did you know about that?"

"I just do. Look what you've done. She wasn't ready yet, and then you had to write that stupid wedding note."

Before he said something he would really regret, he spun and stormed out of Becky's yard.

More than anything he wanted to go to Amber's and try to talk it out reasonably, but he knew that Pamela would stay with her, so there was no chance of that. This was a conversation that needed to happen in private.

He started his truck and roared off home. Halfway there, his phone rang. He checked the caller ID, saw that it was his mother, and threw the phone in the backseat.

CHAPTER Thirty-five

The past three days were the loneliest days of her life.

For three days in a row, she hadn't seen Stan, she hadn't talked to him, they hadn't exchanged any text messages.

Now, as she closed up her store, it was time for Sherry to have a look at her garden, and renew her membership.

She should have been happy, but she wasn't. This was a moment she'd wanted to share with Stan, and she couldn't.

When he'd first told her that he wanted to get married, and she'd thought he meant to someone else, that was when she finally admitted to herself that she loved him, and she probably had always loved him, and that she always would love him. They shared a relationship that very few people would ever experience, and she'd been forced to not pursue it because the timing was wrong—she wouldn't be a liability to him.

How unfair was that?

She arrived at her townhouse at the same time as Sherry, which was good timing. They walked directly into the backyard,

Sherry gave the garden a cursory glance, signed the membership renewal, and tucked it into her folder.

"I heard that you and Stan have had a falling out."

Amber gulped, fighting back the burn of tears, something she'd done a lot over the past three days.

"Yes," was all she could choke out.

"I want to say that we're all really sorry. We didn't mean to make you upset, and none of us have ever seen Stan like this."

"Like what?"

"He refused to talk to Kathy. He suddenly became very silent and left, without a word. Poor Kathy is beside herself. He won't answer her calls, and she won't go to his shop because she doesn't want to bring personal problems up in front of his staff. Then every time she's gone to his house, he's had someone over, so she doesn't knock." Sherry shook her head. "No, none of us have ever seen him act this way, and we've known him almost since he was born."

Amber had known him since he was born, and she'd never seen him like that, either. He'd been angry the day he found out about the matchmaking plot, but this sounded so much worse.

While Kathy had been wrong, she'd meant well. Most of all, Kathy was his mother. If her mother were still alive, regardless of how angry she was, she wouldn't stop speaking to her for so many days. It was probably driving Kathy insane.

Amber checked her watch, even though she knew what time it was. "I'll talk to him about it. I know that he's very upset, but maybe I can talk some sense into him."

"Would you do that? I know Kathy is downright distraught."

Not only Kathy, but she knew Stan had to be just as bad, if not worse. Not only was he so angry that he wasn't speaking to his mother, he also hadn't tried to contact her. Not that she blamed him for that either. But both as a friend, and as more that she couldn't yet understand, she couldn't bear the thought of him being so unhappy.

As soon as Sherry left, Amber drove to Stan's house without calling first.

As Sherry had said, there was another vehicle in Stan's driveway in addition to his truck. However, she recognized it as the car belonging to his neighbor's teenaged son, who usually parked on the street.

Clever. But not clever enough.

Instead of knocking, she used the key that she'd never used before.

She found him laying on the couch, flat on his back, his boots still on, one leg bent at the knee, hanging over the arm of the couch, the other leg stretched straight, sticking out onto the floor. One arm, like his leg, hung down with his wrist dragging on the floor, and his other arm bent at the elbow, draped over his eyes.

His mouth was open, and he was snoring.

It looked like he'd been having the same sleepless nights that she'd been having.

She approached him, lightly shook his shoulder, and stood back. "Stan? Wake up."

His arm jerked up, his eyes flew open, and she could see him struggle to focus. "Amber?" He blinked repeatedly, trying to get his bearings. "What time is it? What are you doing here?"

"Relax. It's Saturday, just after six. I came to talk to you."

Before she could react, he sat up, threw his arms around her, pulled her into his lap, and held her tight. "I'm so sorry. If you don't want to get married, that's fine. We can stay friends. I can wait until you're ready."

She couldn't not return his embrace. She'd missed him so much she felt like she had a hole in her heart, and it was her own doing. "I came for two reasons. First, to say that even though your mother was wrong, she was only trying to do what she thought was best. Whether you agree with her or not, you've got to talk to her and give her the chance to apologize to you properly. The Bible says never to let the sun go down on your anger, and this is one of those times. After my parents moved away, I made sure I was never angry with them, especially over the distance, and I was glad I did. If I'd been angry with them and not speaking to them before they died, the guilt would have eaten me up. Do you understand?"

He sighed, remained silent for a minute, stroked her hair, then nestled his chin in the crook of her neck. "Yes, you're right. I'll call her. Later."

"I also want to tell you that you're right. About everything you said the other day. I don't need to be independent. I know I should have told you all this before, but I knew you'd do exactly what you did. You offered to help and make all my troubles go away. I don't know why I thought that this time I needed to do it on my own. That's what friends are for, and if anything like that ever happened to you, you know I'd help you too."

She felt his smile against her skin. "You have. You dragged me off the road when I was on my bike and got hit by a car, and saved me from getting run over by that bus. Then you did something braver than I could have done. You didn't tell my mother."

Amber smiled back. "That's because she would have grounded you, and you wouldn't have been able to go swimming the next day."

"That's what we do, Amber. We always watch each other's backs."

She stroked his hair. "I know. And this time, you're right again. When we get married, I would move to your house and not have to pay rent, and I'd easily be able to make the payments to Uncle Henry. As well, if you cosigned a loan at the bank, I'd get lower interest and lower payments, and I'd be able to pay it off without it costing you a single penny, so we'd both win. I was being an idiot, and I apologize."

"That's okay, I don't think . . ." His voice trailed off. "Wait. Did you just say *'when'* we get married? Not *if*, but *when?*"

"I'm pretty sure that's what I just said, yes."

Before she knew what happened, Stan kissed her, and she kissed him back.

"I love you Amber," he muttered against her lips, then continued kissing her before she had a chance to say she loved him too.

Until the doorbell rang.

"I'm going to ignore it," he muttered, and he kept kissing her.

The doorbell rang again. And again.

"If it's that crazy kid next door, I'm going to strangle him."

"I saw him parked in your driveway. You did that so everyone would think you had company. Smart man."

The doorbell rang again.

This time, Stan answered it. But it wasn't the teen boy from next door. It was Kathy.

"Mother . . ."

"Stan, I'm so sorry. I'll never do anything like that again. I'll mind my own business and I'll tell the whole garden club to butt out and I'll . . ." Kathy's voice trailed off. "Amber? What are you doing here? How did you get here? I didn't see your car."

"The boy from next door is parked in Stan's driveway, and there wasn't room on the street, so I parked in their driveway. Where did you park?"

Kathy's face turned beet red. "I'm sort of on the sidewalk. I told myself I wouldn't be long, so hopefully Tucker won't notice."

Stan pressed his thumb and index finger into the bridge of his nose. "Tucker will notice, Mom."

"Then I'll leave. Please tell me that everything is okay between you two, that you're friends again."

Amber walked beside Stan and slipped one arm around his waist. He quickly returned the gesture.

"Everything is fine. In fact, it's so fine it looks like we'll be sending out wedding invitations after all."

Kathy squeezed her hands together, pressed them to her chin, squealed, and did a little jig.

Stan stuck one finger in his ear. "That hurt."

"That's so exciting! Are you going to get married at the church, or in my garden?"

Stan smiled and looked down at Amber, ignoring his mother. "Whatever you want."

Amber couldn't hold back her grin. "If we get married in your mother's garden, then we don't have to wait to book the church. I vote for the garden."

Kathy squealed again. This time both Amber and Stan were ready and already had their fingers in their ears.

Kathy made another little dance. "I know who can be the perfect ring bearer for you. Since he's so good at holding the trophy, he'd be even better at holding a ring. He already has the perfect tuxedo."

Stan and Amber looked at each other and smiled. "Gnorman."

Amber nodded. "Gnaturally."

Discussion Questions

1. As in many clubs and organizations, the members first come together as friends. The Bloomfield Garden Club holds contests, one of which is to be the winner of The Spring Fling Early Bloomer, which awards a trophy for the best early garden, putting the members in competition with each other. In times like these, our best friends can become our worst competition. Has this ever happened to you? How did you feel about it?

2. For The Spring Fling contest, when Kathy found out that Becky won, the first thing that came out her mouth was an accusation that her friend was cheating. When a friend gets something you have been striving for, and you get left behind, how do you deal with it?

3. For a long time Amber feared that the Gnapper had taken the trophy as a form of retribution, even though she didn't know what she could have done to hurt someone. Has anyone ever had something against you when you didn't know what you'd done? Or, perhaps someone had a reason, good or bad, right or

wrong, to hold a grudge against you. What did you do to try to make it better?

4. Before Gnorman disappeared from the fountain at the Lake Bliss Retirement Village, Stan had been planning a midnight stakeout, and he had been looking forward to some quiet time alone with Amber. When Gnorman disappeared, his excursion was cancelled, leaving him disappointed. Have you ever had plans you've been anticipating fall through? How did that make you feel? Did you become angry, or did you try to make the best of it? How would God have us deal with disappointment?

5. As Amber went into the theater to get the new note from Gnorman, she remembered a time from her youth that she and Stan had become distracted from the group and counted the lights under the old theater's awning. Have you ever lost interest when you were out with a group? What are some ways to maintain your focus when you become distracted?

6. Amber also recalled a time when she and Stan had made a raft, then the raft fell apart and they had to swim to shore, except Stan's sneakers became waterlogged, and he had difficulty getting them off in the water. Have you ever had a time when a friend was at risk or in danger? What did you do?

7. When Stan thought his friend Hayden wanted to start dating Amber, he couldn't help but feel jealous. Have you ever felt jealous? How did you handle it?

8. When they found Gnorman dressed as a clown, neither Amber nor Stan were amused by clowns in general, but Libby thought that in the right venue, which wasn't her garden, clowns could be very funny. What do you find funny? What do you think are good forms of Christian entertainment?

9. As time goes on, and Amber and Stan come no closer to finding the elusive trophy, Amber becomes more worried about her financial stability. While God is always there for us, often we have difficult times in our lives. What do you tell non-believers, when they see you, as a Christian, suffering, and they ask you where God is, in all your trouble?

10. Out of nowhere Amber got two good contracts to earn some money with her plant-pot flamingos. Have you ever been surprised with some extra income? Did you remember to thank God for it? What did you do with it?

11. Stan had intended to make a game of going out in public with their disguises on, but he didn't forsee how taking Amber out on a date would change his feelings about her. Has this kind of thing every happened to you, when you do something different with someone you thought you knew, you come out with a different perspective on that person?

12. When Amber and Stan witness Edna and Bill having a secret rendezvous at the restaurant, they are shocked; but it seems to be a weekly outing. Do you have a date night or anything similar with your spouse or significant other?

13. When Stan barges in at Andy's house, he is very angry with Amber for not wanting him to be there. Have you ever had a friend do something that left you angry, or hurt, even though he or she had the best of intentions? What did you do to make it right?

14. When Kathy hears about the hidden camera, she dresses up for the camera and acts different in front of it, knowing she's being watched. When you know you're being watched, even if it's not by a camera, do you act different? Do you remember a time that you knew you were being watched? How did you feel?

15. Stan became angry when he found out that Kathy had told her friends in the garden club about the hidden camera. Have you once trusted someone to keep something confidential, and they didn't? How did you feel? How did you handle it? How do you feel about it now?

16. When Stan and Amber found Gnorman dressed like a ghost, he immediately remembered the latest poem, which had stated "a ghost of a chance." Stan was the only one who thought this was funny. Has this ever happened to you? Did you feel embarrassed or try to explain to everyone else why it was so funny? When in a crowd, when you have a different perspective or a comment that differs from everyone else's opinion, do you state your difference or remain silent? Do you consider yourself an introvert or an extrovert?

17. Stan and Amber's first date completely changed Stan's perspective on their relationship, and what he wanted in the future from that relationship. Have you ever had one of those moments where suddenly everything changed? What did you do about it?

18. Even though the Pink Geranium Tea Room was too girly for him, Stan risked his masculine pride and took Amber. Have you ever done something for someone that was something you otherwise would never have done? What did you do? Did you accomplish your goal by doing so?

19. When Amber read Gnorman's last note that intimated there would be a wedding—her wedding—she panicked. Have you ever found out something that completely threw you for a loop? What did you do?

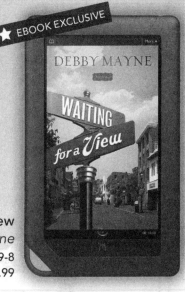